UNLOADED

UNLOADED
CRIME WRITERS
WRITING WITHOUT GUNS

EDITED BY ERIC BEETNER

DOWN&OUT
BOOKS

Down & Out Books
3959 Van Dyke Rd, Ste. 265
Lutz, FL 33558
www.DownAndOutBooks.com

Cover design by Eric Beetner

ISBN: 1-943402-22-1
ISBN-13: 978-1-943402-22-9

CONTENTS

CONTENTS

FROM THE EDITOR
Eric Beetner

I am a hypocrite. You see, I use guns to kill people. A lot of people. And wound them, threaten them, motivate them. I should say my characters do this because I don't own a gun, and this is where the hypocrisy comes in. I personally think guns are too often misused, are too prevalent in American society and are too easy to get. I don't know of any good reason for an ordinary citizen to own an assault rifle or a high capacity magazine. I believe in rigorous background checks and there should be a path to legally get guns away from those deemed unfit or unsafe to own them. I think a lot of things about guns, but it doesn't stop me writing about them.

In the wake of so many recent mass shootings from Columbine to Sandy Hook and far beyond where any rational person would think our government would step in to address the problem, I began to feel conflicted about my writing. Did it glorify the use of guns? I'd say most of the movies I see have gun violence in them, from classic film noirs to modern day Hong Kong action films. And I make no apology for liking them.

But that's fantasy, and so is my writing. When irresponsible gun owners cause deaths of real human beings, a line has been crossed.

I believe in responsible gun ownership. I'm not trying to take anyone's guns away, nor is anyone in this anthology. We don't want the abolition of gun ownership, only a rea-

1

sonable conversation about how to take steps to prevent more mass killings and fewer tragic accidents.

I felt that sitting by and not saying anything wouldn't cut it anymore, especially when the people who seemed to be dominating the conversation were doing nothing more than shouting and threatening one another. To listen to their arguments, the very fabric of America would be destroyed if we limited guns in any way, or we would be destroyed if we left things unchecked. As is always the case, the truth lies somewhere in between.

I began to notice other writers voicing their opinions about how insane the gun problem had gotten in America on social media. Some quoted facts, some voiced frustration, some pleaded for reason. I wondered if they, too, were conflicted about their writing being at odds with their personal beliefs.

And so I reached out and told them my idea. I wanted to put together an anthology of great crime fiction stories, the stories we all love to read and write, but leave out the guns. I knew we could do it. The guns weren't the crux of the story, and if we could show how easy it was to do without for a little while, well maybe it could spark a conversation about guns. Specifically, it could—and I know it does so in a very small way—it could show that the world doesn't end when the guns go away for a time. Maybe a citizen doesn't need to own an assault rifle. Maybe we could all be responsible Americans and accept a limit on how many guns we could own, or how many rounds a magazine can carry. We can talk about concealment, gun locks, background checks, safety instruction and not shout about it or automatically get defensive and reach for the holster to defend our "American way of life."

We could embrace the essence of what the founding fathers meant with the second amendment, without being so literal about it and while acknowledging that they could never have conceived of an M-16 or an AK-47.

The authors represented here responded and wanted to

have that conversation. So they wrote. Original, exciting crime stories with all the thrills you've come to love about a great outlaw story, but without the guns. I doubt anyone will even miss them.

The writers who have contributed include gun owners. They come from all over the country and from both political parties. The unifying factor is a desire for reasoned, sensible change. Anyone who looks at the yearly body count in this nation as a result of gun violence wants the same thing. I don't know anyone, gun enthusiast or not, who wants another school shooting or another rampage where survivors are left asking why and how, never to receive an answer to either.

It is a sad fact that during the time it took to put this book together, more than a dozen more mass shootings took place including killings in schools, churches and movie theaters. The problem isn't going away on its own. Our legislators need to step in, and since they aren't doing so, the people need to speak out.

In addition to being a writer, a father and a non-gun owner, I was almost a statistic. When I was in the second grade—I'll pause to let that sink in: second grade—my friend Danny and I raided his father's unlocked gun cabinet and took a revolver out for a day in the woods. We went around suburban Connecticut shooting at things like tree stumps, frogs we pulled out of the pond and bee hives. It may be obvious that if I were not to meet my demise by a tragic gun accident, then surely I would do something stupid to do myself in, but somehow I've made it this far.

At one point Danny held the gun and had shot a frog we fished out onto the bank of the pond. Why we thought this was a good idea I still don't know. Seeing the frog obliterated I figured Danny's work was done, so I moved on ahead of him. He wasn't done shooting. He took one more shot with me in his path and I felt the earth near my foot shake with the bullet's impact. We laughed about it.

I could have easily been one of the many accidental deaths by children wielding guns without knowing their full power.

We weren't imitating video games, I lived in a Pac Man world back then. We weren't emulating something we saw on TV, it was a *Brady Bunch* and *Mork & Mindy* landscape for me. We were just kids playing with what was available. For us, and for too many kids today, the gun was a toy.

Like I said, I know this is a small gesture. I don't expect to change policy or spark a revolution. But when we are confronted with armed gunmen killing children, gunning down innocent movie-goers, stalking high school hallways, seeking revenge on co-workers, attacking our military bases all with increasing numbers—staying silent wasn't an option for me. And this is how I, and everyone included here, express ourselves: on the page.

Guns have been a part of America since its birth and expansion. Citizen on citizen gun violence is not new. Mass killings are not new. From the shootout at the OK Corral to Dillinger and Bonnie & Clyde, gun violence has been present in our society. That doesn't make it acceptable. There are more guns in America now than at any time in history and, after declining in the 1990s, deaths and violence from guns are on the rise again.

So for a time, let's remove them from the equation and enjoy a good story. For a time, let's do without and I guarantee you America and the American way of life will still be here when you are finished with this book.

We will all go back to writing about guns, I'm sure. They are a fact of life, especially the criminal life we all write about. But I know we can take steps to prevent more tragedies from happening. I know we can let reason win the day. I know we can separate fact from fiction. I know we can listen to each other.

So I thank you for listening, and for reading.

Proceeds from this collection are being donated to States United to Prevent Gun Violence. We felt their reasoned and impassioned approach to sensible gun laws made them exactly in line for the changes we wish to see. Please visit their website http://ceasefireusa.org/ for more information and to make up your own mind on the issues.

"You can have my gun, but you'll take my book when you pry my cold, dead fingers off the binding."

—Stephen King

THE OLD MAN IN THE MOTORIZED CHAIR
Joe R. Lansdale

My grandfather, Stubble Fine, used to work for the cops, but he didn't get along with them so he quit. He opened a detective agency, but he didn't much care for that, even though he was good at it. Well, to be honest, he was great at it. But he didn't care. At heart, he's lazy.

No man in my memory has more looked forward to retirement than my grandpa. And as it turned out, he pretty much had to retire. His legs played out and he spent his days in a motorized chair, in front of the television set. His wife, my grandma, left him early on, well before he retired, and she died of some kind of disease somewhere in Florida. We never met.

On the day I'm telling you about, I was visiting his house, which is a three-bedroom that looks a lot like the three bedrooms along his street and across from it. He and I get along well enough, considering he doesn't really like much of anyone, and hates the human race in general.

But, I get my fill of him plenty quick, and I think the feeling is mutual, though it's more about his personality than about anything I might do or say.

I was pretty close to making my escape, as it was a Saturday, and I wanted to have a nice day on the town, maybe go to the mall, see if any good-looking women were hanging around, but fate took a hand.

Grandpa was watching his favorite channel, one about reptiles and insects and animals. He loved the episodes with alligators and lions, and especially snakes. The ones where adventurers went out and showed off poisonous snakes and told you about them and handled them in precarious and irresponsible ways to show you how knowledgeable they were. Grandpa watched primarily in hopes of seeing someone bit.

So he's settled in with a snake program, waiting on another, cause it's some kind of all-day snake marathon or such, and just as I'm about to put on my coat and go out into the winter cold, the doorbell rang.

Grandpa said, "Damn it."

I went over to the kitchen window for a look. The Sheriff's car was parked at the curb, and behind it was a big black SUV splattered on the sides and all over the tires with red mud. I went to the door and opened it.

Standing there beside Jim was a young woman, who was, to put it mildly, a stunner. She looked like a movie star to me, even though her hair was a little tussled, like she had just gotten out of bed. She was wearing jeans and those tall boots with the white fluff around the tops, and she had on a well-fitting dark jacket with the same white fluff around the collar.

I invited them into the house, said, "Grandpa, it's the Sheriff."

"Oh, hell," Grandpa said.

Jim looked at me. "Cranky today?"

"Everyday," I said.

"I heard that," Grandpa said. "I got my hearing aid in."

We went over to his chair. Grandpa said, "Today is the all-day snake marathon, and I don't want to miss it."

"This is kind of important," Jim said.

"So's the snake marathon," Grandpa said. "It shows next time six months from now. I may not be here then."

I thought: Now that's silly. If you're not here, you're not gonna miss not seeing it.

Grandpa turned his head slightly, looked at me, and said, "I still want to see it."

"I didn't say anything," I said.

"Yeah, but you were smiling, like what I said was silly."

"It is," I said. "Why don't you just record it and watch it when you want?"

"Don't have a recorder."

"I bought you one for Christmas."

"That's what's in the box?"

"That would be it. I'll hook it up."

"Not today you won't."

"Well, it's still silly," I said.

"Not to me," Grandpa said. He put the TV on mute, looked at Jim, said, "Well, get on with it."

"Mr. Fine. Good to see you," Jim said, reaching out to shake hands. As he did, Grandpa sniffed, and smiled.

"Call me Stubble or Stubbs. It's not that I feel all that close to you, but Mr. Fine makes me feel more senior than I like. Besides, I see you from time to time. So we know one another."

"Very well, Stubbs—"

"Wait a minute," Grandpa said. "Never mind. Call me Mr. Fine. It sounds better coming out of your mouth."

"Okay, Mr. Fine."

"What's the problem," Grandpa said. He said it like a man who might already know the problem. But that's how he was, a know-it-all, who, much of the time, seemed in fact to actually know it all.

"This is Cindy Cornbluth," Jim said. "Her husband is missing. I had her follow me here to see if you could help us out. I know how you can figure things, how you can notice things the rest of us don't...Like...Well, you know, there was that time with the murders in the old theater."

"And all those other times," Grandpa said.

"Yes," Jim said, "and all those other times."

Cindy leaned forward and smiled a smile that would have knocked a bird out of a tree, and shook hands with Grandpa. I thought he held her hand a little too long. Before he let it go, he gave her face a good look, and when she stepped back, he gave her a good once-over. If he thought what I thought, that she was as fine a looking woman as had ever walked the earth, he didn't let on. His face looked as sour as ever.

"Give me the facts, and make it short," Grandpa said. "They got a round-up of the top ten most poisonous snakes coming on next, in about fifteen minutes"

"Jimmy...Sheriff. He can't possibly help us in fifteen minutes," Cindy said.

"That's how much time you got," Grandpa said. "You already made me miss the part about where one of the snake wranglers gets bit in the face."

"You've seen this before?" Jim asked.

"He has," I said. "But he never tapes it. Won't hook up the machine. He likes to symbolically capture the program in the wild."

"They got this one snake," Grandpa said, "bites this fool messin' with it, and they can't get its teeth out. It won't let go. The guy is going green, even as you watch."

"You enjoy that?" Jim said.

"Oh yeah," Grandpa said. "Rule of thumb. Don't mess with venomous snakes. Okay now, tell me what happened. Chop, chop."

"I woke up this morning," Cindy said, "and Bert was gone. That's my husband. I don't know where. I didn't think much of it. I thought he might be surprising me with dough-nuts."

"Doughnuts?"

She nodded.

"He do that often?" Grandpa asked.

"Now and again," she said.

"So, Saturday, that's his day off?"

"Not usually. But he decided not to go into work today. He can do that when he wants. He owns his own business. Construction."

"Heard of it," Grandpa said. "Cornbluth Construction. Got some big deals lately. Saw it on the news."

"That's right," Cindy said.

"Would you say he's wealthy?" Grandpa asked. "That the two of you are wealthy?"

"He's been fortunate," Cindy said.

"So, tell me the rest of it."

"I got up this morning, he wasn't home, and I waited around until noon. Then I called the Sheriff. I was worried by then."

"Did you think he might have gone into work?"

"No. It didn't cross my mind."

Grandpa looked down at Cindy's feet. "Nice boots."

"Thanks," Cindy said, and looked at Jim perplexed. Jim smiled. He knew how Grandpa was, knew he had roundabout ways, provided he was in the mood to help at all.

Grandpa called me over, said, "Get your digital camera, go out to her car—" He paused, looked at Cindy. "I did hear right that you followed Jim over?"

"That's right," she said, "but what has that got to do with anything?"

"Maybe nothing," he said. "Get photos of the car, all around."

I found the camera and went out and took photos of the car. When I came back in, I leaned over Grandpa's shoulder and he looked at the digital photos. He took off his glasses and rubbed his eyes and sighed. He put them back on, glanced at the TV and pointed.

"That's a black mamba," Grandpa said.

"What?" Cindy said.

"The snake," Grandpa said pointing at the silent TV. "Very deadly. Hides in the grass, and then, BAM, it's got

13

you. You're dead before you can say, 'Oh hell, I'm snake bit.'"

Grandpa said to me, "Grandson, turn up the heat."

I thought it was pretty warm, but I did as instructed.

"So, you two," Grandpa said to Cindy and Jim, "did you know each other before today?"

"Yes," Jim said. "In high school."

"Date?"

"Once or twice," Jim said. "Just a kid thing. Nothing came of it."

He looked at Cindy, and she smiled like a woman who knew she was beautiful and was a little ashamed of it, but...not really.

Grandpa nodded. "You know, the dirt around here is white. Except up on Pine Ridge Hill. The oil company did some drilling up there, and it was a bust. I heard about it on the news. They had to close it down. They say the old ground up there is unstable, that it's shifting, that a lot of it is going down the holes that were meant for oil drilling. It's like a big sink hole up there, a bunch of them actually. Saw that on the news, too."

"Okay," Jim said, "But, Mr. Fine, so what?"

"Here's the deal. Cindy has a rough place on her hand. Felt it when we shook. But I'll come back to that. She's also got red clay on her boots. The left one. I think she may have stomped some of it off, but there's still a touch on the toe, and a bit she's tracked in on the floor. So, she's been out there to the old oil site. I believe that she's got a bit of pine needle in her hair too, twisted up under the wave there, where it got caught in a tree limb."

Jim leaned over for a look. I gave it a hard look from where I was standing as well. Didn't that old codger wear glasses? How in the world had he noticed that?

"I drove up there the other day," she said. "I was looking for pine cones, to make decorations. I haven't washed my hair since then. I was hanging around the house, didn't have anywhere to go."

"Gonna spray them pine cones gold, silver?" Grandpa asked, not looking away from the TV.

"I don't know," she said. "Something like that."

"On your earlobe there's a dark spot. Noticed it when we shook hands. I'll come back to that"

Jim gave that a look too, said, "Yeah. I see it." Then, appearing puzzled, he unfastened his coat, took it off, dropped it over the back of a chair.

Grandpa grinned. "Warm, son?"

"A little," Jim said.

"Well now, Jim," Grandpa said. "I've known you a long time. Since you were a boy."

"Yes, sir."

"I believe you're a good man, but she didn't call you this morning. She lied and you let her."

"Now wait a minute," Jim said.

"When you shook hands with me I smelled her perfume on your coat. A lot of it. I don't think Sheriffs are in the habit of comforting women with missing husbands with a hug so intense it gets on their coat, and in their hair. And she called you Jimmy."

"Well, we know each other," Jim said. "And I did comfort her."

"Another thing. There's what we used to call a hickey on your neck."

Jim slapped at his neck as if a mosquito had bitten him.

"Not really. Just kidding. But here's what I think. I think you've been having an affair. If she had called the Sheriff's office to get in touch with you, and the two of you were not an item, you wouldn't have come to me right away. You were hoping it was simple and I could solve it without involving the Sheriff's Department. That's why you had her follow you in her car, so she wouldn't be in your car.

"And, Mrs. Cornbluth, that smile you gave me, the one that was supposed to make me weak in the knees. That seemed out of place for the situation."

"People respond in different ways," she said.

"Yes, they do," he said. "I give you that much. Would you like to take your coat off?"

"I'm fine."

"No you're not. You're sweating. In fact, it's too hot in here. Grandson, turn down the heater, will you."

"But you just told me—"

"Cut it down," Grandpa said.

I went over and did just that.

"When you and me shook hands," Grandpa said, "there was a fresh rough spot on your palm. That's because your hands are delicate, and they held something heavy earlier today, and when you struck out with it, hitting your husband in the head with whatever you were using…A fire poker perhaps? It twisted in your hand and made that minor wound."

"That's ridiculous," Cindy said.

"It certainly is," Jim said, "Okay, Mr. Fine. Me and Cindy had a thing going, but that doesn't mean she killed her husband."

Grandpa said. "Jim, you came by her house. Just like you were supposed to. I don't mean you had anything having to do with Mr. Cornbluth, but Cindy was expecting you. You had a date with her because Bert was supposed to be at work, but when you showed for your date, she told you he had stayed home, and she hadn't been able to reach you, and now he was missing and she was worried. That it wasn't like him. Right?"

"How could you know that?" Jim said.

"I guessed a little, but all the other facts line up. After she hit her husband in the head with something or another, she wiped up quick."

"But why would I kill him?" Cindy said.

"That's between you and your husband, but if you were having an affair, it might be you weren't that fond of him, and he found out, and you didn't want to lose all that money, and thought if the body wasn't found, you'd get insurance money and no jail time. The murder was quick and spontaneous, done in anger, and afterward, because Jim was coming, you had to do on-the-spot thinking, and it was stupid thinking.

"You drove the body out to the old oil well site this morning, dumped it, drove back and cleaned the car, the house, and maybe you were cleaning yourself when Jim showed up. You had to wipe yourself down quick. But that spot of blood on your ear. You missed that. And one more thing, Mrs. Cornbluth. You're sweating. A lot. That's why I turned up the heat. To see if you'd take your coat off on your own. You didn't. That made me think you had something to hide. Like maybe the blood that splashed on you from the murder wasn't just a drop on your ear, and you didn't have time to change before Jim showed up. So, you threw a coat on over it. Was she wearing it in the house when you showed, Jim?"

Jim nodded, looked at her. He said, "Cindy. Take off your coat."

"Jim, I don't want to."

"Jim isn't asking. The Sheriff is. Take it off."

Cindy slowly removed her coat. She was wearing a gray, tight-fitting wool sweater. There were dark patches.

Grandpa said, "Those wet spots on her sweater. I think if you check them, you'll find they're blood. And if you check up at the old oil site on Pine Ridge Hill, you'll find her husband at the bottom of one of those holes. You know, they were supposed to fill those in next week. If they had, good chance that body would never have been found. That's how you got the pine straw in your hair, wasn't it? When you were draggin' Bert from the car, through the pines, to the top of the hill? And, Jim, when it all comes out, that you were dallying with a married woman, while on the job…Well, I hope you keep your job."

"Yeah, me too," Jim said taking out a pair of cuffs. "Put your hands behind your back, Cindy."

"Jim. You don't have to do this. Bert found out about us—"

"Shut up! Just shut up. Put your hands behind your back. Now."

She did. He handcuffed her. She looked at Grandpa. "I hate you, you old bastard."

As they went out the front door, which I held open for them, Grandpa said, "Lots do."

Grandpa turned up the sound on the TV. Just in time. The countdown of the world's most poisonous snakes was just about to begin.

BABY PIGEONS
Reed Farrel Coleman

Fuckup: He's such a fuckup.
Fuck up: Please don't fuck up.

Look either of 'em up in Webster's and you'd understand Tommy Dushane. Tommy, as they liked to say in the Gravesend neighborhood he'd grown up in, was a royal fucking fuckup. With him it went beyond the anatomical, biological, or psychological. It was downright metaphysical, though he would have been hard pressed to pronounce the word let alone define it. He was a buffoon wrapped in a flag. His neck was red, his collar blue, and his skin a trashy white. These days he lived in a place that gave shitholes a bad name: a rickety firetrap of an illegal apartment in Central Islip that began its existence as a tool shed. Not even the illegals who had fairly overrun CI, Brentwood, and North Bay Shore would've lived in that shitbox.

To be a real fuckup, though, was to understand highs *and* lows. Fuckups weren't losers. Losers go down for the count and never get up off the mat. They live out their lives, such as they were, below the radar screen. That wasn't Tommy. Nuh uh. Tommy knew highs, several of them, a countless number. Whether it was a bad choice, an ill-timed word, or a stupid bet, he always self-destructed. Always. One of his old friends used to say that Tommy Douchebag could fuck up finding a genie bottle. When Tommy went down, he went down in flames. It got so he developed a sixth sense about it, like how animals know when an earthquake is coming. As Tommy stumbled down the aisles of the 3:14 to Ronkonkoma, blue hard hat in hand, he got that feeling. The big fuckup was at hand.

It was odd how you never saw the Tommy Dushanes of the world on their way into Manhattan, only on the trains back to Long Island from Penn Station. It was like how you never see baby pigeons. It was kinda like those fuckers just appeared whole, all grown up and ready to shit on your head. The trick was that the construction guys took the pre-dawn trains into the city, so it left the stockbrokers to ponder the baby pigeon problem of where the construction workers had come from. Although their wardrobe was strictly, Dickie and Carhartt, their shoes steel-toed Red Wings, they did not lack for quiet desperation. Some sat wondering where the money for their kids' college tuition would come from. Some would fall off scaffolds tomorrow or the tomorrow after that or...Some would die of cancer. And some would happily hold their great grandchildren in their arms.

Tommy didn't believe in silent despair. Good thing, too. He might've drowned in it. No, he was one of those guys who put his faith in Budweiser. *In Anheuser-Busch he trusted.* He had finished a six pack by the time the train had reached Bethpage and had bummed a seventh off a fellow hardhat. Never much for introspection, he didn't bother ascribing today's accelerated consumption of alcohol to that gnawing fuck up feeling in his belly. Nah, it was nothing a hot shower—his landlord let him use the basement bathroom for an extra ten bucks a month—and a few cups of coffee wouldn't fix. But right at the moment all he was worried about was finding a place to unload the seven cans worth of excess fluid.

"For fuck's sake!" he screamed loud enough for the whole car to hear. Tommy slammed a wind-chapped hand into the locked bathroom door. "What the fuck you lookin' at?" he slurred, pointing at a Wall Street type who had turned to see what the commotion was about. "Fuck you and fuck this!"

Tommy stepped into the next car and the car after that one. The handle to the bathroom in that car had been removed and replaced with a steel plate.

"How the fuck am I s'pposed to get in there?"

"Use a can opener, ya prick!"

Tommy didn't exactly recognize the voice, but it had a vague familiarity. The vagueness only enhanced by the seven beers and the distraction of a bursting bladder. But he smiled at the man who had just called him a prick, showing his chipped front teeth

"Hey, man," Tommy said as if the guy was his favorite uncle. He didn't have a favorite uncle, but if he had one, he would have greeted him like this. "What's the good word?"

The guy smiled back at Tommy, but not like an imaginary favorite uncle. No, it was more the smile of a shark. He knew Tommy didn't quite remember him and that was all to the good...Well, except for Tommy.

"Come on, I'll show you a car where the bathroom's working."

Riding the elevator up to the 27th floor of the Carillion Park West, Picassa—her "stage" name—stared intently at the cleanly shaven nape of the elevator operator's neck. For his part, the elevator operator stared at her ample cleavage reflected in the mirror-lined car. As she stared she wondered about the night ahead, what preliminaries the client had in store before the matter at hand. A show? Christ, she hoped not. She'd already sat through that inane *Finding Neverland* and the incomprehensible *The Incident of the Dog in the Nighttime* so often she knew the stage blocking better than the understudies. She never understood why they insisted on Broadway. Half of her clients didn't understand six words of

English. And the words they knew other than hello were usually: fuck, blow job, tits, and anal.

Would dinner ensue at Masa or Eleven Madison Park followed by drinks at the Algonquin or some hot rooftop bar where they could behold the skyline? Or would the client skip the prelims and go for the old suck, hump, and run? Sometimes she could tell what the night ahead held in store by what she was told to wear. Not tonight, though. Tonight could go either way. The instructions were to dress for an evening out, but not in anything with too many buttons or clasps.

The elevator slowed. A quaint, old fashioned bell chimed.

"Twenty-seven. Your floor, ma'am," the operator said, turning to have a direct view of her cleavage. He was unable to hide the smile at the corner of his mouth.

Although it was just the two of them in the large elevator car, she brushed her breasts against him as she exited. His smile grew wider still.

Stepping out of the car, the doors closing behind her, Picassa turned left as she had been instructed to do. She was now to walk down two flights and go to room 2512. *Clients*, she thought, *could be such children.* Some were just desperate to be seen with beautiful Anglo women. Some were so fearful about blackmail, about their business rivals using proof of their dalliances against them. It was bad enough she had to fuck some of them, but she especially disliked it when they made her jump through hoops to do it.

Presumably, she could have been horse-faced and dressed like a char woman as long as she could follow instructions and had breasts, lips, and a functional vagina. Checking her makeup in the hall mirror and smoothing her strapless indigo gown, she decided she more than met those prerequisites. She added a spray of perfume to her cleavage, blew herself a kiss, and walked to the stairwell door. She pushed it open.

Clients my ass! From the day she had gone into the life, she had been schooled to think of these men as clients. Never johns. Never.

If you think of them as johns, then you will think of your-self as a whore. We do not employ whores.

Those words went round and round in her head as the stairwell door slammed shut at her back. But playing pretend, regardless of profitability, had a limited shelf life. Just lately they were all johns to her, these little Asian men with their big bankrolls and eager yellow cocks. She kept telling herself she could make it a few more months, that just a few thousand more was all she needed to stake her. She could get Tommy Jr. back from her mom and get the fuck out. Out of the business. Out of New York. Out of the same atmosphere as that jerk-off who'd knocked her up and fucked up her life.

"Shit!" she whispered to no one, noticing the light was out on the landing below. Stairs of any kind were treacherous enough, decked out as she was in a form fitting gown and nosebleed stilettos. Picassa hitched up her gown with her left hand, the same hand that held her matching clutch, and took a firm hold on the cool banister with her right.

Almost fully to the dark landing, she heard a man's breathing. She froze. She let go of her gown and the rail in order to reach for the canister of pepper spray she carried in her clutch. She stumbled forward to the landing and in reaching reflexively back for the railing to catch herself, the clutch and spray vanished into the vacuum of the dark stairwell. The man in the shadows seemed to sense her fear and to reassure her, jingled his room key. She exhaled and an audible sigh of relief escaped her lips. She noticed she was panting and felt the sting of sweat against her freshly shaven underarms.

"*Konichi wa, Ichiro-san,*" she said in perfect Japanese. It hadn't been easy for a girl from Gravesend, Brooklyn to master the proper inflection. She waited for Ichiro-san's reply.

His response was universal. A strong hand shot out of the dark, grabbed a handful of her hair, and forced her to her knees. She was a little unnerved by this, but not because it had never happened before. On the contrary, she knew that sometimes they enjoyed a little danger or wanted to play out some long held masturbation fantasy. She had once doubled her fee for letting a Saudi prince watch one of his wives go down on her in a private box at the Met. He said it was a wife, but for all she knew, the woman might've been another escort. Probably was because she was awfully good at it and Picassa hadn't had to fake her orgasm.

No, there was something else about this client. His hands were too big and powerful, his palm too rough and calloused. But maybe not. His pants were expensively made and when she reached for him through the open zipper, she felt that his boxers were silken. From that point on it was automatic. She made the proper coos and sighs and placed him in her mouth. Then she showed off by taking him all the way, deeply into the back of her throat, keeping him there for quite some time. They all liked that and it usually earned her extra gratuities. Many of them would ask her to spend the night afterwards, no matter the expense, so that she might reprise the performance over and over again. Men were such uncomplicated animals.

It was only when her client's thighs stiffened and his back arched that the unease fell over her again. It was too late now. He yanked on her hair so hard her eyes teared up. It was done. Again, she made the proper ego building coos and sighs. But as she tried to stand, he held her down, pulling her hair harder, tugging her head back. Then in a flash, it came to her.

"Show me your room key!" she said, even as some of her hair pulled away from her scalp.

He showed it to her and laughed. Although the Carillion Park West was a grand old hotel, it had gone keyless last year.

Her eyes got wide with fear, her heart pounding so hard she might have been able to see her chest vibrate had there been enough light. He pulled her up off her knees, keeping her head tilted back. She opened her mouth to scream, tried to scream, but she felt a slight breeze, heard a swishing sound, felt a pinch in her neck. She gasped for air. She grabbed for her throat. Her heaving chest was warm and soaking wet, yet she was desperately cold inside. She was losing consciousness when he finally let go of her hair. She pitched forward, gravity and inertia pulling her body down. There was a dull thud when her near-lifeless body smacked onto the concrete landing below. Outside the door, in the hallway, she heard a man bitching to his wife about a grown man having to go see a silly play about Peter Pan. If she wasn't already dead, Picassa might've laughed.

After his new friend, Bobby—he said his name was Bobby—had showed Tommy where there was a working bathroom, they'd sat together for the remainder of the ride to Central Islip. Bobby was a helluva guy. He was from Gravesend, too, the old neighborhood in Brooklyn. Tommy was relieved to find out where he recognized Bobby from.

"I'm a few years older," Bobby said, "but we used to see each other around like on Avenue X sometimes or by Spumoni Gardens."

"Yeah, yeah, sure," Tommy said, still feeling the buzz from all the beers.

"Hey, Tommy, let's you and me go have a drink for old times' sake and maybe get something to eat. On me, of course."

Tommy Dushane was a fuckup, but he wasn't a stupid one. He was also a poor one because even though he had a good paying job, he was into every guy who put money on the street. He bet on everything that was bet-able and lost on everything you could lose on. He owed so much vig that he would never live long enough to see the light of day. That's why he lived all the fuck the way out here and in a shitbox the size of a half bathroom.

"Free meal. Free booze. Hell, yeah."

Now Tommy was a fucked up fuckup, maybe drunker than he had ever been and still been semi-conscious. He didn't really recognize where Bobby had taken him, though he figured it was somewhere near the railroad tracks. He didn't guess he would recognize much of anything in the state he was in, but so what? Bobby was cool. He'd treated him all night, brought him to a bar, bought him a few Jack Daniels, a cheeseburger and fries, and another JD for dessert. After that he'd given Tommy cash to go buy them a bottle of whatever he wanted at a liquor store on Suffolk Avenue.

They'd polished off the bottle of JD, sitting together on the grounds of the old college, north of the new minor league baseball stadium. They'd talked a lot about Gravesend and some of the people they knew in common. Talked about the girls they had fucked. Tommy had gone on about one in particular: Pattie Petrocelli. Talked about how she was the hottest girl in the neighborhood even when she was young.

"Man, I was fucking her since she was twelve. Taught her how to suck cock so that no one ever did it no better. Wasn't nothing I didn't teach her," Tommy bragged. "I taught her how to do it all, man. And I mean all."

"Come on, Tommy," Bobby said after Tommy had described a particularly interesting encounter with Pattie P. in the boys' bathroom at Lafayette High School. "Let's walk some of this shit off."

That was before. They had walked for what seemed like forever and Bobby had been really quiet. Tommy just figured that the booze had finally gotten to Bobby. Shit, they'd had enough to drown a freakin' elephant.

"This is good here," Bobby said, stopping in place.

"Good for what, huh?" Tommy slurred.

Bobby didn't answer. He just kind of smiled like he had on the train. Then he said, "I thought you woulda remembered me by now, Tommy Douchebag."

"Hey, man, there's no need to—"

He didn't finish the sentence because Bobby's left fist connected with Tommy's gut so hard he puked. When Tommy was done puking, Bobby grabbed Tommy by the hair, stood him up and broke his jaw with another left. Bobby was writhing in pain at Bobby's feet, making tortured squeals and screams. Bobby checked his watch and yanked Tommy by his jacket collar past some bushes, up some stairs, and onto an overpass.

"Still don't remember me?" Bobby asked again, putting his fist into Tommy's rib cage so hard that many of his ribs snapped. "You should. You sure remember a lot about my sister, Pattie."

Tommy's eyes got wide as he remembered Bobby. But Pattie's big brother was named Nick and he had been in prison when...*Oh shit!*

Bobby saw the look in Tommy's eyes and knew Tommy knew. A train whistle blew in the distance, maybe a mile or two away from the overpass.

"That's right, Tommy Douchebag."

Bobby stopped talking while he proceeded to beat Tommy into unconsciousness. Then he lifted Tommy up over the railing and dropped him right in front of the oncoming train. Bobby, Nick actually, watched as the train shredded Tommy Dushane into little pieces of fuck up beneath its wheels.

As he made his way down the steps, he noticed a bunch of sleeping pigeons on a horizontal metal beam on the underside of the overpass. He shook his head and wondered why you never saw baby pigeons, ever.

SWAN SONG
Hilary Davidson

It wasn't quite noon but Celina was on her third mimosa. I'd made them weaker than I would've for other guests, but that only made her gulp them down faster. "Alice," she stared at me intently. "If you were a man, would you want to fuck me?"

I glanced at the sunroom. My three-year-old twins, Aimee and Ava, were busy finger-painting something—hopefully paper—on the floor. They gave each other a curious little glance and went back to pretending to ignore us.

"You can't talk like that in front of the children," I whispered.

Celina took another drink, running one hand through her long platinum hair. She heaved a sigh, but her awe-inspiring chest barely deflated. When we were in our twenties, Celina's breasts had made her a favorite with *Maxim* magazine and earned her walk-on parts usually described in the script only as "the babe." Her agent had mined that hoary old trick, insuring her pneumatic assets with Lloyd's of London. A decade later, her chest was larger than ever, but no one in Hollywood seemed to care anymore. That didn't stop Celina from trying. On a quiet Sunday morning in New York, she had her extreme hourglass figure squeezed into a low-cut gold lame confection.

"Why are you asking?" I added, my voice still hushed. "You're not thinking of more surgery, are you?"

"Maybe I need to. It's not like I'm getting work. You

29

know what I was offered on Thursday? Playing a mother on some lousy sitcom. I'm thirty-six and I'm not up for leading roles anymore." Her voice was getting louder. "The juicy, sexy parts are going to twenty-two-year-old airheads who are screwing anything with a fat wallet. No wonder Marilyn Monroe killed herself when she was thirty-six. Can you picture her playing someone's mother?"

"Mommy, we don't have orange." Aimee looked over. "We need orange."

"Daddy's going to bring orange paint with him when he comes home," I promised. "He said he'd pick it up." My husband was a specialist in rehabilitative medicine at New York Presbyterian Hospital. Sunday mornings were a busy time for him.

"We need it now," Ava yelled. "We need orange!" Turning three hadn't done away with the Terrible Twos. The twins were worse than ever.

"Why don't you mix red and yellow?" I said. That earned me glares from the twins.

"Ugh, rug rats, you're giving Auntie Celina a headache." Celina's voice seeped through the room like poisonous gas. The twins settled back onto the floor, murmuring between themselves and casting furtive glances at Celina. They were fascinated by her, but never spoke to her directly.

I stood and walked into the sunroom, annoyed at Celina but unable to say so. She was so bitter these days that I could only take her presence in tiny draughts.

"Alice, where's that pitcher of mimosas?" called Celina.

"On the table," I answered, but as I glanced over, I saw that it was empty. Had Celina guzzled it down the second I'd moved away from my chair? I backtracked into the living room, picked up the pitcher, and went to the kitchen. Celina followed.

"It's so frustrating. I don't know what to do anymore," she whined. I wasn't about to press more oranges for fresh juice, so I extracted the ready-made kind from the fridge. "I'm no saint. I've slept with plenty of producers. But now, it's like I have to get on my knees just to get an audition for a shitty part I don't even want, you know?"

I poured champagne into the pitcher and stirred. "Mmm-hmm."

"I know I've got what it takes," Celina went on, pacing. "My acting coach says that she hasn't seen anyone since Cate Blanchett with talent like mine. She says the depths I can get to, the emotional honesty in my performances is just overwhelming. But how do I get to show that off? I don't have much time left if I'm going to be famous."

"It's getting harder out there all the time for actresses." I reached for the Grand Marnier. The mimosas needed just a splash. Maybe two.

"Easy for you to be smug. Not all of us can marry rich doctors and sit around all day doing nothing." Celina poured champagne directly into her glass. "Of course, I'm not saying you have it easy," she added slyly. "My grandmother always said that people who marry for money have to work hard to keep it. I wouldn't take on your life for anything."

"There's nothing I miss about Hollywood."

"You would've been a star if you stayed. But you threw it all away. For what? To be a house-mouse? This is your prize." Celina turned in a circle, lifting her hands at the stupidity of it all. My children, my husband, my Brooklyn brownstone, there was not one thing she could imagine wanting.

Sometimes it was hard to remember why Celina and I were still friends. I was fond of her when she was at her home in Los Angeles, but when she visited me, she grated on my nerves. She was my only connection to my former life as an actress. I'd met her when I'd first come to New York, a starry-eyed eighteen-year-old who'd just taken her first plane ride.

We'd been classmates at the Lee Strasberg Theatre and Film Institute and roommates at the Parkside Evangeline, the Gramercy Park residence for young single ladies that the Salvation Army used to run, before it sold the building for condos. Back then, Celina had awed me. She was just two years older, but I was from Battle Creek, Michigan, and she was the granddaughter of a Russian countess. "My family died in the Russian Revolution," she announced the day we met, speaking as dramatically as if her mother and father had just been shot by the Red Army, not four generations back. That it took me several years to even question her claim was perhaps a tribute to Celina's acting talent, or proof of what a rube I was.

"The problem with you, Alice, is you're a quitter," Celina said at lunch a week after our mimosa-fest. She'd disappeared for a few days, without telling me where, and now she was crackling with energy. "You could've been the next Naomi Watts. You could've had an Oscar! Instead you gave it all up to change diapers."

I took a bite of sea bass and tried not to grimace. Back in the day, I'd starred in a few plays so far off Broadway the cast risked falling into the Hudson. I remembered years of auditioning when I was always hungry, partly because I had no money, but usually because I was starving myself for a role. Then I'd gone to Hollywood, and all I wanted to do was forget what happened there. I forced my brain away from that unwelcome memory. It was a terrible time I'd never visit again.

"It's not like acting was the be-all of my existence. I was ready for a change," I said. "I was exhausted by trying to make it happen. Not the acting, but all the...other things." That was quite the euphemism, but I hoped Celina would pick up on what I was inferring.

"You didn't have what it takes to bask in the limelight. That's the bottom line." Celina signaled to the waiter to bring her another glass of wine. I shook my head to indicate the round was only for her. "If you did, the desire would burn through you like a thousand stars. It would be the only thing that mattered."

"There are a lot of things that matter to me. That's no one of them."

"Well, I have news," Celina said. She stared at me, waiting for me to drag it out of her. "Because I have finally made it."

"Really?"

"You can't tell anyone this," she whispered. "But Edgar Ravovitch is casting me in his next film."

"The Hippopotamus?" My mouth went dry suddenly. Celina was smiling and nodding at me. The waiter put a fresh glass of white wine down in front of her and I turned my eyes toward him. "Actually, I'll have one of those, too, please."

"I knew I'd break you out of your little house-mouse rut," Celina said. "Cheers, sweetie."

Edgar Ravovitch had been making movies for thirty years. There were two rooms in his Hollywood Hills mansion devoted to the countless awards he'd won for writing, directing and producing. But there was another, more twisted accolade he'd earned over that time. He didn't just sexually exploit women, as so many film executives did; he humiliated and degraded them, and then he sometimes destroyed them.

"Celina, you can't be serious."

"I know, he's repulsive in every way. I don't think he's taken a shower in the past decade. He's so ginormous now he has to use one of those motorized scooters to get around. Imagine having your ass grabbed by that."

The waiter put a glass of wine in front of me and I drank half of it down in one gulp. It was clear that Celina had completely forgotten what had happened to me when I'd tangled with Edgar Ravovitch. That, or my friend was actually a far better actress than I'd ever realized.

"He's a dangerous man," I said.

"He's incredibly disgusting, but he makes stars. Look at

his track record! This is the project that could put me over the top." She took another drink and shuddered. "And, Alice baby, I will have earned it. You have no idea."

"Please don't tell me you spent the past few days with him."

"He took me to Paris. Which I never really got to see, because those cobblestone streets are a bitch with a scooter." She rolled her eyes. "You're going to say that every girl sleeps with him for a part," Celina said. "That's true. That's how some of the most famous actresses in the world started out. He makes them famous. It's a trade." Celina finished the rest of her wine. "It's just business, after all. And that's how you do business with Edgar."

"There's no guarantee he'll do anything for you," I said.

"Of course he will." She narrowed her eyes at me. "Didn't he come through for you after your little interlude with him?"

I could feel my heart beating in my throat. She remembered, after all.

"Only somehow, you didn't have the nerve to go through with it. He offered you a starring role in that nineteenth-century hospital drama he made. You would've won an Oscar for sure." She peered at me with her fierce, feline eyes. "Maybe you were a little house-mouse then and just didn't realize it?"

Celina was, in many ways, the same woman I'd met at eighteen, only sharper around the edges, a diamond cut and faceted, smaller but undiminished, revealing more of the fire within. It was entirely possible that I was wrong to fear for her. She was stronger than I was, more determined. Bitterness had made her ruthless. It was quite possible she could deal with Edgar and win. I couldn't talk about what Edgar Ravovitch had done to me, so returned to her favorite subject.

"What's the film you'll be in?" My voice cracked on the question.

"It's a ghost story. You know that guy they're calling the new Brad Pitt? He's starring in it."

"And you are?"

"The ghost. The movie is going to start with the scene where I get murdered. I'm an eighteenth century English Duchess. The costumes are going to be so beautiful!" Celina hugged herself quickly. "I know it's not a big part, but it's a *prominent* part, if you know what I mean. I have the weirdest feeling, like it's going to change my life. My psychic says it will. It's finally going to happen for me, Alice! I'm going to be famous, at last."

Celina returned to Hollywood for the filming. She sent me a purloined clip of the murder scene. It was brief, but a show-stopper, and my friend was the perfect icy goddess on celluloid. When she finally came back to New York, she was wearing a new ruby ring.

"You're not engaged?" I asked, horrified.

"No! It was a treat I bought myself, for all I've been through."

"Suffering for your art."

"More than you know," she answered. "Where's the champagne?"

Celina told me more than I wanted to know about Edgar while I watched my daughters playing in the sunroom. Their latest game seemed to involve barnyard animal noises, a blessing since they didn't hear a word of what Celina said. It was also darkly appropriate, given what she told me.

"You didn't," I gasped. "How could you stand it?"

"I kept thinking if it didn't kill Catherine the Great, it wouldn't kill me," Celina shuddered. "But it was horrific. It wasn't even a full-grown horse."

"How could you do it?"

"It takes a lot to impress Edgar. He gets bored easily."

She stared at me. "Isn't that something like what he made you do?"

"No." I shook my head, pushing the memory as far from my consciousness as I could. "Not even close."

"He tied you up in his basement," Celina said, her eyes widening as she remembered the part of the story I'd been able to tell her.

I nodded slowly. "I thought I was going to die."

"Because of some light bondage?"

"It wasn't that. He opened up my veins. I thought I was going to bleed out."

Celina sat ramrod-straight. "I remember now. You were gone for days. I was worried about you! There were a couple of other blonde actresses who went missing back then. I thought you'd be another one."

I closed my eyes, forcing back the tears. "It was torture," I whispered.

"That's grotesque," Celina said, slumping back. "No wonder you ran away from Hollywood."

I couldn't tell Celina the worst part of the story. I glanced at Ava and Aimee, who were engaged in a furious exchange of oinks. If any man ever did to them what Edgar Ravovitch had done to me, I would murder him. There wouldn't be a hesitation. I wouldn't even feel a moment's guilt.

There was a long gulf of silence that opened between us.

"What I need to figure out now is what to wear to the premiere," said Celina, carrying the conversation over the terrible fault lines I'd opened up. She was oblivious to anything but herself, and I somehow found it endearing. A better friend might have pried. Celina didn't care enough to. "It's got to make a statement. It has to be memorable."

"Versace?"

Celina gave me a disapproving look that might've been a frown if she hadn't just been botoxed. "It can't be something a starlet would wear. It has to say that I have arrived. A star is born."

"Vintage Halston?"

Celina sighed. "I need to really cement myself in people's minds. Hardly anyone noticed Jennifer Lopez until she wore that dress cut down to her navel." She drank more champagne. "I need a dress that will make me famous."

The dress that Celina ultimately chose was breathtaking. She wouldn't tell me where she'd found it, or who the designer was, but it consisted of layer upon layer of sheer silk tulle with a peach body stocking underneath. There were hundreds of tiny, winking crystals sewn into the fabric, making the dress shimmer like a constellation on a summer night. On the night of the New York premiere, she got ready at my brownstone. The twins were at their grandparents' house in Queens so they wouldn't be underfoot. After her hairdresser and makeup artist left, Celina studied her reflection in the Cheval mirror in my bedroom. "Seriously, Alice, what do you think?"

"You're like some impossible combination of Jayne Mansfield and Jean Harlow. Is that even possible? You look absolutely beautiful." She truly did. Her platinum hair and pale skin made her ethereal, and no one could help but stop and stare at that dress. While I was reassuring her, the doorbell rang.

"That'll be Harry Winston," Celina said, as if the jeweler's was a personal friend. "They're letting me borrow some diamonds. Earrings worth fifty thousand dollars, or something like that." She beamed. "Just wait till I'm really famous. Then I'll get the good stuff. Necklaces worth millions." She stared at her reflection and smiled, as if envisioning her neck encircled by ropes of priceless stones. "They let you have anything you want when you're famous."

But it wasn't armed guards with jewelry, just a messenger

with a note for me. I set it on the hall table and went back upstairs to Celina. Her cell phone rang. "My agent," she sighed before answering. "So where's my bouquet?" she said to him.

There was a pause. Then all Celina said was, "What?"

She was silent for a long time, her face frozen. Her eyes were wide as the first woman to be sacrificed in any horror movie.

"He can't do that. He can't I'll sue the bastard." She listened again, her teeth gritted. "Yes, I understand. Yes, I said I get it."

She shut the phone and threw it at my mirror, shattering the glass. "I'm going to kill that bastard!" she screamed.

"Celina, what...?"

"He cut me out of the movie. He replaced me with another actress."

"I'm so sorry," I said, and I meant it. This role was everything to Celina, and it had vanished. More than that, it was an opportunity for Edgar Ravovitch to demonstrate how cruel he could be on a whim. "Can you sue for breach of contract?"

Celina turned away and her voice was muffled. "Apparently it's all kosher with the contract. That bastard Edgar even made an extra payment. Hush money. The notation on it was *Pony Express.*"

Her anguish and humiliation hit me in the chest. I went to hug her, but she pulled away. "I need to be alone, Alice."

I muttered a few words and left the room, feeling sorry for my friend, and hoping that this would be the push she needed to get out of a business that ate beautiful women alive.

The freshly delivered envelope was sitting on the hall table, where I'd dropped it. When I opened it, a blue piece of stationery fluttered out, curving through the air and landing at my feet.

It's such a shame, Alice. You would have been perfect for this role. Not the ghost, but the lead. If you'd stayed the course, you would have one at least one Oscar by now.

I recognized the handwriting, but even without that cue, I would've recognized the stench of Edgar Ravovitch anywhere. There was a heavy musk of sweat and blood desperation that hung around him like a shroud. It was in everything he touched. Suddenly, I was twenty-eight again, trapped in Edgar's basement dungeon for days. I'd thought I would die. Instead...

I rushed up the stairs. Celina was on the floor, sobbing as if her heart might break.

"How badly do you want to be famous?" I asked her.

She stared up at me. "You know I'd do anything."

"I can make it happen for you."

"Alice, have you lost your mind?" She made a strangled laugh through her tears "You're a Brooklyn house-mouse with two little rugrats. What on earth could you do?"

"I can give you exactly what you need. You can take my story and make it yours."

"I don't understand what you're saying."

"When I was trapped at Edgar Ravovitch's house, I wasn't the only actress in his dungeon. There was another girl there. Remember Contessa Kruzic?"

"Of course I do. That little witch stole a part right out from under me. I hated her." She stared at me, uncomprehending. "When she went missing, I felt kind of guilty, like maybe I'd caused it by hating her so much."

"Edgar had both of us tortured. He tied us up, starved us, and then had us both bled until we were weak as newborn kittens. Then he left us with nothing but a knife."

Celina's face went white as the ghost she'd played. "A knife?"

"He told us only one of use could leave the room alive.

The one that did would star in his next film. Remember the one about the nineteenth century nurse? The one that won five Oscars? That was the film." I sank to my knees in front of her. "I killed her, Celina. I crawled to the knife before she got to it. With the last bit of strength I had, I stabbed her in the leg. She'd already lost so much blood. She died quickly."

"You?" Celina breathed, her eyes fixed on mine. "You did that?"

"Not for the role. I didn't want to die." I stared at her, desperate. "Can you understand that? I just wanted to live. That's why I ran away afterwards. I didn't want fame after that."

"I thought Edgar was just a sexually exploitative freak..." she breathed.

"Edgar's sexual peccadilloes are just a little hobby on the side," I said. "His real lust is for blood. The actresses he's helped are the ones who came out of his little torture chamber. There are at least two others in freezers in his basement. He showed them to me when I was there. Mila Montgomery and Petra Jordan."

"Edgar killed them?"

"I think they were trapped in the same way I was. He has the girls kill each other, but the blood is all on his hands." I took a breath. "Look what he sent me tonight."

I handed her the note and watched her face morph from sorrow to rage. There was enough competition between us, even now, that the idea I could have been the leading lady in the film made her soul burn.

"That bastard," she seethed. "I really am going to murder him."

"That's exactly what I was thinking," I said. "Go to the premiere. Stick a knife into him. You'll be arrested, but when you are, you're going to tell the police what happened to you. How Edgar tortured you. How he killed other girls. How he's responsible for the death of Contessa Kruzic."

"But they'll blame me."

"You're the victim, Celina. You're like a hostage with Stockholm Syndrome. Edgar terrorized you to the point where you couldn't tell up from down, right from wrong."

Her tears were dry, and she was nodding. "I've been the victim, all this time." She was mentally preparing in the way we'd learned at the Lee Strasbourg School, internalizing a role until it rang true, until we were inseparable from it.

"Maybe he told you he wouldn't hurt other girls if you did what he said," I suggested. "I don't know. That's your part of the character to fill in. But the bottom line is, he's a monster and you're the one getting justice for all the women he's destroyed."

She nodded, now deep in thought, and got to her feet. "I need to fix my makeup," she said.

That night, Edgar Ravovitch's sensational murder dominated the news. The first headline I saw was, *Larger-than-life director Edgar Ravovitch attacked by deranged diva at premiere.*

It was a fortunate thing that the twins were staying at their grandparents' house. That meant I could stay up late, watching the news come in over a hundred different websites, each building a new detail on what that last one had. When my husband came home, he peered in as me, hunched over my laptop.

"What's so interesting, babe?" he asked, coming into the room and kissing the top of my head.

"There's a director, a monster who abused Celina for years. She finally struck back. Here, read this." I turned the computer so he could read the latest on TMZ, and I watched his face. He was so handsome, not at all like a leading man, but in a slightly rumpled, bespectacled way that made me feel safe.

"This is horrifying," he said. "Do you think it's all true?"

"They say the police have already gone to his home and found the bodies in freezers in his basement." My voice was shaky. "He made actresses literally fight to the death for starring roles in some of his films."

I could feel a shudder run through him. "That's insane. How could anyone..."

"I don't know," I said, standing to hug him. "I can't understand it. But I believe Celina. I know this guy is guilty. I've met him. He is evil personified." I took a couple of sharp breaths. "I'll have to testify for her in court. I don't want the girls dragged into anything, but I'll need to..."

"Don't worry about the girls. They're too young to understand whatever craziness Auntie Celina got herself into." He glanced at the screen again. "I'm so glad you left La-la-Land when you did, Alice. Those people are out of their heads." He kissed me again. "Do you want to stay up and talk?"

"Let's just go to bed. Give me a couple of minutes."

He left the room and I looked at the screen again. The front page of the *New York Times* had loaded again. There was a huge photograph of Celina at the preview, just after she'd been arrested. Her platinum hair fanned out around her like a halo, and her sheer dress made her look almost as naked as a Roman statue. But her face was the most mesmerizing thing of all. Her perfect features were in stark contrast with her haunted eyes, brimming with loss and sorrow. *Avenging Angel*, read the headline. Under it were the words *Celina St. Cyr Slays Monster Who Murdered Missing Starlets*.

In the space of a few hours, the director with the household name had fallen and a new star had arisen. I touched the screen, my index finger at the hollow of Celina's chiseled cheekbone.

"I always knew you'd be the famous one," I said, and closed the screen.

THE STARRY NIGHT
Grant Jerkins

One

The stars. My God, the stars.

Is what Mr. Landay thought as he looked out the living room window and contemplated his plan. The swirling night-time sky. The universe expanding. He imagined Vincent van Gogh, in all his self-injurious, bugfuck crazy glory, had gazed upon much the same sight outside his asylum window those many years ago.

Mr. Landay had given his plan a great deal of thought. He was a careful man. And a patient man. He learned patience from the stars. The stars abide.

Mr. Landay had no intention of ever getting caught.

For starters, Mr. Landay never perused his interests online. Never. That was the number one no-no as far as Mr. Landay was concerned. He simply did not understand these men who pursued their hobby in chatrooms and message boards, or via instant messages and texts and photo exchanges and the myriad other electronic ways in which children could be had. Tricked, mislead, blackmailed, et cetera. Why, you couldn't even turn on the news without seeing some weak-chinned schmo with an uneven goatee blinking under the hot lights. Caught. Caught red-handed meeting up with a child he'd enticed online. Why weren't people more careful? Discreet?

If it wasn't that, then it was footage of FBI agents carrying hard drives out of homes to catalog the caches of thousands upon thousands of illegal images their forensic technicians divined from the digital depths of said hard drives. Then the feds sifted through your contacts and next thing you knew they would say you were part of an organization. A child molestation ring. And if one of your fellow hobbyists happened to live in Canada or something, then they would be crowing about you being the lynchpin in an international ring of child pornographers. And when would people learn the simple art of discretion? The stars, the planets. They were discreet. The universe was discreet.

Mr. Landay was a big believer in discretion. Discretion was an art, and Mr. Landay an artist.

The Internet was not safe. It had never been safe. If you used the Internet, you would be caught.

The downside to discretion was that one did not get the opportunity to wallow in one's basest desires. Chances to indulge those proclivities—safe chances—were few and far between.

Over the years, Mr. Landay had experienced some mild successes. Nothing epic, though. He was still waiting for the one experience that would define him. Someone to be Ryan O'Neal to his Ali MacGraw. There had been a neighbor boy whom he'd caught setting fires. Blackmailed him. That had lasted almost three months. Until the boy's family had moved away. Even though the boy remained emotionally detached (perhaps clinically so), Mr. Landay missed him. He had been deeply troubled, and Mr. Landay hoped he would find peace in this world.

There were the twins. Alicia and Alice. His sister's girls. But he'd never felt right about that. It had been wrong. And he was certain they'd been too young to remember. If they did remember, they certainly gave no indication when he saw them over the holidays. Although Alice was apparently a lesbian now. Transgendered. Something like that. And Alicia was filling her skin with tattoos. Just filling herself up, inking herself like she thought human beings were blank coloring books in need of a crayon.

Unlike some, Mr. Landay did not differentiate between boys and girls. All that mattered was their essence. Their goodness. Their scent. The smell of children. He inhaled it. Savored it. He was driven. Compelled. Even though he knew he would spend eternity in hell (deservedly so,) it was worth it.

He could not stop. But he could be careful. Safe.

Mr. Landay had worked at the hospital in a janitorial capacity for all of his adult life. Environmental Services. It was a good job with decent pay, and he had taken on more and more responsibilities over the years, so that he now oversaw the safe disposal of biohazard and infectious waste materials—he ran the incinerator.

He oversaw the destruction by fire of bloody gauze, pus filled dressings, urine soaked pads, biopsied tissue samples, excised tumors, aborted fetuses, amputated fingers toes hands breasts limbs etc. He went from floor to floor gathering red bags and sharps boxes onto his special cart. During busy times, when the combustion chamber never even got to cool down between loads, the different departments brought the red bags down to him. Delivered them to him. And all he had to do was keep the temperature up to state regs and keep an eye on the exhaust readouts and keep the numbers within BACT and MACT air standards.

The blue Moss Incinerator had been upgraded and computerized some few years back, so that now much of those environmental and regulatory standards were kept within limits by the computer. Fluid levels, air injection, HHV's, airborne particulate. All of it was automated. But Mr. Landay had had the higher ups thinking that he alone was qualified to keep the fire breathing dragon in line. Job security. He called himself a specialist in the field of biomedical waste management, but in reality he was nothing more than a bumpkin with a pitch fork and burning barrel.

It had crossed his mind that if he ever got into a situation in which things got out of control—for whatever reason—then he would have an out. He would have a way to destroy the evidence. It was funny. Even though Mr. Landay understood that he was a diseased human being, he was still essentially human, and most people's initial reactions were just like his when viewing the incinerator for the first time. They had the same thought that he'd had when he'd first seen it. Invariably they asked Mr. Landay if he thought the big blue steel Moss Incinerator could be used to destroy the evidence of a murder. And Mr. Landay always told them what old Mr. Kennestone had told him in his shaky old-man voice when he trained Mr. Landay on the pre-upgraded machine many years ago: It would cook you. Cook you down to bones.

Mr. Landay did not think it would ever come to that. Hoped not. He was not that kind of man.

Although there had been opportunities over the years, chances for quick and unseemly grope sessions, or even long cons to build parasitic relationships with ill or injured children and their parents (single mothers were prime opportunities, single mothers of sick children were begging for exploitation), Mr. Landay had not sought to indulge his peculiar proclivities via his position at the hospital. Don't shit where you eat. Don't get high on your own supply. Et cetera and so forth.

Play it safe. That was his motto. His parents were still alive. And the thought of his mother or father becoming aware that their son was a monster, well, that was just too much. Play it safe. And that's what he had done. Until just recently.

He had seen an opportunity. A glorious opportunity.

Since there were times when orderlies and aides and the like in various departments throughout the hospital were tasked with gathering the red bag biohazard materials from their respective departments and delivering the infectious waste items to Mr. Landay for incineration, he was brought into contact with a wide range of low-level employees.

There was one young woman in particular, a little retarded girl who worked in the Children's Cancer and Blood Disorder Clinic. A sweet thing. Retarded. A little short plump roly-poly of a thing. Amy. Her mind was as simple and clear as the sky over a Nebraska cornfield. Mr. L was drawn to her. To her innocence. To her childlike nature.

A friendship blossomed between them. She often came downstairs and ate lunch with Mr. L, scribbling in her diary while the two of them ate near the cardboard baler, their table a compressed cube of empty boxes. She just scribbled away in her hot pink Hello Kitty Dream Diary. That's what she did. "I a writer," is what she told him. Cute.

And he could tell she was sort of dressing up for him. Bright pink eyeshadow with sparkles in it. Pink sparkly polish on her nails. Stardust. That's what she called it. Pink stardust. Poor thing. Looked garish. Clown-like. Stardust indeed. Billion-year-old carbon.

And it would have been a simple thing to capitalize on that friendship. To gain and then betray her trust. To convince her to do things for him in the name of their friendship. She would do anything to avoid offending him. To avoid hurting her friend's feelings. Oh, the things he could make her do by manipulating her emotions. It would have been so easy. But, in the end, although she was innocent and like a child in so many ways, she simply was not a child. Physically, she was an adult woman. She did not smell like a child. She did not have a child's body. A child's mind, yes, but Mr. Landay required the whole package. He was not one to settle.

And so Mr. Landay was unable to perceive how his position at the hospital could help in that particular area of his life. Until last month. Something had happened when staffing was tight, and Mr. Landay was required to go up into the hospital and retrieve the red bag materials from the various floors.

He had been pushing his stainless steel cart through the Children's Cancer Clinic, gathering red bags like a migrant field worker, plucking up a bumper crop of sharps boxes. He stopped and chatted with Amy. And he lingered. He lingered because the entire floor smelled of children. It was an olfactory overload. He could happily live his life out in such an environment.

And as he lingered and chatted and savored, Mr. Landay noticed something. Something caught his eye. He'd seen this thing many times before, but the ramifications of it had never struck fully home. Until now.

Mr. Landay noticed that inside this fortress of a hospital with its privacy and security measures firmly in place, inside a children's ward in which a single adult male would be eyed with suspicion, would be asked countless times, May I help you, sir? Within all of this, there was a certain group of individuals who had free rein. There was a class of people on this floor who could come and go as they pleased, unchallenged. A type of person who had complete access to every child in the clinic—no ID or employee badge required. They were allowed to approach children and interact with them and build relationships and gain their trust. To forge alliances with children who were sick and completely dependent up adult intervention and guidance.

There was a way that Mr. Landay could walk onto this floor in complete and utter anonymity and never be questioned as to the nature of his presence here. And if by chance he ever was challenged, asked to provide ID, he could say that he left it in his street clothes, go out to retrieve it, and never come back.

It took him a month of carefully examining his plan from every possible angle before he actually accepted that it was as foolproof as he believed it to be. This was the opportunity of a lifetime, the stars had truly aligned, and Mr. Landay was damned if he was going to let it pass him by.

Once he was sure, he went out and purchased the necessary supplies. And he placed "emergency kits" in various hidey holes throughout the hospital. Just in case. Always have a plan B.

And if anyone ever did become suspicious, if there ever was any danger of detection, why he had an eye on the inside, didn't he? He had Amy. She wouldn't let him down.

Two

I a writer. Down sindome. I a writer. I a retarded. I work here. I Amy. I work here hospital little kids. I a retarded. I used work to the workshop with other retardeds. Put together piece metal make things. Miss Brooks-Lane she get me job hospital. I love the little kids. I love babies. I love Miss Brooks-Lane. Thank you Miss Brooks-Lane.

I love the babies the little children. They sick. My god they sick. The little children. They have the cancer. I a retarded. The little children they love me. They have the cancer. In they blood. In they brain. In they bones. Lukeemia. The little kids be bald no hair. I work here. I help them. They say I help them. They love me. I get paid. Paycheck. Twice week month. Mr. Crandell my supervisor. He nice. Funny. Make Amy laugh. He bald too no hair like children. But no cancer. He say his hair fall out. He say his hair saw his face got scared run away. He funny. I love Mr. Crandell too. He married man name Kip. Funny.

I get paid. Paycheck. No more workshop. I get paid. Sometime I hold the hand little children when they put the needle. Little children no like needle. Amy no like needle. Amy be brave little children. It hurt. It hurt bad. The little children cry. The Mommy Daddy cry too. They all cry. I hold they hand too. They feel better. I get paycheck. Paid. Twice week month. I have bank account. Checkcard. Visa.

Sometime no stop baby mommy daddy cry. I no stop. I take picture my phone. Everybody smile picture. That my secret. Everybody smile picture. Get it? Mr. Crandell say delete HIPAA. Privacy. No picture break rule privacy HIPAA. I say okay delete. But it work. Stop little children crying mommy daddy too. Smile.

Mr. Crandell funny. Ha ha. Jokes. I love him. Bald.

The cancer everywhere. Little children. My god they sick. I sad. Cry at night alone sometime I think about it. No cry at work. I strong. Get paid.

The clown come to the cancer clinic. Lots of clown. Boy clown. Girl clown. Sometime I no tell boy or girl clown. Just clown. I no like the clown. Why clown? Sometime little children cry see clown. Scared clown. Why clown for cancer? No understand.

One clown come in. Bad clown. Man clown. No see his face. You no see his face. He be anybody. Nobody ask see his badge. Nobody ask see his picture card who he is. Nobody ask see band on wrist. No band. He could be anybody. Why nobody ask who that clown? I ask. Who that clown? Who that clown? I no like that clown.

The mommy and daddy and little baby go in tranfoosion room. Where they stick the needle good medicine that kill the cancer make hair fall out. Hurt make baby sick but kill the cancer. The mommy daddy they worried about they little baby no see they little child daughter go off. She go walk around. No want to see needle. They have video game all over place. Ms. Pac-man. Galaga. Free. No quarter. It free. And anybody can play for free and sometime I play Ms. Pacman for free and Mr. Crandell say we no pay Amy to play video game. He say get back to work. But it okay for Amy to play video game with the little children. That why I here. Make friend. Make feel good. Make no think about cancer.

Sometime too I empty trash and take BIOHAZARD downstair Mr. Landay burn it up. Safe. He my friend too. He no funny but talk Amy make feel good. Important. He no treat retarded. And too I put toilet paper bathroom. Sometime rubber glove give nurse pee-pee cup left in bathroom. Rubber glove. Latex. But I hold people hand picture take make feel better. Smile. That my job. I get paid. Help people. Check. My name.

The little girl daughter she walk around. The mommy daddy worry about baby boy needle in his arm bag of likwid medicine take long time put all that medicine in little arm. Sad. I sad for them.

Daughter she play Ms. Pac-man like me. I play with her little bit. That okay. I be friend to her. I make people feel good welcome Mr. Crandell say okay.

Bad clown he watch us.

I have the down sindome. I say that already. Eyes slant look in mirror. Chinese. I a retarded. I know.

Mr. Crandell say go downstair get more special wipe they use to clean. BIOHAZARD. Mr. Crandell say get more. I get more.

Bad clown watch me get on elevator. He watch the daughter girl. Her mommy daddy no watch her. They no watch her. I no watch her. Elevator. She alone.

I come back. Special wipes. ANTIMICROBIAL. The clown he gone. The daughter girl she gone. Then Amy see daughter girl. She cry. She sad tears. The mommy daddy they think tears baby cancer. No baby cancer. No. Daughter girl cry clown. Daughter girl cry clown.

Bad clown gone.

Bad clown back. Another day. Bad clown back. He bad.

Nobody see clown. Notice. They think normal. I no think normal. I think bad. Amy notice. Amy see.

Boy with cancer. Brain. Bald head stitches. Boy head stitches like baseball. Clown friend boy. Galaga. No boy. Clown no friend.

I tell Mr. Crandell bad clown. I say Mr. Crandell that clown bad no good. Mr. Crandell think I scared clowns. I no scared clowns. He bad clown. I tell. I tell him. Mr. Crandell no understand retarded words. Amy not talk good. Some people scared clowns he say. It okay he say.

It not okay.

I spy clown. Amy watch. Follow.

He in bathroom with boy. Little metal door in bathroom wall. I know. Sometime Amy get pee pee cup for nurse. Rubber glove. Universe precaution. Use metal door. They leave pee pee cup in wall.

I go other side of metal door. Nurse area. I open little metal door. No pee pee cup. I no supposed open both door see inside bathroom. Wrong. Privacy. HIPAA.

I open both door. See inside. No see anything. I put my phone camera through. Stick arm through. All the way. Amy take picture.

I do wrong. Amy do bad wrong. Privacy. HIPAA. They told me privacy. Respect. I look at picture. Bad picture. Bad wrong. Nasty.

What do? What do? I break rule. No want get fire. Miss Brooks-Lane disappoint in me. She get me job. No want get fire. Amy love my job. Paycheck. Help people. I a writer.

Clown see me look at picture. I look at him. He look at me. He know. I know.

He try talk me. Say see pretty picture. He say he help little children feel good. Like me. He no like me. He say what your name. Amy. He say you pretty Amy. You want go get candy. He talk like I a retarded.

I scared. I think Mr. Landay.

Three

This was very, very, very bad. Likely the worse ever. Mr. Landay had been caught. Red handed. Caught by his friend, Amy. In flagrante delicto. Photographic evidence. In blazing offence. The retarded girl need only push the wrong button and that photograph would be bouncing around in outer space, circling the globe ten times over before Mr. Landay could draw even a single breath. Very bad indeed. Mr. Landay had never been in such a predicament.

Of course he recognized Amy's sparkly nail polish (*stardust*) as soon as the hand holding the phone had emerged cobra-like through the sample pass-through door. The dual-access biological safety cabinet. The chart room, he knew, was on the other side. The pink iPhone with its sparkly skin. There was even time to see the phone display the captured image on its four-inch widescreen high resolution retina display. It was strikingly clear. A little off center. A bit tilted. But the focus was spot on, the clarity alarming. It was bad, very bad indeed.

He left the boy behind. No need to smooth the edges. No need to speak to him one last time of that special bond they shared. The need for secrecy. Of how his parents were already under unbearable strain worrying about the boy's cancer, et cetera, et cetera, so forth and so on. No, no need for any of that refinery. The jig was up. What he needed was to get the hell out of here before sweet precious Amy started showing that photograph to anyone who was willing to indulge the demands of a little retarded woman.

The immediate task at hand was to get off this floor before he was stopped and questioned. He would never be back here again. This was a dead socket to him now. A black hole. The immediate task at hand was damage control. First get off the floor. And it might be that was all he needed. For, really, what did Amy have? She had a photograph of a boy and a clown. Engaged in inappropriate behavior. A clown and a boy. It had nothing to do with Mr. L. He still had his anonymity. He was pretty sure. It all depended on Amy.

He was an unidentified man in oversize floppy shoes, an orange shock wig, red bulbous nose, Liza Minnelli eyebrows, and heavy white greasepaint. Unrecognizable. Untraceable. Unless. Unless Amy had somehow recognized him. As he had recognized her sparkly fingernails. Unless there was a tell of some kind. But he didn't think there was. He was a careful man.

She was retarded, but she was perceptive in her way. He had to know. Before he got off this floor, he had to know if she recognized him. And it wouldn't be a bad idea to destroy that phone.

Mr. Landay walked past nurses and aides and phlebotomists and oncologists and hematologists and he took the time to toot his little plastic horn at some of the children. And even in his current state, he was aware of the fragrance they were giving off. Then he saw her. Ahead, in the elevator vestibule. Amy. Looking at that damn phone. She looked up at him. He looked at her. There was fear in her puffy, slanted eyes. Anger too, it looked like. And maybe recognition. Was that recognition? Did she recognize him? He had to know.

Mr. Landay knelt down beside Amy and asked if he could see the pretty picture. She shook her head in defiance. And Mr. Landay had a sense that this girl could be capable of violence. Amy. Violence. Not possible, he once would have thought.

"What's your name, pretty girl?" Mr. Landay asked. Soothing.

"Amy." It was a bark. A bark from a dog warning off a bigger predator.

"There's a candy machine downstairs. Can I buy you a candy bar? I was only trying to help the sick boy. Like you do."

The control panel dinged and Mr. Landay and Amy both looked up to see the elevator doors whoosh open. Then, without realizing what had happened, Mr. Landay was flat on his back, sprawled across the floor. Amy had pushed him. Hard. She had, as they used to say back in school, knocked him on his ass.

He tilted his head to watch her walk into the elevator. Her Hello Kitty Dream Diary and pink-skinned iPhone clutched to her bosom. And those mongoloid eyes of hers were heavy lidded with defiance.

The doors closed and Mr. Landay picked himself up. There were people around, but no one seemed overly concerned with a fallen clown. He watched the lighted display cycle through the floor numbers as the elevator descended. Cycling lower and lower. But it did not stop at the first floor where Hospital administration was housed and Amy could have found any number of interested parties with whom to share her multi-media presentation. Nor did it stop at M where security officers and other Personnel milled about and the cafeteria drew all manner of people. And on past L it went, where once again the good people of the world would be anxious to hear her tale. The elevator ultimately stopped at the very last destination available. LL.

Lower Level. Landay Land.

And it finally dawned on him. As though God had intervened on Mr. Landay's behalf. God loved all his children equally. Mr. L understood that now. A smile perched on his blood red lips. Not only did she not recognize him in the clown makeup, but Amy was actually going to the Lower Level to seek comfort and solace from her good friend, Mr. Landay.

He punched the wall button with his white-gloved finger to call the elevator up. He had to hurry. He wasn't even sure where the stairs were. He wasn't a young man anymore, in any case. A little Mexican girl and her family wandered up

and waited for the elevator with him. Probably going downstairs for a bite to eat. The little girl was pushing a rolling IV
stand. Her chemotherapy. The elevator arrived, but he didn't
want them witnessing his destination. As he pushed the girl
out of his way, the IV tubing popped free from the venous
catheter in her arm, spraying little droplets of poison. She
started crying.

Mr. L's eyes twinkled with genuine delight under his arc
de triumph eyebrows as the elevator descended. He got off
on seven, where he had stashed a bag of necessities in the
acoustic tiled ceiling of a seldom-used bathroom just outside
Bariatrics.

He was already feeling better. The situation could be contained. He thought of the swirling stars, the universe expanding, and he knew that in very real sense the outcome
had already been decided. Poor Amy. This had already happened and would happen again. Faulkner was right. The
past isn't dead. It's not even past. Van Gogh knew it too.
And so did Mr. Landay.

Poor Amy. Maybe she knew it too.

Four

I think Mr. Landay. He help Amy.

It cold down here. Amy scared. Nervous.

Mr. Landay help me. He my friend. Mr. Landay listen
Amy. Where Mr. Landay? He no here. I sit. I write. I look
picture on phone. Bad picture. I put it Facebook? No. Nasty.
I wait Mr. Landay. He help Amy.

I get lonely. Scared. Where Mr. Landay? Me leave. Show
Mr. Crandell. Mr. Crandell mad about HIPAA. Patient pri-
vacy. No picture. I tell. I better not show Mr. Crandell nasty.
I write. I wait. Long time. Need help.

Somebody come. I hear. I see. Mr. Landay. Everything be
ok. Amy feel better.

"Amy! How you doing, sunshine?"

Mr. Landay call me sunshine. I like. "Mr. Landay, I got trouble. Big trouble."

Mr. Landay understand retarded words. Some people no understand Amy.

"Big trouble? Oh no! Maybe I can help. I bet I can. You just sit right here at my desk."

Mr. Landay desk piece wood two block. He funny sometime. Sometime no. He burn trash. BIOHAZARD. I give Mr. Landay phone. He look see.

"Bad clown touch boy."

"Bad clown, indeed. Although I don't think he's actually touching him. No, it looks to me more like he just wants to be close. Yes, I think that's all it is. He just wants—now, Amy, did you get permission to take this photograph?"

"No sir, no permission. Bad clown hurt boy."

"No, no, I really don't think he's hurting the boy. Are you sure the clown wasn't just a doctor dressed up like that?"

"Doctor?"

"Yes, they do that sometimes. Dress up like clowns. I thought you knew. Did you show this to anyone?"

Mr. Landay hand me back phone. "No. I no show."

"Not even Mr. Crandell?"

"No. He get mad. HIPAA."

"There's something wrong with his hip? He hurt himself? I hope he and that, uhm, Kip fellow, didn't overdo it."

"No. Not hip. Hip-ah. Private. HIPAA."

"Oh, yes, yes, yes. Health Information Privacy something something. I'd forgotten about that. I'm afraid this photograph is a clear violation of HIPAA policy. A clear violation. I hate to say this, Amy, but you could lose your job."

"Love job. Paycheck. Help people. Love job."

"I know dear, but if anybody ever found out you took this photograph, it would mean automatic termination. You just can't take pictures of people using the bathroom."

"Termnation?"

"Dismissal—you'd be fired. No job."

Amy grab Mr. Landay. Hold him. I cry. I cry. Can't help. I cry. Say, "Please no tell, Mr. Landay. Please no tell. I do anything. No tell. Amy do anything."

Mr. Landay push Amy back. Look in Amy eye. He say Amy I no tell. He say Amy I no tell but we break phone camera be sure.

"You see the wisdom, don't you? If we destroy the phone, no one will ever know."

Delete, I say. Delete. Easy. Show how.

"No, I'm afraid that's just not good enough. These things hold onto information. You just can't trust them. Believe me, I know, Amy."

Mr. Landay walk across room. He push button on big metal fire maker. Loud buzz. It whoosh. Rumble. Fire.

"I'm afraid we have to burn it, Amy. It's the only way to be sure."

"No want to."

"You want to keep your job?"

"Yes. Job keep."

"You want Mr. Crandell to call the HIPAA authorities?"

"No."

"Because if he does, and they confiscate your phone and find that photograph, you could end up behind bars."

"Bars? Amy?"

"What I'm saying is Amy go jail."

Burn phone I say and give phone. No want phone. Want everything be okay again. Be over. Bad day. Bad clown. Over.

Mr. Landay throw phone in fire. Metal door bang shut it scare Amy.

"That's it, Amy. It's all over. Like it never happened. Every-thing normal. Never speak of this again. If you pretend that it never happened, then it never did. Okay?"

Okay okay okay I say okay grab hold Mr. Landay love

him happy he help Amy no trouble gone. Give big hug. I squeeze. He no like touch. It okay. I give big hug. I see white paint behind Mr. Landay ear. I touch. I show white finger Mr. Landay. Oh my he say. He say oh my.

I say white like clown. Bad clown. Mr. Landay?

Oh Amy Mr. Landay say. He sad. I see he sad. I no wish you do that he say. I say sorry white paint like clown face.

Then I no breath. Amy no breath. Mr. Landay he choke Amy. Hands hurt. No breath. Hurt. Why? I no understand. Amy a retarded. Why? He squeeze. Amy no breath. Face hot. Tired. Sleepy. No breath. I look. I see Mr. Landay eyes. They dark. Amy sleepy. Eyes like night. So dark. I get lost. Mr. Landay eyes. Dark. Swallow Amy up. Amy lost in the dark. See specks light. Dots light in the dark. They stars. Amy see the stars. They swurl turn. The stars. My god the stars.

Five

Mr. Landay was crying. It was just so unutterably sad. Poor Amy. Poor dead thing. He never thought any of it would ever come to this. Yet on some level, he must have, because he had planned for it, hadn't he? He planned for everything. Plan B. Plan C. Plan D. So forth and so on. But even though he'd planned for it, given it thought, he'd never considered himself capable. He in fact had no idea if he was capable of that kind of violence until right this minute. But he was. He was. Poor Amy. A sweet soul.

Mr. Landay cracked the torpedo-hatch door on the big blue Moss. It was still hot inside. He set about cleaning off some carbon deposits clinging to the walls of the combustion chamber. He wanted Amy to have a clean burn. Carbon. That's all we are. Stardust.

He set the solution level to the hottest burn possible. Everything looked good. The Old Blue Lady, that's what he called her. She could handle a lot. But she couldn't handle a whole adult body just tossed in there. No. He would have to feed it smaller pieces. Break the load down and send it in inside the stainless steel cart. He put on his surgical mask and gown as was correct protocol when dealing with bio-medical waste. In the toolbox he found a hacksaw and a hammer that would be good for the bones. That should do it. Whatever was left after incineration he could run through the sharps shredder.

It was just that his parents were still alive. Mr. Landay simply couldn't risk getting caught. Bringing shame to them. He was sorry for Amy. So sorry. But it wasn't like killing a regular human being. Amy was Amy. Maybe they would meet again. Out there in the universe. Their carbon mingling.

He went to check the solution levels and air feed to the secondary chamber one last time before he set about the task of reducing Amy.

Six

I wake up. Floor cold. Dirty. I miss the stars. Stars wake me up. Stars make me sleep. Swurling. I alive. I Amy. Throat hurt. Bad. Mr. Landay stand over fire door. Buzzing. Whoosh. Loud. He bad. Kill Amy. Choke hurt. No breathe. Dark eyes. See stars. Touch boy. Touch girl. Bad clown. Kill Amy. Burn me up. I know. He burn Amy. Gone.

I get up. Amy get up. Amy not scared. Amy mad. Mad. I mad. Little children. Cancer. Throat hurt. Swallow. Hurt. See Mr. Landay. Mr. Landay stand front fire. Senterator. I run. Push. I push. Push hard. Mr. Landay look at Amy. He surprise. Eyes big. Dark. No stars. Him fingers grab hold edge door. Hold on. I push again. Harder. Mr. Landay hold on. He scared. He say Amy. No Amy. Amy stop. Please Amy stop. I hurt. He say I hurt. Mr. Landay hurt. Please Amy. Sweet girl. He call Amy sweet girl. I let go help Mr. Landay. He my friend. He kick Amy. Trick. Kick Amy private part no man touch tell Mama. It hurt. Hurt bad. Amy private part no man touch tell Mama hurt bad. Mr. Landay smile. He say word Amy no understand. Ugly word. He come at Amy. Hit kick punch swing. Mean. Crazy.

I see hammer floor. Amy pick up hammer. Amy swing. Hit. Right between the eyes. Hit hard. Blood. Bone break. Mr. Landay fall backward. He fall. Fall into metal door. Senterator. Fire. Mr. Landay fire scream. Shut door. Amy shut door. But Mr. Landay loud. Scream. Clown scream. Burn him up. HIPAA okay. I tell Mr. Crandell. He funny.

Amy sad. Amy happy. Amy tired. What happen? Amy sit down. Tired. Throat hurt. Finger hurt. Finger broke. Fingernail broke. Broke off. Stardust. Burn up.

I Amy. I a retarded. Down Sindome. I Amy. I a writer.

COPPER
Keith Rawson

You know what I find most interesting about you, Cole?
What's that?
Fear of failure. You're afraid that no matter what you do in life, you'll fall on your face and humiliate yourself.
Is that right?
Don't get me wrong, it's just not you. Most people suffer the same. That's why America is nothing but a nation of slaves. A people so afraid of failure that they scramble their entire lives to make billions of dollars for people who weren't afraid to fail. Do you know how sad it makes me to say that, Cole?

This is the third time I've heard this speech. The first time, I was in awe. His words were cryptic, but relevant, near prophetic. The second time, I gave a low snort. I'm not the type of person who needs to hear the same thing twice, it sticks, even if it's something simple like wipe the shit off your shoes before you come inside, or remember to hold your pinkie up when drinking tea with your great aunt Bertha. I'm good at orders. I don't forget, ever.

With this third time, I've finally figured it out, this is his version of a pep talk. A way to get my blood pumping. The thing is, Bob doesn't have a fucking clue.

* * *

There ain't nothing in there.
  Sure there is, you just don't know where to look.
  Fuck...Fuck, man, there ain't nothing but skeletons.
Fuckin' nothing but raw wood.

I've never liked Jerry all that much. I mean, he's my brother and all, but he's a know it all little shit. Been that way since we were kids. I'd be trying to tell him something...you know, nothing important, just little kid bullshit about superheroes or baseball players, something, and he would start in: No, that ain't right. That's wrong! You're wrong, Cole! And then he'd give me his explanation. Back then, he was usually wrong. Usually he was doing nothing but blowing smoke and trying to one up me.

The best part of spending time with Jerry when we were kids was getting to go home at the end of the day. Knowing that I didn't have to put up with his bullshit, and that he got to stay with his Ma, and I got to stay with mine, and I wouldn't have to see him again for a whole month. It's still that way, except he goes home to his wife, and I still go back to Ma's house. Difference being I have to see him the very next day. The only thing that makes life bearable with him is every morning he has a cup of coffee and he lets me bum smokes out of his pack. Soon as he opens his mouth, though, my day's ruined.

He's right about this place. It's nothing but bare frames; rotting timber. There ain't gonna be no copper here, but we drove all the way the hell out here, so I'm not leaving until I've had a look around. Plus, I ain't willing to admit that he's right.

* * *

What the fuck are you doing?
I get out of the car, grab my crowbar and hammer out of the backseat.

You can stay in the car if you want to, I'm taking a look around.
I'm gone two hours. When I come back, he's sleeping.
Thank God for small favors.

I decided a while back that I needed to get on with my life.

The problem is I don't have anyone around to tell me what my life should be. That's the problem with life in the Army, you get used to people telling you what to do: When to eat, sleep, shit, piss, run, walk, work, blah, blah, blah. I know the best way to move on is find myself a wife, maybe have a couple of kids so it'll motivate me to find regular work with a boss staring over my shoulder letting me know when I'm doing something wrong. I figure the wife and kids will serve the same purpose: To tell me I'm wrong. To shame the shit out of me, make me feel small, less than a man. Only praising me when they've seen that I've sunk too low, and my work is suffering for it.

As sad as that sounds, it's what the Army taught me, and I miss it. But I ain't quite ready to find its replacement yet, I just need something other than what I've got.

Anything.

It's real power. The way it makes you feel, like there's electricity coursing through you. Have you ever experienced anything like that?

I shrug. He knows I have, but I ain't going to give him the satisfaction of my words. He wants my words more than anything. They're power to him, real power. He wants his words to be coming out of my mouth. He can't have them, because his words are pointless.

Of course you have. You felt it the moment I met you.

It was Mom who talked me into the service.

Mom wasn't much for the government. She'd bitch about it every chance she got even though she got all her money from them. It was in her blood, her dad was a union copper miner who had lived through more than his fair share of strikes and his fair share of being forced back to work government men who always sided with the bosses. Which is what made it such a surprise when she handed me the brochure she picked up at the Camp Verde recruitment center.

Maybe it wouldn't be such a bad idea, you know. Go travel, make some money, maybe go to school after you're done.

Her hands were shaking when she handed the papers over to me and left without her turning her back to me. I didn't blame her, I was a bad fucking kid, and I knew the real reason she wanted me in the Army was so she wouldn't have to lock her door when she went to sleep at night.

I dream of fire.

It's been that way most of my life. When I was six or seven, or maybe a little older or a little younger, but still just a baby to this world, the house we lived in went up in flames. I remember the fire as a cold sweat, my body dripping from head to toe, my hair matted against my scalp, my lungs filled with soot, hitching, trying to catch my breath. I remember it as darkness suddenly filled with flickering yellow light and the roar of some huge animal. Outside of the sensations, the only thing I remember seeing is Ma filling my eyes. Her lips were broken, split, blood ringing her teeth. She was screaming, telling me to get up, but I was stiff as a board, holding my breath. She finally yanked me out of bed, rushed me out into the front yard.

I remember she laid me down in the gravel, and turned to stare at all the yellow roaring and heat, her tears streaming tiny rivers down her ash covered cheeks. The old house belonged to my great grandfather and had been passed down from generation-to-generation. My mother and I were the last to sleep under its roof. The land was still ours. Three acres that used to be fifty of barren orange Arizona. I never asked what happen to the other forty-seven the family used to own?

It don't matter.

A few years after the fire, Ma put the first of three trailers that we'd live in until I went into the service. Most nights, I think about building a house out here make it like the one before. I picture myself working under the sun, pouring the foundation, hammering out the frame, hanging the roof. I see it all right before sleep snatches me away.

I forget about it in the morning and tell myself none of it was my fault.

When Ma handed me the brochures, I knew she wasn't making a suggestion. I needed to go and the sooner the better. It hurt some, but I did what I usually did with hurt: Buried it and waited for what the seeds of it would flower.

Ma gave me two brochures, one for the Army, one for the Marines. Ma was convinced I should be a Marine. The way I saw it, the government sent the Marines in first. They sent

Marines to die. I didn't want no part of dying. I wanted to fuck around, shoot a badass gun once in a while, but stay in the back. Maybe learn how to fix diesel engines in the motor pool, work in the kitchen. I knew I'd have to take some shit in basic training, but the way figured it, the Army was my best bet for just fucking; my best chance to be a hump.

Of course, there ain't no difference between the Army or the Marines. The Army didn't want humps, they didn't want to teach you how to be a mechanic, or cook food. They wanted meat. They wanted meat creeping through the sand, waiting on turbans and beards to pop up with guns folded in their robes, grenades strapped to their chest, a shitty home-made donator sweat stained in their palms. That's all the Army was, what Iraq was, meat vs. meat.

Bob lets me bum his smokes like Jerry does. I think that's mostly why I keep hanging out with him, so I can keep pre-tending I'm a non-smoker just because I don't ever spend money on them. Bob's name really ain't Bob, just like my name ain't Cole. Bob's real name is Michael Jerkins. He goes by Mike and works as a car salesman at a Prescott Valley Mercedes dealership. He's hot fucking shit over there and has his picture up with three little brass plaques attached to the frame. All of them read: Salesman of the Year followed by the years he was awarded: 2010, 2011, 2013. I don't know what the fuck happened in 2012?

He owns a nice little place in Prescott city proper, right in the downtown historical district. The house is over a hun-dred years old and was originally built by some dipshit silver miner. He shares the house with his wife and two sons. The wife has the look of a woman who used to be considered pretty but fucked herself up with cigs, booze, child birth, and the lethargy of being a stay-at-home mom for too long. She owns a touristy candle shop a couple of blocks from the house. I'm pretty sure Mike's income is what supports their house and the shop is just a way for her to get out of it a few hours every day.

I don't give a shit about their kids, they just look like a couple of teenage assholes, which I'm sure they are.

How would you get into the house, Cole? Through a window, or would you try to snap the lock on the backdoor?

I call Mike Bob because I think he looks like the killer from *Twin Peaks*. He doesn't mind me calling him Bob because he likes to think there's a certain level of ambiguity to our relationship. That by not knowing the details of his life, he'll be somehow harder to find. Bob's one of those assholes who thinks he's smarter than everyone else because he earns a good living. Bob thinks his money insulates him and that I don't know any of these things about him. I'd like to think it's willful ignorance on his part, but I know it's because he thinks he's superior to me. And he's right in some ways. I don't have all the American conveniences that make it so easy for people to find out who you are. It makes me a little sad because I want these things, but in the same breath, I don't want these things because there's a certain amount of comfort in being a ghost.

An open window would be best. And open window on a beautiful spring night. All we would have to do is cut a screen and we would be free to do whatever we wanted.

I grab a fresh smoke from the dashboard and try to avoid looking at the pictures Bob has spread across it.

* * *

Ma got sick while I was gone. Her heart gave out, or one of the pumps in it did. She didn't have the money for a doctor to find out for sure. She died the first time at work. She flat-lined and everything. The paramedics who brought her back to life at the bar she worked at used their paddles and brought her back. She was in the hospital for only one night and was discharged the morning after. She went home after filling her new prescriptions, laid down, and had a second heart attack. There wasn't anyone there to shock her back to life. Her boss at the bar was the one who found her when he came to check and see how she was doing. He ended up breaking a window to her bedroom when he saw her sprawled out.

The Army let me come home for two weeks. All I did the entire time I was home was sleep. I'd wake up at ten, be conked out on the couch by one with a movie playing in the background. I kept Ma's bedroom door closed, I didn't need anything out of it, and the window was still busted. I didn't have a funeral for her, we were never the most social of people, and I think she would've been embarrassed if it was only me and her boss watching her get lowered into the ground. I had her cremated and put her in her bedroom once I boarded up the busted window. I locked the door behind me, it felt appropriate.

After my two weeks of leave was up, I didn't go back, and they haven't come looking.

I go out on my own on the days when Jerry has real construction work, that's how I met Bob.

Land developers thought Prescott Valley was going to be where the next big Arizona housing boom was going to be. They were wrong. The boom stayed in Phoenix, but it didn't stop them from building a few thousand track homes on the city outskirts near the RV dealerships and the scuzzy self-storage facilities. They sold some, but it was a bust, and most of the folks who bought the mass produced tinder boxes ended up giving them back. The developers made tracks, left the homes to rot and be picked over by scavengers like me and Jerry.

When we first got started salvaging, we went for the high-end items: Air conditions, sliding glass doors, toilets, dishwashers. The thing is we weren't the only smart fellas in our little corner of red dirt nothing. All the high-end junk went fast until all that was left was what was buried in the walls. The thing with scavengers is they're lazy. They don't mind busting their humps lifting a two-thousand-pound air-conditioner, but if they have to tear up some drywall to get at some copper wiring or aluminum pipes, they get all jiggly in the knees. This left the salvaging playing field wide open for more industrious types like me and Jerry.

It was December 2nd, Jerry was a month into a three month job slapping together an enormous apartment complex in Phoenix. He offered to try and get me on the crew even though he knew I'd say no.

The Mexicans work without ID. They don't pay 'em shit, but they don't pay no taxes neither.

He was offering because he didn't want to be lonely. Phoenix is a two-hour drive one way, and with the price of gas, he was going to rent a cheap room close to the site during the week. Even though I barely saw them speak a word to one another when I was around Jerry and his wife, I knew he'd missing having a body to share space with. I was an adequate enough body, plus I would chip in on the cost of the room.

I didn't want the job, though. Not because I thought the

Army would come looking, but because I didn't want to leave, ever. So instead of waiting out in front of my trailer for Jerry to come and pick me up, I used Mom's old Dodge. It was a gas guzzler and it leaked oil, but the tags were current and it got me up to Prescott Valley just fine.

I was working a development that they were going to call Mountain View. Three square miles of crackerbox track homes, most of them complete. It was hog heaven for salvagers when they abandoned work on it. Jerry told me when we first started coming up here that fellas would get into fights over the flat-top ranges and air-condition units. It got so bad that there was even a couple of shootings. By the time we made it up, there was nothing left but the copper in the walls, quiet for miles around, and the occasional security man who seemed to never got out of his patrol car. We'd hump our gear in and lug it and our spools out, so we never gave him a reason to stop. Not like he seemed able enough, the old boy looked like he was in his seventies and carrying a hundred pounds of heart attack weight.

I was working near the center of Mountain View, a couple of blocks away from where the dry Olympic size swimming pool and clubhouse were. It was a risky spot because the security guard kept his station there. But I was working at four a.m. with a headlamp strapped around my hat. If I was the sort who spooked easily, I would've been in a cold sweat.

I was pounding through the drywall of in the master bathroom of a two story place. When I started work on it at two a.m., I was surprised to find no one else had gotten around to tearing the place up. The range, microwave, and stainless steel refrigerator were still in place. It was a gold mine. But I wasn't there to pick up major appliances—I'd have to come back over the weekend when Jerry was back in town—I was there for copper and pipes.

While I was yanking the toilet away from the wall, I felt something touch my shoulder. At first I thought was just a piece of drywall crumbling off and hitting me in the shoulder, but then it tapped me again, the distinct slap of a hand. The army gets you weird. It gets you jumpy. Not so much from the time out in the desert, but from other guys constantly fucking with you. You get touchy and mean.

I turned without thinking and buried the claw end of my hammer in a woman's skull. Her mouth and head were wrapped in duct tape, silver ribbons of it hung from her wrists. Her forehead and cheeks were dusty, dimpled with shallow cuts. My eyes went glassy as the woman fell backwards, my hammer still in her head.

A couple of seconds or a couple of hours later, there was Bob, sweaty, holding a box cutter.

After we buried the woman, I thought I'd found my anything in Bob.

I've killed plenty. Enemy soldiers, civilians, my fellow soldiers.

Lots of those shitbirds.

No one wants to ever say it, but I've got no problem with it because I was one of them: Just because you're a soldier don't mean you're hero. It don't mean you're a good guy. It just means you're some asshole who loves raping and killing, and the Army pays you to do it to as many brown people as you can.

I thought Bob was the answer because he loved raping and killing, or at least said he did.

The woman we buried was his first, and he hadn't gotten around to doing either.

I listened to his spiel the first time over a cup of coffee at a Denny's out near the I-17. The spiel made sense.

Maybe what I was missing wasn't the order and discipline?

Maybe it was the killing?

We agreed to meet at the same house in Mountain View two weeks later. We went back to the same Denny's, and I listened to his bullshit again. This time I figured out the only reason Bob wanted me around was because he didn't have the balls to actually kill anybody, he needed me there to do it.

He needed me there to take the fall in case we got caught.

I started follow him after the second meeting, gathered my intel.

When we met again at Mountain View, we didn't go back to Denny's, we came to this house in Prescott Valley. We parked across the street and Bob spread his pictures of the three women who lived in the house across the dash, and he told me what he'd do—what I'd do—to the three women.

I smoked half a pack of Marlboro's, and when I was done with my last one, I grabbed Bob by his stiff, jelled down hair, and I pushed the orange cherry into his cheek.

I held him steady while he tried to hit me.

I blocked out his screams.

I savored the old favorite smell of burning.

I slammed his head into the steering wheel and then showed him my pictures.

The pictures of his house and car.

Of his wife.

His sons.

I told him about grabbing the boys when they were walking home from lacrosse practice, or whatever fucking privileged sport they played.

I talked about Mountain View, anal rape, and how much I missed it.

I talked about inserting candles into his wife.

I talked about dousing him with gasoline and how he'd smell while he was on fire.

I told him it wouldn't smell like the puddle of urine he was sitting in.

I told him if he ever came back to this house, to these women, I would do everything I'd just told him I would do to him and his family without a second of hesitation.

I broke his nose before I left the car and stole the rest of the cigarettes.

CREAMPUFF
Rob Hart

People called him "Creampuff."

No one knows if it was a nickname thought up by the staff, or if he actually called himself that. That's just what people called him.

It could have been like when you call a big guy "Tiny." Cognitive dissonance. Here's this big black guy, and he answered to Creampuff, like it was John or Paul.

There were a lot of things people didn't know about Creampuff, but here is what is known: He was huge, like a recurring childhood nightmare. People say he was nearly seven feet tall, but that's just the way truth gets warped by word of mouth. He was more like six-three, which is still pretty big. He had gauges in his ear wide enough you could fit your thumb in, and a thick beard like a jumble of cables that reached down to his sternum. And always he was wearing a gray wool skullcap, even in the summer.

He had one tattoo. A series of black lines running parallel down his left forearm. It started with five lines. The last time anyone saw him, when the morning shift found his body in a thick pool of blood, throat cut ear to ear, there were seven lines. No one knew what they stood for. Nearly everyone had a theory. Most of those theories had to do with how many people he had killed.

Which is a little heavy, and not really based on anything. Creampuff was only a bouncer.

Granted, he was a special kind of bouncer, with a skill-set tailored for these strange modern times. He was required to deal with a hugely diverse range of people—brain-dead tourists to rich yuppie jerks to bridge-and-tunnel trolls to the most dangerous animal in New York City: Moms pushing baby carriages.

Creampuff was a bakery bouncer.

The kind of job that didn't exist ten years ago and suddenly is in such demand, colleges should teach a course on it.

You know what a canelé is? It's this little pastry that originated in Bordeaux, in the southwest of France. It gets cooked in a copper mold, which forms a deep bronze crust on the outside. Inside is light custard flavored with vanilla and rum. They're the perfect little mouthful, barely bigger than one bite, and you can get them in a lot of places in New York, but only a few places actually do them right.

Patiserie in the East Village is one of those places, going back to the 1940s, when the store first opened. But as with any business that isn't a bank or a real estate agency, one day, they found themselves struggling to meet their rent. Their canelés, being a thing of legend, did good business, but still, were barely keeping them afloat. It's hard to keep the lights on when your star product sells for three dollars a pop.

So the owners of Patiserie brought on a hotshot pastry chef—a kid with half his head shaved and cooking utensils tattooed up and down his forearms—to put a new spin on the menu.

And this new chef considers the canelé.

It's classic, but as a canvas, a little blank. He tinkers with it for a few weeks, and eventually figures out a way to get rum-infused ice cream on the inside.

Think about that.

Instead of a warm custard, it was still-cold ice cream. To properly caramelize the crust of a canelé you've got to hit it with a ton of heat. Plus, introducing alcohol into the mix screws with the melting point of the ice cream. All that, and there was still cold, perfectly-unmelted ice cream on the inside. This thing was a marvel of modern kitchen engineering.

Word spread, and within a week of it hitting the menu, the chef was on *Good Morning America*, the plastic-faced anchors making a show of begging him for the secret to his cooking process, which of course, he wouldn't reveal. They did come up with a new name for this treat: The Creamelé.

So that goes viral, and the next morning, there's a line down the block and around the corner. Everyone wants a creamelé.

Suddenly all the employees who are supposed to be cooking and baking are working crowd control. That's no way to run a business. Especially since three people needed to be assigned to the creamelés, which were made in a back room with blacked-out windows that no one but the chef and his helpers were allowed inside.

Enter Creampuff.

Nobody knows where he came from. He just showed up one day, arms crossed over his chest, his eyes cold and unmoving like blocks of chipped ice. Some people thought he was the embodiment of order, attracted by the gravity of chaos, here to bring order to an entropic universe.

Truth is, it was probably a job posting on Craigslist.

Patiserie only had the capacity to make two hundred creamelés a day, and you could only buy one at a time. There was no calling ahead to reserve them. You had to wait on the line. And they were a ten-foot treat, meaning you had to eat them within ten feet of the bakery. Wait too long, and the ice cream would melt.

Every single day, people who wanted ice cream for breakfast would line up as early as four a.m., when the first shift of bakers would arrive.

Doors opened at seven a.m.

By nine a.m., that day's allotment of creamelés was gone.

So you've got a line to control. There are people running outside the bakery to eat their creamelé. And then, there are all the people trying to game the system and get in without waiting on line.

This is what Creampuff faced, every single day—because he worked seven days a week. But he had a system.

If you were there for a creamelé, you got on the creamelé line. Five people were allowed inside the store proper at a time, and only five people. One person in, and one person out. Even if you were with a group of people, even if you were with your husband or wife, you got split up to go inside. Creampuff only made an exception when parents had their kids with them—not that kids could have a creamelé, because there was alcohol in it.

In front of the store, on the sidewalk, there was a sign on a pedestal explaining how the line worked. Plus a lengthy explanation on Patiserie's website. Not that it helped much. Because people in New York think they are the center of their own little universe, a lot of Creampuff's job consisted of dealing with people who didn't want to wait.

There were the Richie Riches who would stride up to him and wave a bill under his nose. Usually a twenty, sometimes a hundred. Creampuff would take it, stick it in a pouch on his belt that read "donations for charity," and cross his arms.

No one ever asked for their money back.

Two celebrities and the chief of staff for the mayor walked to the front of the line like it wasn't even there. Creampuff surely had no idea who they were, but it wouldn't have mattered. Even after they pitched a fit, invoking the "don't-you-know-who-I-am?" protocol, Creampuff shrugged, put his hand up, and waved them toward the back.

Pregnant mom pushing a stroller, arguing she couldn't wait because her precious little thing had toddler yoga in fifteen minutes?

Back of the line.

Tourist on his last day in New York City, and he'll never be visiting again, and this is his last chance to try a creamelé? Back of the line.

A man diagnosed with cancer, a week to live, and a creamelé was his final wish?

Creampuff offered to let him cut if he presented a doctor's note. The guy never came back.

The line was sacrosanct to Creampuff. The way he figured it, the people who dragged themselves out of bed in the middle of the night to wait for a pastry—they were idiots. They had some gaping chasm inside their souls that they tried to fill with food, and honestly, the whole thing was a little sad.

But they made the effort. Creampuff had to at least respect that much, and not let anyone who didn't make that effort cut in front of them.

In a city where chaos is the accepted norm, a line has to mean something.

Creampuff had a memory for faces, too. More than once a line-cutter would come back, a day or a week or a month later, and when they finally made it to the front, Creampuff would shake his head. He didn't even have to say anything. They knew what they had done. And each one of them shuffled off, cradling their shame.

Same thing with the non-creamelé line. The store had a separate line that led to another counter for people who didn't want a creamelé. Some people thought they were being clever, sneaking around to that side. They also found themselves blacklisted.

This is the new face of New York City. Living here used to be a game of survival. Now it's about conning your way into frozen treats.

Creampuff was a product of the way things used to be. He rarely spoke. When he did, he never raised his voice. The only time he ever smiled was when there was a child waiting with a parent, and for a fleeting moment, he would soften. For the most part, he would nod, or shrug, or point toward the back of the line. And people listened. The kind of people who on a different day you'd expect them to be a problem, they fell in lockstep.

Creampuff carried with him that aura of not-to-be-messed-with. He was one of the people this city couldn't manage to chew up and spit out.

It got to be where Creampuff became part of the creamelé story, like a member of the Royal Guard in front of Buckingham Palace. People would want to take pictures with him. They would tell him jokes to try and get him to laugh. Girls would flirt with him to try and make him blush, but he never did.

One guy said with a name like Creampuff he must be a homo. That was the only time anyone can remember Creampuff laying a hand on someone. He grabbed the guy by the back of the neck, pulled him close, whispered something into his ear, and the guy took off at a full sprint, blanched white as a field of snow.

It was around this time, that Creampuff's legend was growing, that the first break-in happened.

Rival bakers had been trying to replicate the creamelé without success. Either the crust would be soggy, or the ice cream would melt, or they would burst during the cooking process. It was one of the most sought-after recipes in the city, and some people even offered to buy it, but the owners of Patiserie wouldn't entertain offers.

They had gone from just another bakery into one of the hottest destinations in New York City. The prime minister of Mozambique queued up on three separate occasions until he was finally able to get a creamelé. Why sell off the keys to that kingdom?

The morning of the first break-in, Creampuff arrived to find that the front door had been pried open. The register hadn't been touched, but the door to the creamelé kitchen was ajar. Luckily the chef always brought the custom bake pieces home with him, so all the perpetrator found were a few standard ovens and raw ingredients—nothing that couldn't have been guessed at already.

This is when Creampuff began sleeping in the store.

No one asked him to. Just one day there was a cot. Once the evening shift had been cleared out, he would show up, lock the front door, and disappear into the back. People began to speculate, about whether he had a place to go, or even had a home. Some people thought he might have been homeless. He only seemed to own a few shirts, a few pairs of pants. He never spoke of life outside the bakery, and no one ever came by who seemed to know him.

For a while, with Creampuff living in the bakery, things were calm. Business continued to boom. The owners made so much money they were able to buy the building the store was housed in, ensuring that future generations of the family would be secure. They even thought of expanding to another storefront, in the West Village. The creamelés were the star attraction, and the chef was their most valuable player, but still, Creampuff was given a share of the credit, for maintaining order and appearances.

For being part of the story.

Then came the day they found his body.

No money had been taken. The creamelé room hadn't been touched. There was just his body, sprawled out on the white tile, blood cutting geometric trails through the grout.

There were some theories about who had done it. Maybe one of the rival bakeries, in a robbery gone bad. There was also a multi-national dessert corporation that waved a seven figure check in front of the owners, and were told to bug off. A corporation certainly would seem capable of murder in the pursuit of profit.

Some wondered if it was revenge. Someone who wanted a

creamelé and didn't get it, come back to make Creampuff pay for the slight. Or something else from his life, catching up with him. Rumors began to circulate that he was in witness protection, and the fame achieved by the bakery had blown his cover.

How else to explain the savagery of a murder like that, in a town where people have forgotten what it means to be savage?

After the crime scene had been processed, the owners learned that Creampuff's body had been unclaimed. Having paid him in cash, there was no address for him on file. He had become another anonymous death in an anonymous city.

So the owners and the employees put together a collection for the funeral. The costs were eventually completely covered by an anonymous donation. Some person of means who had stood on that line, and decided the man who maintained it deserved a bit of dignity in death.

The funeral was a quiet affair, around the corner from the bakery, at St. Mark's in-the-Bowery. A few dozen people showed up. Mostly employees, though some loyal customers, too. In the back of the church was a frail black woman, a shroud around her face, weeping softly into a yellow handkerchief, and many assumed she was family, though she left before anyone could ask.

When it came time for the eulogy, the owner of Patiserie, a slight old man, was helped to the dais. He stood there for a long time, looking down at his hands resting on the podium. Then he looked up and told a story.

One day Creampuff had finished his shift and was getting ready to leave, when he saw a woman across the street, struggling to carry groceries into her apartment building. He didn't know her. But he walked across the street and said something to her and then took the bags from her hands and disappeared inside. He came back out and walked away and went home.

It was a small moment in the immensity of this man's life, but it was a measure of the kind of person Creampuff was. Someone who did the right thing when the right thing was required. He didn't seek thanks or reward. He did it and he moved on.

After the funeral, things slowly returned to normal.

The owners of Patiserie hired a new bouncer. This one not as reliable, not as steadfast. If someone handed him a hundred, he would allow that person to cut the line. He was prone to anger and berated people for not walking inside fast enough. He was high on the allowances of his power.

He was no Creampuff.

Occasionally someone would ask about Creampuff, not having heard the news, and would be disappointed for a moment, before returning to their quest for a creamelé.

Something no one was able to prove was that after he was gone, the line got a little shorter. Patiserie always sold out of the day's allotment of creamelés, and the offers to buy the recipe never stopped, but it seemed like there were less people waiting.

And, eventually, people forgot.

In New York City, the space left by a memory is a vacuum. It won't be long before something fills that space.

But even then, there are people who fight against the vacuum.

On the one-year anniversary of Creampuff's body being found, early in the morning, the employees opening the store found a gift-wrapped package leaning against the closed door of the bakery. Inside was a framed photo of Creampuff. It was a candid shot, taken with a cell phone camera in the early morning hours, when the sun wasn't yet strong enough to push away the shadows.

Creampuff, staring off toward the end of the line, his arms crossed, like they were always crossed. A statue, solemn and unmoving, with the hint of a smile spreading across the boundary of his lips. His face a portrait of contentment.

That's the story of the photo hanging behind the register at Patiserie. The owner thought it important that the photo hang there. It means you can't buy a creamelé without seeing it.

You might not know the significance, but at least you will see it.

THE ESCAPE
Kelli Stanley

She could hear the dogs barking, behind her with the other guards. Three cavernous, slobbering jaws, lifting up in the darkness, baying at the light, the light so far ahead. She rushed through the darkness hurriedly now, can't let the dogs find her, can't go back.

How long had she been running? How long since she'd been seized with rough hands and pushed quickly into the fisherman's boat?

Hours, minutes, days...

The hull was black, blacker than the water and redolent of river bottom, and her fingers clutched at the bottom planks. Then a sudden lurch and moan of the moldered wood, and she was picked up and thrown on the ground, spongy damp clinging to her until she shook herself free. The old man watched her, jagged grin the only light in the dark.

Dogs snarled and barked in the distance, not yet across, a gelid sound that crackled against the brackish, lapping water.

They were on the other side of the river. They would not be alone for long.

The girl was confused, uncertain, pain and cold an unfamiliar memory. Was she leaving? But there was comfort in the confinement. Safety in the routine. And no one ever escaped.

The fisherman's eyes devoured her body. She wrapped her

arms around her breasts, thin linen stiff and frozen to the touch.

"He's waitin' for you." The rot of his breath made her flinch. "Your lover—run along, he's up ahead. The dogs'll be here soon."

She left him then, backing into the darkness, legs no longer held prisoner. The woods bent their roots around her ankles, ivy vines clawing at her sheath. His cackle echoed through the stillness, punctuated by barking. Closer now. She turned to the black of the forest. She did not look back.

The mossy ground was damp, unforgiving. Tendrils tripped her and she fell, surprised at the blood on her skin.

Keep going. Don't look back, the dogs will find you. Keep going. If the fisherman wasn't lying—and why would he?—she knew who was ahead, waiting for her.

He'd arranged this, planned the escape. The only man she ever loved.

The dogs howled again. She shivered, and started to run.

Springtime is the season for lovers, and it belonged to them. They left the city often, finding each other reflected in the countryside. Hyacinths danced along the river's edge, fragrance making their heads as light as their feet. Daffodils trailed and leaned over the small pond, mourning their reflections. He'd sing to her, songs for her alone, and it seemed like the birds stopped their own song to listen.

They were far away from the city, the noise, the constant arguments.

"When can we get away?"

"After you speak to my father."

"I don't need to speak to him to do this."

And then he would kiss her, stroke her breasts beneath her dress, and they would roll the wine down their throats, luxuriating in the sense of secrecy that enveloped them.

On a bright, cloudless day in May, she escaped the confines of the house. The girl could feel the eyes of the servants, knew the housemaid had seen who it was she met. Had seen him, had wanted him, because one was the other.

That day they made love. So many times before he had held back, though she'd begged him to take her, to brand her as his own. Even then, when their bodies came together, and they lay on the grass with the sun shining on them, for the girl, it was still too much of a barrier.

"I love you. Don't ever, ever leave me...I want to be with you, in you, all the time."

He'd laughed and stroked her hair, surprised at the ferocity in her face.

"I'll talk to your father."

They drank more wine and made love again, blending, merging into one. They didn't see the man on the hilltop, watching them.

The black was ceding to a dull iron grey, metallic color of worn armor and sharp knives, grasp of ivy giving way to coarse grass and thin trees with white trunks, landscape a monotone palette. The grass cut her feet and she was cold, the damp of the river still clinging to the linen that wrapped her, and occasionally tripped her, as she willed her legs to move faster along the path.

Feeling again. And memory. They rushed through her, propelled her forward. A nearby bark made her jump. Too close. She ran again.

The trail was hard to follow; seemed to constantly switch back, and it was only through careful watching that she was able to make out the right direction.

He was up there, somewhere, safe at the border. Waiting for her. She couldn't see him—not yet. But he was ahead and she would find him. Before the dogs found her.

She fell as she climbed over a fallen branch, the path slippery beneath her feet, breath in shuddered gasps. She didn't touch the cut on her cheek or the blood on her left leg, ankle bruised and swollen, limp already slowing her down.

He was waiting!

She froze against a tree, bark clawing her skin. Harsh, quick panting, a yap and a whine, as one dog bit another. The one with the guttural growl began to bay. The others joined him, voices triumphant. She picked up a sharp rock.

They were nearly upon her.

"But, Father, I love him!"

The words poured out of her along with anger, and the old man looked surprised at the shock on her face. Was she really that young?

"It's out of the question." He was late to the courts, and glanced along the street to make sure no one could hear them. He seized her arm, and led her into a small, dark alcove, where they were less likely to be overheard.

"Go back home to your mother."

The girl was usually obedient, but he'd missed the flush of womanhood in her cheeks.

"No, Father. I won't."

The old man breathed hard, wondering what he'd done to deserve such a child. He had a case to hear this afternoon.

"I've told you, and I won't tell you again. He is unsuitable in every way. A musician, a traveler, a...a preacher. He's not the kind of husband I want for my only daughter."

"And what about what I want, Father? Or is that not important?"

He slapped her across the face. The thing in her eyes grew stronger, and he looked down, then toward the bustling street and the court in the distance.

"Go home to your mother."

She watched him walk down the pavement, an old man struggling to stand upright. Her eyes never left his back.

She pressed herself tight against the spiny wood, hoping the trickle down her arm was sweat. No blood, not now, not this close.

The rock in her hand wasn't heavy enough. No reason to hold it. Nothing could make a difference. She trembled. Their teeth, the iron jaws. How many times had she been told there was no escape?

She shut her eyes. They were just on the other side of the tree. The large paws clawed the ground, the panting tongues licking the air for her scent. She prayed for her lover. Prayed it would be quick.

The guards murmured something unintelligible. A language of their own, one even the Matron never understood. She strained forward. Frantic, confused yapping. Heavy feet crushed the dead leaves, rustling and ripping. The head closest to her whimpered, then howled in frustration.

They were leaving. As if they didn't want to find her. At least not yet.

She counted heartbeats, waiting until the barks and growls were distant and behind her again, muted by the wind. Then she dropped, slid to the ground, her back still braced against the tree. One escape already.

She laughed aloud, tears on her cheeks, a strange sound in the forgotten wood.

Her mother was beaming. The servants were serving dinner, and even her father looked impressed, despite himself.

Her lover was singing.

It was a voice so sweet in sound that the maid froze to watch with a dish in her hand, forgetting her life-long training, forgetting everything but his voice, his hair, his face. Even the cook drifted out of the kitchen, mesmerized.

After the song, he spoke with her father, serious subjects, related to worship and law and other things that meant nothing to her but everything to her father. She watched from the other room, conspiring with her mother, and they both hugged each other when the old man smiled and nodded.

The housemaid's face fell, and grim lines of age formed around her lips and eyes. She muttered words, soft syllables of hate and revenge, curses worse than death itself...

At the end of the evening, smiling broadly, her father counted the money. Then he held out his hands, and she ran to him, throwing herself into his arms like a little girl. He held her tight, relinquishing her to the charismatic young man with the beautiful voice. And the generous bride-price.

They all smiled at one another, and that night, when she watched her lover leave and melt into the night, she knew she would be his forever.

She'd seen him!

Heart pounding frantically against her chest, she floundered through the swamp, gray, rough grass retreating to a bog of brown decay. The light was coming up, growing brighter. They were closer to the border.

Patched clothes, worn and dirty. But they hung on the straight, lean back and athlete's body, his blond hair longer and unkempt, still curling like the tendrils of a vine on his white neck.

She fought for another glimpse, mud heavy on her burning legs. He walked unevenly on higher ground, first fast, then slowing almost to a stroll.

He was all that mattered. Not the hungry dogs, still barking in the distance, not the grim, implacable guards, not the Ice Queen herself, the Matron with the cruel smile who delighted in her suffering. He was all that mattered.

She pushed herself faster. Her ankle finally buckled under the weight of the thick sludge, plunging her into the water. She pulled herself upright, brushing the mud off her arms. The green-brown stripes stayed fixed.

Leeches. Their tiny teeth stabbed her flesh, burrowing holes in her limbs. There was no time to remove them, no time to stop them from sucking the remaining strength from her legs.

No time.

Escape...

They'd gone back to the place where they'd first made love. It was June.

The girl was busy figuring out the food, the guests, the singers—oh no, he couldn't do his own singing, he was the bridegroom, besides—she laughed at his easy smile, as he propped on an elbow on the grass—besides, she wanted people to notice her dress.

She was thinking about lying with him, making love in the afternoon sun, when a shadow fell across the glen. She looked up, startled, but her lover smiled and rose, greeting the youth as if he knew him.

He was a farmer, a bee-keeper, the son of a rich and powerful man. He owned the adjacent fields, near the river, and had heard of the wedding plans. He brought them honey from the hives, for good luck.

The young girl accepted it, smiling at first, but grew troubled by the look in the bee-keeper's eyes, and most of all by the brush of his finger when she took the honey jar from him.

It burned.

"Please come for the wedding," her lover was saying.

"When is it?" The young man's eyes continually darted

toward hers, and she shivered, thinking of a snake's tongue. "Tomorrow."

His mouth looked broken when he smiled. "I will be happy to come."

Her lover laughed, that easy music that made her mother love him and her father yield. She moved closer, and he put his arm around her and kissed her, and still she felt the bee-keeper's eyes.

The girl turned to him reluctantly, looking at the honey, glowing like the sun in the pot. "Thank you for the gift, and for coming to the wedding."

The bee-keeper nodded, his face on fire. Then he turned abruptly, leaving them alone in the clearing.

Her lover tried to draw her to the floor of the meadow, kissing her lips and cheeks. But she shook her head, troubled. The bee-keeper's eyes followed her. Scorching her soul.

She matched her movements to his, a mirror, a shadow. They were climbing a hill, a rocky dry peak with jagged stones and prickly, scrubby bushes that hid the precious path. At least they were out of the swamp.

The trail turned in on itself, like a snake biting its tail, heading always for the light, the dogs and the guards, behind and close, growling for her scent.

He was still hesitant, resting now and then to wipe his forehead, looking up as if for a sun that would never shine again. She stopped when he did, looking at him, not noticing the leeches had dropped from her legs or the fresh blood on the rocks from her mangled feet.

Cross the border. Keep going. Escape.

The words timed themselves to her intakes of breath, ankle dragging behind her, useless except for the pain.

She willed him forward. Don't stop. Don't look back. He must know she was there. The dogs smelled her again, the shrill yaps bouncing between the dagger-like crags of the hillside.

The guards. And with them, perhaps, The Ice Queen herself. She shuddered, despite the heat. In the distance, her lover rested against a tree.

She wouldn't go back. She couldn't.

The Warden let his wife do what she wished. And the guards...the murmur, the rustle, words not understood, but only felt...

Had she really thought of staying, back there with the fisherman? Memory drowned her, a flood of sound. The cries, the agonized cries...

Never. Never go back.

"Escape," she whispered, startled by the urgency, the fear in her own soft voice. "Escape."

The morning of her marriage was the second happiest day in her life. The sun shone with a gentle warmth, bathing the revelers in the lovers' sense of joy. Her father stood proudly, her mother cried. The singers didn't make the fine ears of her husband ache too badly, and everyone enjoyed the feast, eating and drinking into the late afternoon.

Her lover—her husband—entertained a small throng of admirers heading back to the city. She looked at him proudly, knowing he was hers. Not wanting to interrupt, she took some of the containers to the river for washing, the honey pot of the bee-keeper among them. It glowed red in the slanting rays of the late afternoon, but she was too joyous to pay attention.

She was kneeling near the edge, smiling at her own reflection, when she saw him behind her.

His eyes glowed like the honey.

She scrambled on the bank, stood up rapidly.

"Is—is there something you wanted?"

Her husband was too far away to hear her muffled scream, to see the wedding garment ripped from between her legs. He couldn't see how she pounded his chest and tried to scratch his face, twisting as his hands covered her body and threw her to the ground. He couldn't smell the odor of fear and sweat and semen, or taste the blood that poured from her body or feel the invasion, the rape of her body and soul.

The bee-keeper carried her back to the glen, washed. He claimed she'd fallen and stepped on a snake.

Push aside memory. Pain of her legs and hands and arms held strength. Focus on pain, on the man in front of her. Pain. Love. Life. Full and terrible and hard to bear, but all there was, all she wanted.

The top of the hill. Lush meadow stretched before them, encircled by a stand of laurels. Almost there.

He was walking listlessly, hesitant and slow.

A long, deep growl made the laurel leaves tremble. The guards. They would not be denied again.

She started to run. Her ankle buckled and she tottered, just managing to stay upright. She strove forward, forgetting pain, forgetting everything except escape.

Don't look back. Don't wait for me. I'm here. Keep going!

Exhaustion and dejection weighed on him like mourning clothes. Sweat dotted his brow, his cheeks hollow and stretched. Doubt twisted his face.

She fought her breath, struggling to catch him.

Run, I'm behind you! Run, Run!

Light streamed through the green canopy, a full, rich sunshine, and she could hear the birds, the small animals waiting.

The border. Safety. Life.

The dogs bayed and lunged, the hot stink of their breath burning her legs. Still he wavered.

She wanted to scream, but her throat closed, as if the bee-keeper's hand was still around it. She wanted to run faster, but she froze, as though his arms were still wrapped around her and his weight was trapping her to the ground. She wanted to yell, to shout that she was there, to tell him she was alive.

Run, damn you, run, don't wait for me, don't look back, don't look back!

...their screams rose and joined in the air, her voice finally free. And for a heartbeat he saw her, bloodied and torn and suffering.

"Orpheus!" she cried. "Orpheus!..."

And Eurydice died again.

The Ice Queen smiled, and somewhere above a granite boulder cracked open with the frost. The girl sighed. In the laurel grove, a leaf withered on a stem, dried and curled, and floated to the forest floor.

She sat by the river, watching the fisherman. She thought she was looking for someone in the boats, but she couldn't really remember. Someone new asked her once how long she'd been there, and she couldn't remember that, either.

She knew she couldn't leave. Not ever. But why would she want to? There were things to do. The same things, every day, but that was all right.

Sometimes in the dark forest men and women looked at her, tears on their cheeks. She was always surprised when she felt her own face, and found it, too, was wet. She remembered tears. And songs, though they wouldn't let her sing them.

Once in a while she thought she'd hear music, the sound of a lyre and a voice, somewhere in the forest. Once she'd caught a glimpse of a young man, blond, with curling hair like ivy, so beautiful...

But then the Ice Queen sent the Furies after her and they didn't let her go back to the forest for a long, long time.

THE SHY ONE
Alison Gaylin

Cody was the cute one. Max was the intellectual, Dean the bad boy, Terrence the clown...That's what the magazines said, but you didn't need the magazines to know it. All you had to do was look at them—the clothes they wore, the way they moved in their music videos, Terrence puppy-dog bouncing, Dean swaying his hips...All you had to do was watch and take note: The hair, for instance, could tell you a lot. The smiles—dimpled or wicked, ironic or sweet. The way their eyes locked up with yours—one gaze knowing, the other questioning, the other somewhat blank, as though he were searching for his own reflection in your pupils.

Katie Flynn knew those four. Loved them, just as everyone in the Fandom loved them. But there were five boys in the band, and Sean was the fifth.

Sean was the one you'd die for. Sean was the one who could make you kill.

The rest of the band had dark hair, but Sean's was sandy blond. The other four were Australian, while Sean spoke with a soft Kiwi accent, each sentence a song. In interviews, Cody, Max, Dean and Terrence all answered fast, jostling for the right answer, the clever quip. "Terrence never shuts up," Cody would sigh. And he was right.

But Sean rarely spoke. Sean was The Shy One. "The others

are cleverer than me," he once told *Tiger Beat*. "I let them do the talking."

Katie had an autographed poster of the whole band on her bedroom wall—a big glossy shot on the beach, sun shining through their hair. There was a kiss print in the corner, which embarrassed her a little. It had been done with a computer; she'd never wear that shade, let alone kiss a poster. Still, it was one of the most special things she owned. In it, all the boys were smiling and in their bathing suits, each bare chest tattooed with a for-real Sharpie signature. Katie had bought it off e-bay. They'd signed it personally, while on their most recent European tour. She liked running her fingertips over the signatures, feeling the imprints that the pen had made. If she held it close, Katie swore, she could even smell the ink. (To be fair, that could have been just her imagination.)

Under her pillow, though, was something even more special: another picture, unsigned, of Sean, The Shy One. In the photo, he wore a black T-shirt, half-closed eyes and a crooked, uncertain smile—as though the picture, his life, *all of it* had happened a few moments before he was ready. He was sitting on a blue fluffy chair that could have been Katie's own chair in Katie's own living room in White Plains. She had one just like it. That had to be a sign.

Every night, when her parents were asleep and they thought she was too, Katie would slip the picture out from under her pillow. She'd shine the light from her phone into Sean's green eyes until they glowed back at her and they could share each other's loneliness.

"Someday," she would whisper. "Someday, Sean."

Katie didn't much like the other girls in the Fandom. Besides the band, she didn't have anything in common with them. She followed the most popular accounts on Instagram, but only to see the dumb pictures they posted—screen grabs from music videos, pictures of cats and baby brothers and sisters wearing T-shirts that read "I heart Cody" or "Max is my Man." Really dumb stuff, not to mention the comments posted beneath. (*OMG what a cuuuttteeee BaeBae! And such good taste!!! What's your kitteh's name? His name is Cody lol!*)

Katie liked looking at the pictures, though. And the comments, dumb as they were, were full of feelings she that she shared. She loved all the Boys as much as anyone in the Fandom loved Terrence and Cody and Max and Dean. But what she and Sean had was different. It was special. In the whole world, he was the only person she could talk to. Strange, yes. The one friend on earth she could confide in, yet she'd only seen him in two dimensions.

She didn't find that sad, though. Some people didn't have anyone at all.

For ten months, Katie spoke to that picture every night. She would slip it out from under her pillow before going to bed and tell Sean about her hopes, her dreams, the funny things she'd seen on YouTube that day...She'd tell him about the moments she felt glad to be alive and the long, aching stretches when she yearned for something different, something better. At the end of the tenth month—at midnight on September 30 after a solid hour of talking to him, Katie told Sean she loved him.

One week later, he started talking back.

"You should go out," Sean said. It wasn't the first thing he'd said to Katie. The first had been "*Hello, you,*" and that had been a day ago, in a voice so soft and whispery she'd thought it was the wind.

"*Over here,*" he'd said. "*Look here.*" And that had been the second thing—the thing that made her jump back, for when she'd looked at the picture, she'd caught his lips moving.

Then came Sean's final words that night: "You're stronger than you know."

It had made her cry, but in a good way. Not so much because of the words themselves, but because it proved to her that it was really Sean speaking, his lips really were moving; it wasn't in her head. *You're stronger than you know.* Katie never would have had that thought on her own.

The next day, all day, she'd gone without looking at the picture. Her parents were keeping an unusually close eye on her. Or at least that's how it felt. She'd be watching TV, and she'd catch her mother staring at her. Or she'd be on her iPhone, scrolling through Instagram and see her dad's shadow in the doorway. They watched Katie through breakfast, lunch and dinner. "Anything interesting happen today?" her mother had asked over dinner as she was slicing the roast beef. And when Katie replied, "No," they had stared at her for what felt like a full minute. It had taken all of Katie's willpower not to scream at the top of her lungs.

After her father had gone into the living room to read his newspaper, Katie had helped her mother clear the plates, just like always. At this point, it had been close to sixteen hours since she had seen Sean's lips moving. She longed to be with him again, so much so that she could physically feel it—little parts of her dying and crumbling and turning to dust.

Soon, she kept thinking. *Soon.*

But then her mother spoke. "Katie." Her voice was a sheet of ice. "Last night, in your room…"

"Yes, Mother?"

"I thought I heard talking."

Katie's heart started to pound. "You heard wrong," she said. "There was no talking."

"You're alone in there?"

"Yes, Mother. Of course I'm alone."

"You aren't skyping or—"

"Who would I skype with?" Katie said. "I have no friends."

Not the whole truth—not now, anyway—but at least it made her mother shut up. After they finished clearing the dishes, Katie went into her room, and slammed the door behind her. *Now, Sean.*

She couldn't wait until after her parents went to sleep— she was too keyed up, those words scrolling through her mind, that gift he'd given her: *You're stronger than you know.*

She flew at her bed and slipped the picture out from under the pillow and shined her phone on his beautiful face. "Sean," she whispered. "We almost got caught."

His eyes glowed. "You should go out."

"What do you mean?"

"You know," he said. "You know what I mean."

She did, of course. But it made no sense. She didn't leave the house. He knew that. She hadn't left the house since the boy down the street, and that had been such a long time ago.

"You don't leave the house," Sean said, "because they won't let you."

"They do it for my own good."

"How could that be for anybody's good?"

"They're keeping me safe."

"They're keeping you prisoner, love," he said it in that Kiwi accent, the words scented like beach sand, wrapping her warm like a lullaby. "They let the cat wander about the neighborhood, but not you. Does that seem fair, Angel? Does it?"

"It's...it's a dangerous world out there, and—"

"You're stronger than you know."

"Katie?" it was her mother's voice at the door.

"Crap," Katie whispered.

"Escape," Sean said.

"Who are you talking to, Katie?"

"I'm reading from a book, Mother."

"Out loud?"

"I'm praying."

Silence.

Katie held their breath. Sean held his along with her, both of them waiting, both hanging from the tensest of threads until they heard Mother's retreating footsteps, her parents' bedroom door closing softly.

"Close call." Katie started to slip the picture back under her pillow, but then she stopped.

Sean was staring into her face, green eyes blazing in a way they never did in real life. She watched his lips curl into a smile—a secret one, just for her. "Katie," he said. "My Katie."

She nodded.

"You know what you need to do to set yourself free."

Her cheeks felt hot. She turned to the poster on her wall—to Dean and Cody and Max and Terrence. And Sean. The other Sean. The one who didn't talk.

They had a song, the Boys did. It was called, "Set Yourself Free," and it unfurled in Katie's mind like a bright flag. *If you love me, darling, you'll set yourself free/ We'll be free together, you and me...*

She turned back to Sean's picture, to those soft, twisted lips, to those green eyes, twinkling. "Ready?" he said.

"Yes."

Carol Flynn woke up with a start at four a.m. *Bad dream*, she tried to tell herself. But it wasn't a dream, it was life, her life. Every night, waking up like this.

Years ago, Carol used to be such a sound sleeper. But all of that changed with motherhood. First it was the mysterious kicks of pregnancy that roused her from slumber, and then, after Katie was born, the slightest shift in her baby's breathing could jolt her awake. It was a common problem for new mothers, one that Carol assumed would right itself once her daughter matured. But as it turned out, their daughter blossomed into something neither she nor Bill had ever imagined, and as a result her sleeping only grew more fitful.

These days, Carol longed for the calm of new parenthood, for the days before she and Bill knew there was anything wrong with their daughter. *Not wrong. Different. Fine as long as we stay alert, as long as we watch her...*

Bill snored like a bear. She couldn't understand how he could sleep like that, but he was only a father, after all. He'd never felt the kicks. He didn't share Carol's intuition. Bill expected that life would go okay if he worked at his job, if he paid his bills, if he put healthy food on the table and kept the doors locked and a baseball bat in their bedroom closet, just in case. He'd always been that way, and he still held by those tired old rules, as though nothing had ever happened to them. As though healthy food made any difference at all.

As though a home could only be invaded from the outside.

Carol tried listening to Bill's snoring, the long intake of breath and the sawing release, a door opening and slamming. It usually soothed her, the familiarity of it, the rhythm. But not tonight. *How can he not see?*

Carol nudged him awake. "I think she's off her meds," she said.

"Huh?"

"Katie."

He dragged an arm across his face, wiped sleep out of his eyes. "No," he said. "I watched her."

"So did I."

"I counted the pills."

"And?"

"And," he said. "She's on track."

"She could be hiding them."

Bill moaned. "Carol."

"I heard her talking to herself."

"Probably chatting online," he said. "About that band

she likes."

"She said she was praying."

"So? She was praying then."

"I'm going to check on her."

"Leave her be."

"I'm just going to peek in." Carol slipped out of bed, put on her robe.

Bill said it again, more insistent this time. *"Leave her be, Carol."*

Carol sensed the anger in his voice, and she knew why. Katie acted out when she felt "too mothered." The therapist had told them that, back when Katie was still living at the treatment facility. "You need to watch her, but you must give her some space," the therapist had said, as though that therapist knew anything. As though Carol's love, and that alone, was what drove her only daughter to do what she had done to that boy down the street.

"I know you have the best intentions, Mrs. Flynn," the therapist had said. God, how Carol had hated her, how she'd hated all the staff at that treatment facility, those people in her neighborhood, writing in to the newspapers, standing outside the courthouse, busybodies all of them, telling her she had no right to be a parent, that her daughter was a murderer, a monster who should be put down or institutionalized forever. It was why she kept Katie inside—not for *their* protection, but for her own, for Katie's own.

"If she's talking online, that's a good thing," Bill was saying. "She needs some freedom. She needs to socialize."

Carol stared at him. "You don't remember."

"It's been a long time."

"It was a fight. Over a singing group."

"It was a chemical imbalance. She's on her meds."

"I need to check on her."

She started out of the room, padded down the hall, Bill's voice trailing behind her. "For God's sakes, Carol." But then, he was next to her as he always was, hand on her shoulder. Protecting her.

She wished it didn't have to be like this. So dearly, Carol wished that they could be like other parents, that they could look in on their sleeping daughter without that gnawing feeling inside, that they could watch the rise and fall of her chest and listen to her soft breathing and see only an angel.

Carol flicked on the light in the hallway. As quietly as she could, she turned the doorknob.

"Honey," Bill whispered. "You have to back off."

"I'm just checking."

"Last time, okay? You promise, after tonight, you'll give her privacy? Treat her more like an adult?"

"She's our daughter, Bill."

He squeezed her shoulder, too hard. "Carol," he said quietly. "She's a forty-year-old woman."

"Where is she?" Katie's mother asked her father as Katie came up behind them, Dad's baseball bat clutched in both hands, the metal cold against her palms and Sean's voice in her head, urging. *"Don't be frightened, love. It will be over soon and you'll be free."*

Katie wasn't frightened though. She was amazed, in fact, at how small her parents had become in their old age, small enough so that she could see right over both of them and into her bedroom, the hall light illuminating her neatly made bed, Sean's picture propped up on the pillow, lips curling into a smile.

"What the hell is going on?" Dad said. "What's that picture?"

But Katie heard only the voice of Sean The Shy One. "I love you," the picture said, Sean said, as Katie raised the bat over the tiny heads of her wrinkled parents.

"I love you too," she said, as the bat came down.

LORELEI
Joyce Carol Oates

Please love me my eyes beg. My need is so raw, I can't blame any of you from looking quickly away.

Not you, not you, and you—none of you can I blame. *Only just love me, can't you? Love me...*

That Sunday night, desperate not to be late, I had to change trains at Times Square, and the subway was jammed, both trains crowded, always I knew it would happen soon, my destiny would happen within the hour, except: it was required that I be at the precise position when you lift your eyes to mine (casual-seeming, by chance) as you turn to face me. I must be there, or the precious moment will pass, and then—so lonely! In the swarm of strangers departing a train, pushing into the next train, pushing to the gritty stairs, breathless and trying not to turn my ankle in my spike-heeled sandals, my hair so glossy black you'd suspect it must be dyed but *my hair is not dyed, this is my natural hair color*, and my skin white, exquisite soft-skinned white, and I'm wearing a black suede short skirt to mid-thigh and black diamond-patterned stockings with a black satin garter belt you can catch a glimpse of when I'm seated and I cross my slender legs in just the right, practiced way; and a white lace camisole, and beneath the camisole a black satin lace bra that grips my small breasts tight lifting them in mute appeal.

Please love me, please look at me, how can you look away? Here I am, before you. My shiny-black hair I have ratted with a steel comb to three times its natural size, my mouth that's small and hurt like a snail in its shell I have outlined in crimson, a high-gloss lipstick applied to the outside of the lips enlarging them so I'm breathless smiling making my way to the far side of the track being pushed against, collided with, rudely touched by—who?—sometimes I feel one of you brush against me light as a feather's touch, purely by accident, or almost-accident, sometimes it's a hurtful jolt, I could step aside if I'm alert enough but a strange lassitude overcomes me, this one isn't the one, and yet!—the shock of him colliding with me as he hurries past, scarcely aware of me, doesn't slow his pace or apologize, not even a murmured *Excuse me,* the touch is like an electric shock, half-pleasurable, though meant to hurt. As if he knows, this stranger, that he isn't the one. Not tonight.

That Sunday night, not late—not yet ten p.m. And not so crowded as the previous nights, those wild weekend nights, but still plenty crowded at Times Square, you can be sure. And I was the desperate girl you saw hurrying to make the downtown train. Before the doors closed. Stumbling in my high-heeled shoes so you might have thought there was something wrong with me, the over-bright glisten in my black-mascara eyes and parted crimson lips, the look in my feverish face of anticipation and dread, you'd have felt a stab of pity, and maybe something else, something deeper than pity, and more cruel, and possibly you'd offered to help me, offered your seat to me at least. And possibly, I'd have accepted.

Always in the subway I think *On this train, this train is my destiny: who? Which one of you?* Tremulous with excitement. Anticipation. Pondering through my lowered eyelashes the possibilities. Mostly men of course but (sometimes) women also. Young men, middle-aged men, occasionally older men. Young women, with a certain sign. But never middle-aged, or older women. Never. I tried not even to look at them. Resented them, their raddled faces and tired eyes. And sometimes in those eyes a look of hope, which I particularly despised. For in the hopeless, hope is obscene! And when out of sheer loneliness one of these women smiles at me, moves over inviting me to sit beside her, like hell I will sit next to some old bag like she's my mother, or grandmother!

As if I would ever be one of *them.*

On the train that night a woman of about forty-five took shrewd note of me as soon as I entered the car, out of breath and laughing to myself, my hair just slightly disheveled, fallen into my face. The woman was wearing a green uniform, and ugly dirty-white nurse's shoes they looked like, and her dirt-colored hair flat against her head in a hairnet, staring at me not with sympathy or pity but with disapproval I thought, prissy fish-mouth I tried not to look at. Hate that type of person observing me, judging me coolly. Not to the hairnet woman was I pleading *Look at me, love me! Hey: here I am.*

In the subway the trains move so swiftly you can never catch your breath. Outside the grimy window that's a reflecting surface like a mirror mostly there are the rushing tunnel walls, that slow as the train slows for a station, and the doors open with a pneumatic hiss like the sigh of a great ugly beast, and passengers lurch off, and new passengers lurch on, and I lift my eyes hopeful and yearning *Who will be my destiny? Which one of you?* At 34th Street one of you entered the car, sat near me, I could see that he'd chosen the seat beside me deliberately, for there were other, unoccupied seats. The way his eyes trailed over me like slow slugs, my crossed legs in the patterned black stockings, my mouth in a dreamy half-smile, as if I'm expecting to recognize a friend. A friendly face. Like a child hoping to be pleasantly surprised, for I am not a cynical person by nature. And he stared at me appraising. His mouth moved into a kind of smile. He was many years older than I was, one of the bad-Daddys of the subway. In the underground are the bad-Daddys, you know one another. Staring rudely, with that smile at the edge of a sneer, or a sneer at the edge of a smile. In his early forties, pale coarse pitted skin attractive in that battered way some men are, that would be hopeless laughable ugliness in a female. Sand-colored hair crimped and wavy like a wig, and in his right ear lobe a silver ear cuff looking as if it might hurt, like something clamped into the flesh. *The sign* that took my eye immediately was that he was wearing suede, which matched my skirt: a black jacket with chrome studs. (The jacket was not "real" suede of course. My skirt, that strained at my thighs just inches below the fork in my legs, was not "real" suede of course.) He was wearing dark trousers and (fake) ostrich-skin boots. On his (hairy) left wrist, a heavy I.D. bracelet. When he opened his mouth to smile, there was the shock of a gleaming tongue-ring winking at me. As if he knew me he spoke a name, had to be a name he'd invented at that moment, or maybe it was a name known to him, of a girl he'd known and had not seen in years, and I smiled at him saying no that is not my name, I am not that girl, and he asked *Which girl are you, then?* And the tongue-ring winked at me in a nasty way, unmistakable. And I told him Lorelei—I am Lorelei. And he cupped his hand to his ear as if hard-of-hearing in the noisy subway train and he repeated the name *Lorelei* and added *A beautiful name for a beautiful girl.* It was not clear to me if he spoke these words truly or in jest but I saw that he was excited by me. I saw the light come into his eyes, that were ordinary small mud-colored eyes. In a lowered voice he began speaking of himself, said he was a lonely pilgrim searching for something he could not name, been searching for all of his life, would I like to have a drink with him, please would I like to have a drink with him, we could get off at the next stop and have a drink together, he knew just the place, and all this time I was quieting observing him, through my mascara-lashes I was observing him, his eyes that were ordinary and mud-colored and hopeful and the truth came to me *No: he is not the one.* So politely I told him I could not get off the train with him, no thank you. Told him that I was meeting someone else. And he stared at me not-so-friendly now, and spoke to me in a low crude voice not-so-friendly now, exposing the spit-gleaming tongue-ring not-so-friendly now, called me *Lorelei* like it was *Loora-Lee* and some kind of stupid name, cow-name, he didn't think so much of. All this while other passengers in the train were trying not to observe us, trying not to hear the man speaking to me, the way you'd speak to (maybe) a retarded girl in the train, a girl her family ought not to have let ride the train alone, that kind of girl, but I am not that girl of course. One of those eavesdropping was the hairnet woman in the ugly green uniform, I saw now was food-stained, had to be a cafeteria worker probably, so I could pity *her.* The hairnet woman was frowning at both of us like we were the scum of the earth, so I could despise *her.*

Shutting my eyes then, and not opening them until later, several stops later, the hairnet woman was gone and the tongue-ring man in the seat beside me was gone and I checked my reflection in my little gold mirror compact seeing a shiny nose, anxious eyes for I had almost made a mistake. *That one was a test. In your ignorance you might have gone with him.*

For my life at that time was a continual testing. That in ignorance or desperation I would make a terrible error, and would not realize my destiny.

Slamming into the car from the car ahead was a big girl of about thirty with no eyelashes like she'd plucked them all out or shaved them, and she'd shaved most of her head so just stiff platinum-blonde quills remained, so striking!—everybody in the car stared at her even those who'd been nodding off woke to take in such a sight. The girl's face was glowing and shiny as if made of some synthetic material like flesh-plastic, with no pores, and her lips were swollen and pouty, and moved as if she was talking to herself. For in the underground, some of us sometimes talk to ourselves, and you are (maybe) meant to overhear. Seeing me, her eyes latching onto mine, she stopped in mid-stride and stood swaying above me holding the rail about two feet from me, observing me and a slow smile broke over the plastic-face like something melting. Big husky girl six feet tall in khakis and tight-fitting black T-shirt with DRAGO FREK in red letters. *The sign* was a bullet-shape silver ring on the middle finger of her left hand which was the bullet-shape of the silver buckle of my belt cinching in my waist tight. Her eyes on me restless as those minnow-sized fish that devour living things in seconds—piranha. Leaned down to ask did I know what the freak time it was and I laughed saying no I did not know what the "freak time" it was, I was sorry. After ten p.m. I said, this is what I thought the time was up on the ground where there were clocks. This made Plastic Girl laugh too, and a smell of spicy meat came from her opened mouth. She asked didn't I wear a wrist watch?—and I said no, and she laughed again saying Hey, was I a girl who didn't give a shit about the time, and I frowned at this, I did not like to hear profanity or nasty words, not even from a girl who stared at me in a way that was flattering. All this while Plastic Girl leaning over me and breathing that meaty smell saying, I guess you're the kind of girl who knows her own mind. That is fucking cool.

Raising her voice to be heard over the racket of the train Plastic Girl started telling me about this place she was expected at, some kind of residence she wasn't going back to, halfway-house, *halfway-to-Hell house*, except somebody there owed her, had clothes of hers and personal documents so she'd have to return except not by any fucking front entrance where you had to sign in, she'd get back inside by a window and it wouldn't be broad fucking daylight, it would be night. I listened to Plastic Girl's voice like it was a radio voice. It was a voice beamed to me that had nothing to do with me. Distracted by Plastic Girl's heavy breasts swaying inside the T-shirt, and her belly above the zipper-crotch of the khakis pushing out round and hard like a drum. The bullet-shape silver ring that was *the sign* between us, that (maybe) Plastic Girl had seen also. And the thought came to me *Is this the one? A female?*

But at the next station a swarm of people entered the car. A man pushed between us like Plastic Girl didn't exist. Rude behavior but he was taller and bigger than Plastic Girl and knew she would give him no trouble. Smiling sidelong at me like he knew me, or was pretending to know me, this was a game we'd played before, him and me. (Was it?) A woman seated close by decided to move to another seat, uncomfortable with Plastic Girl and now this new guy hanging above her, each of them drawn to me, as eyes were drawn to me generally, and right away the guy took her place before Plastic Girl could sit down. You could see that Plastic Girl was angry. Baring her teeth like she'd have liked to tear at someone with those teeth. I looked up at her appealing with my eyes, sorry! I was sorry!—but Plastic Girl shrugged and moved off, took a seat farther down the car that had just opened up. As the train lurched I could see her shaved head glowing like a bulb and the platinum-blond quills quivering like antennae. I knew: Plastic Girl would keep her eyes on me, she would not let me go so easily.

The man beside me nudged me—it was the first actual touch of this night, I reacted with a start—asking did I remember him? Huhhh?

Did I remember him? Dunk's the name.

Dunk! I did not remember any *Dunk.*

Laughed to hear such a silly name—*Dunk.*

Sure you do, sweetheart. You remember Dunk.

Then realizing yes I'd met Dunk before. More than once

before. Why I'd felt sort of strange seeing him, sort of protect-
ed-by-him, the way you do with some individuals, though
not with most men, not ever. A few weeks ago we'd got to
talking in the subway and he'd taken me for coffee (at Union
Square). Possibly I'd been dressed then as I was dressed now.
And Dunk in the fake-buckskin jacket he was wearing now,
and his steel-gray hair pulled back in a little pigtail at the
nape of his neck as it was now. (Had to smile at this little
pigtail since Dunk was near-bald except for a band of hair
around his bumpy-looking head he'd let grow to pull into a
pigtail.) There was something old and comfortable about
Dunk, pothead hippie from long ago. Dunk said he remembered me, yes he remembered Lorelei, hey, did I know I'd
broken his heart? Dunk made a weepy jocular sound like a
wheezing heart might make but mostly he was needing to
blow his nose which he did in a dirty tissue, making a honking noise so I laughed. That was Dunk's power: to make you
laugh. The dirty wadded tissue in his hand was *the sign* for
in my pocket was a dirty tissue stained with blood.

Dunk had been a psychiatric social worker for the city.
Had to quit after twenty-three years and take disability pay
to save his soul, he said. In the coffee shop at Penn Station
he told me of his life lapsing into a singsong voice like a lullaby. You could see that Dunk had told his story many times
before but Dunk had no other story to tell. He was very
lonely, he would confide. His skin exuded heat like a radiator.
Made me laugh—almost—how his right eye drifted out of
focus while his left eye had me pinned. In the coffee shop
Dunk paid for my coffee and for something to eat, Dunk believed that I was too skinny. He said that I would never ma-
ture if I was malnourished. He said that my organs would
age prematurely and that I would die prematurely. He told
me of his patient who'd threatened to kill him and he'd said
what difference did it make, we're all going to die anyway
aren't we. He'd been so depressed. And something terrible

had happened to his patient, and Dunk was to blame though no one knew. Though Dunk would not confide in anyone except me.

Then, Dunk said, he got bored with being depressed. I was listening with just half my mind. The other half yearning for you. By this time I'd realized that Dunk was not my destiny.

This night, Dunk is asking would I come with him, we could have a meal together. Politely I said thank you, but I have an appointment with someone else.

Who is my destiny? You?

Whoever it was, I didn't see. Never saw his face. Never saw but a shadow in the corner of my eye. Great bird spreading its wings. (I believe it was a man. I am sure it was a man. But even that fact, I can't be one hundred percent certain of.) At the 14th Street station. My plan was to take the uptown to 57th Street. Past Times Square. I'd been disappointed in Times Square lately. The area around Carnegie Hall is very different. Lorelei would be more visible there. Now standing at the edge of the platform a little apart from a small crowd gathered for the next train. A few yards maybe. I didn't believe that I was standing dangerously close to the edge. Something on the sole of my high-heeled sandal, something sticky and disgusting like a large wad of gum. And this gum was like a tongue. Ugh! Trying to scrap it off my shoe when I saw, or half-saw, your shadow in the corner of my eye, advancing upon me from the left. The thought came to me swift and yearning *Please touch me* because it was such a familiar thought, I did not believe that I was in danger. *Touch me even if you hurt me. Oh please.*

Then I was falling. I was screaming, and I was falling. It happened so fast! Faster than I can recount. Though even then thinking *You touched me at last. It was a human touch. You chose me because I am beautiful and desirable and young. You chose me over all the others.*

But already my happiness has ended. I have fallen onto the track. I have fallen helpless, on my back. A smell of oil in my widened nostrils, something musty and cold. Out of nowhere the train is speeding. Oncoming headlights. My body is a boneless rag doll flopping and being crushed by the train. The emergency brakes are thrown but it's too late, it was too late as soon as you moved up stealthily behind me smiling whispering *Lorelei! Lorelei!* in your way of cruel teasing. You pushed me from behind, hard. Swift and hard the palms of your hands flat against my back between my shoulder blades. As if you've planned the act, you've rehearsed the act numerous times to perfection, and in the very act of pushing you are turning aside, to the left, taking care that the momentum of your act doesn't carry you over the edge of the platform and onto the track below with your screaming victim. And you are running, you are pushing past bystanders running and gone with your mysterious cruel smile as below the platform on the tracks inside the terrible grinding wheels my body is caught up, my legs severed at the knees, a wrenching of bone, my left arm is torn off at the shoulder, my skull crushed as you'd crush a bird's egg beneath your careless feet, scarcely knowing you'd crushed it. The silly high-heeled sandals have been tossed from my feet and will be found a dozen yards away. My blood is rushing from my body to congeal with the cold oil and filth of the tracks. My body is crushed, disfigured. You would no longer stare at my beauty. You would no longer recognize Lorelei. On the platform above, strangers are screaming. I want to cry, these strangers care for me. In that instant, they care for me. Fellow passengers who'd disapproved of me in the trains have now forgiven me and are crying Help! Get help! Oh God get help! A tall husky girl who might be Plastic Girl runs to the edge of the platform, can't see me because my body is hidden by the train skidding to a stop.

And Dunk, slack-mouthed in horror. Dunk with his bald-hippie pigtail gone gray. Dunk stunned and sick with grief he has lost me for the final time.

And you others who never knew me except to glimpse a girl pushed in front of a speeding train to her death, these others grieving for me, too. Never knew me in life but will never never forget me as I am in death.

Please love me? My eyes beg. Glancing at the window beside your seat, uptown train flying through the tunnel, lights in the car flickering off, back on, off again and back on like the sensation before sleep. Lights in the car so bright you can't see outside, only your reflection in the grimy window, my own face, and sometimes you don't recognize that face.

Please love me? I love you.

SEESAW SALLY
Alec Cizak

She sat outside his house in her driver's Town Car. Duran Duran or some other pop shit crackled on the radio. Holmes, the driver, shut it off. "Rock and roll took a dive the day Bonzo choked on his fucking vomit," he said.

"Yeah, sure," she said. She worked on a Carlton 120. Mr. Lime said the client sounded old, said he claimed he had never called a service before. Either way, the job would suck. Were the client being honest, he would be coy and act ashamed, or something dumber. And, more than likely, had he lied, he'd be some geezer expecting her to roll over like a dog every time he peeled more cash off his dirty palm. She took one last puff and tossed her cigarette onto the street.

"Need some weed?" said the driver. He opened his chubby hand, showed her a joint that had been soaked in his sweat.

"I burned one down at home," she said. Getting stoned helped her leave her body while a client made use of it. She'd close her eyes and see stars and planets and comets.

"Cool." He opened his door. "Let's make some money."

She got out on her side. In her head, she repeated, over and over, *They're all chumps.* The clients, the driver. Her father, of course. *Only thing better than flying through space would be going back in time and throttling the bastard before he got his hands on me.*

"You okay?" said the driver.

"Give me a break," she said. After checking her small,

kidney-shaped purse for mace, she tugged on the bottom of her skirt. Made sure no one could see her panties without permission. Client might get a glimpse, think that's enough to spark his imagination, and slam the door on her. Holmes would pound the windows, promise to break the guy's legs. If the client threatened to call the police, she and Holmes would have to book. And she'd be out of an hour's pay and possibly subject to a slap in the mouth from Mr. Lime.

Just looking at the client's house revealed he had no wife. No girlfriend to tell him to fix the chain link fence out front, bag the dog shit on the lawn, and for Christ's sake, wash down the white, aluminum siding covering what she suspected were rotted, wooden walls. Hounds barked inside the client's garage. At least he had been kind enough to put them away. On her third or fourth job—she couldn't remember—her driver had to tear off a Doberman's jawbone.

The gate leading to a walkway of cracked cement blocks hung crooked, one of its rusty hinges missing a bolt. She waited for Holmes to open it so that she wouldn't get her hands dirty or break a nail, or worse, cut herself on some vagrant sliver of metal. As she stepped through, Holmes said, "I'll hang back."

"Cool," she said. The straps on her high heels dug into her ankles as she hobbled up the front walk. She pulled a screen door back and knocked. The client fumbled with a chain on the other side. She assumed he had taken it off, but then the door opened a smidge and a man well over forty poked his snout through the crack.

"Mercedes?" he said.

He looked familiar. She couldn't place him, though. "The one and only," she said.

The man swept the chain aside and opened the door to a living room cluttered with magazines and newspapers stacked like buildings on a hardwood floor. Against one wall was a ripped, mustard colored couch, against the opposite, a slim piano with no bench. The man stepped away, allowing her to enter. She looked him up and down, still wondering where she had seen him in either of her previous lives. "You got to pay Holmes," she said.

He didn't move.

She nodded over her shoulder. "Holmes," she said. "My driver. He collects the fee."

"Oh." The man produced a thin, faded wallet. "Um," he said, "Hundred-fifty?"

"That's right."

"That covers everything?" He counted the bills twice.

"Excuse me?" she said.

"One-fifty, that's for everything?"

"That's the fee, honey," she said. "What we do now depends on how much you want to tip."

"Really?"

She motioned with her fingers, hurrying him to fork over the dough. Best to get it to the driver. If the client chickened out or squawked about the tip schedule, she and Holmes and Mr. Lime would at least get something for the trip. And the risk.

The man gave her the once-over. As all men did, he stopped for a moment too long at her breasts. "Okay," he said.

This fat ass hasn't been laid in a century. She marched down the walkway to give the money to Holmes.

He told her he'd be in the car. "Shout if things turn to shit," he said.

"No sweat," she said. "He's a chump."

The man did what all rookie johns did—he offered her a drink and a seat on his grungy couch. "Thanks," she said. She sat so that she wouldn't wrinkle her skirt.

He called from the kitchen, "Wine okay?"

"Sure." She had no desire to see what kind of pigsty the

man cooked and ate in. She hoped he wouldn't want full service. At least, not in his bedroom. Not on his bed. He probably hadn't washed his sheets since the 1970s. She scanned the magazines and newspapers. Stacks of browning, folded copies of *The Indianapolis Star* and *The Indianapolis News* and education magazines.

A fucking teacher.

Of course.

The man returned. "Carlo Rossi," he said as he handed her a plastic wine glass.

"Perfect," she said. A little alcohol on top of the weed would give her a nice spin. When she closed her eyes, she would see roiling star clusters and supernovas. Before she got it to her lips, however, he stopped her.

"A toast?" he said.

"What for?" she said.

"Who knows?" he said. "Momentary romance?"

"This isn't romance, ah," she paused, "what's your name, by the way?"

"You can call me Sam."

Mr. Duncan.

Her sophomore lit teacher. Benjamin Harrison High.

Fuck.

Please don't recognize me.

"Well, Sam," she said, "this is business. It has nothing to do with romance."

He smirked. "Sure."

Mr. Duncan had been one of the saints, one of the sorry sons of bitches who tried to save her when it had already been too late. He had told her that he knew what the students called her in the hallways and bathrooms and locker room—*Seesaw Sally*. She couldn't help it. Spreading for any boy who asked seemed an appropriate revenge after what her father had done to her. Mr. Duncan told her the best medicine was success and the stones in that path were set by education. The real American Dream, he said, required physical and mental labor. Once upon a time, maybe. Against Mr. Duncan's pleas, she dropped out in the middle of the semester and started dancing at Sugar Cookie's, a strip club on Madison Avenue. Didn't take long to get to the next, obvious step, mostly thanks to Mr. Lime.

"So," said Mr. Duncan, "how does this work?"

Why doesn't this bastard recognize me? When she was in his class, he sure put on a good show, pretending he cared. That was only four years ago. *Whatever.* She went into her sales routine—"Your entertainment depends on your investment, Mr.," she stopped herself. "Sam."

"Okay."

"So, for instance, if you want me roll the top of my dress down so you can look at my tits and get yourself off, well, that's going to run you a hundred dollars."

"Really?" He looked offended.

She continued. "I'll lose my dress and panties for two."

"And I'm supposed to take care of myself?"

She nodded toward a box of tissues on a stack of *Life* magazines. "Yes, sir," she said.

"I don't mean to be rude," he said. "You see, I haven't actually, you know, done it, since my fiancée left me."

"Jerked off?"

"No," he said. "*It.*"

As much as she hated chumps, she knew they couldn't be happy if they didn't plow a woman at least once or twice a year. Even the ugly ones, the fat ones, and the old ones. "When did your fiancée leave you?"

"Nineteen-sixty-eight. November. Seventh. Thursday. Somewhere between eight in the morning and four-thirty."

"Wow," she said. "You haven't gotten laid in fifteen years?"

"Right," he said.

Crap. The chump wanted full service. Hell, he *needed* it.

125

Who knew where he worked these days. She'd heard that Harrison High closed a year ago. Wherever he taught, his students might benefit if he got some trim, shed some stress. She imagined what he looked like naked. Glanced at his paunch. Most of these middle-aged guys had loose skin in bad places. Some of them could barely get it up. And then they complained if they didn't get off. Refused to pay. She didn't want Holmes breaking Mr. Duncan's arm.

"Well," she said, "we're really not supposed to do that. This is an entertainment service." Standard bullshit designed to protect Mr. Lime.

Mr. Duncan's shoulders slumped.

"However," she said, "if we agree that the arranged date is over, then we can make a deal on the side." Mr. Lime claimed this piece of dialogue would fend off any charges an undercover pig might stick her with.

"Okay, good," he said. "Good, good."

Putting her hand on his knee, she said, "It's quite a bit more expensive."

A puppy couldn't have nodded faster. "That's fine, really."

"One time on the Love Boat," she said, her hands hovering over her breasts and her thighs, "will run you six hundred. Twice, well, that's a thousand."

He sat back. Grimaced.

"And I'll spend the night," she said, "with unlimited access, for two g's." She tapped her thigh, made little white circles that disappeared right away.

Mr. Duncan sighed. He put his forehead in his palm. He opened his wallet and counted the remaining bills. "Could we do one time for four hundred?"

"I don't haggle, Mr.," she stopped herself again. "*Sam.*"

"Well," he said, "if I'm going to spend a fortune, might as well be worthwhile." He stood and started for the hallway. "I've got some money stashed away."

"Shall we do it here?" She patted the couch. *Please?*

"The bedroom's the appropriate place for that." Then he disappeared down the corridor.

She made her way to her feet and weaved through stacks of newspapers. On top of one heap, a headline announced, "Reagan by a Landslide." Atop another stack, "Bussing Riots Turn Violent." Halfway in the living room and in the corridor, an *Indianapolis Star* headline said, "Mission Accomplished." A giant picture of Neil Armstrong saluting next to a flag planted on the moon took up the rest of the page. She remembered watching the first landing on TV with her family, telling her father she wanted to be an astronaut. The bastard laughed and said, "Girls don't do that stuff." Mr. Duncan had asked her, once, what her goals were. Just to make him happy, she'd slipped in the bit about how she wanted to walk in space, fly to Mars.

"You good with math?" he'd said.

"I'm not terrible," she'd said.

"What's stopping you?"

Not too long after, she dropped out and moved in with her friend Heather, who told her how much money she could pull at Sugar Cookie's. Those were the days when anyone who had the audacity to be nice to her *needed* to be punished. And she disciplined them the best way she knew how— she hurt herself. If they cared so much about her, surely they'd suffer along with her.

As she pushed aside the door leading to Mr. Duncan's bedroom, she held her nose. Dirty laundry, mostly socks and briefs, covered the floor. She saw him put a shoebox on a shelf in a closet filled with sports jackets and short-sleeved, button down shirts.

"A thousand for two rounds?" he said.

"That's right, honey." She took the money from him and folded it into her purse. "Get undressed, sweetie." She set the purse on a nightstand next to the unmade, twin-sized bed. The tiny table was the cleanest piece of furniture in the house. The only thing on it was a picture in a heavy, brass frame. A younger, more handsome Mr. Duncan, his arms around a brunette with a poofy, 1960s haircut and a bullet bra under her sweater that made her boobs look like rockets. She picked it up. "She's beautiful," she said.

He looked away as he unbuttoned his shirt.

What a crock of shit. *Life.* They were putting shuttles in the stratosphere now and women were on board. Too late for her. She ran a finger along the frame of the picture of Mr. Duncan and a woman who had obviously fucked him up. "Hey," she said, "did you hear me?" She crossed the room, the picture still in her hands.

"Yes," he said. He removed his shirt. Judging by the sick, lemon shade of his undershirt, nobody had ever taught him how to separate colors from whites.

She smiled and waited for him to do the same.

He looked at her, paused, and said, "Sally?"

She drew the picture back and slammed it into his face. He hit his head against the wall as he fell. The glass covering the photograph cracked and cut his cheek open. He slumped between the bed and the wall, motionless. She put her ear against his chest. His heart beat, his lungs filled and collapsed. "Pleasant dreams," she said.

The shelf in the closet was just high enough that she had to drag the bed over and stand on it to reach it. She pulled the shoebox down and opened it. Gobs of money inside. As she left the house, she flipped furniture and kicked over stacks of newspapers like Godzilla, crushing Tokyo.

She hurried down the front walk, looking left and right to make sure nobody saw her. Holmes leaned out the passenger window. "What's going on?"

"Early Christmas," she said. She held the shoebox up.

The driver nodded. He sparked the engine and opened the door for her.

They booked out of the neighborhood and onto the freeway. She showed him the cash.

"Holy shit," he said.

"Halfsies?"

"Right on."

"We'll slide a couple of bills to Mr. Lime," she said. "Tell him I let the chump splooge on my tits."

"What if this guy calls the cops?"

"Are you kidding?" she said. "He's a public school teacher."

"Sweet."

She rested her head against her window. Streetlights reflected in the glass. Looking past them, she searched for the sky, for the stars. Nothing but clouds and pollution. No planets, no comets, no moon. Then she took the lid off the shoebox and counted the money.

TATTOO
Joe Clifford

You never claimed to be one of the good guys. But this? This will probably go down as one of the shittier things you've done. If there's a heaven and hell, you're ending up on the south side. No doubt about it. But that's a pretty big if. What you do know is that pretty girls shouldn't go around breaking hearts.

There's a contract you enter into when you date someone. An unspoken, mutually agreed-upon understanding. Might not be signed and legal, no lawyers shystering their fifty percent cut. But it's binding just the same. And Karah fucking knew that. She knew that when she'd lie there, both of you spent after a long night of fucking in your trailer, still a little drunk, high, naked, talking about a future together; she knew it every time she'd trace the outline of your tattoos, asking why the pretty things always cut deepest, as the big rigs rumbled on the concrete overpass above, quaking the park. With each lilted word she was asking for a piece of your heart. Might not have been explicitly stated. But that's what she was doing. And you gave it to her, said, "Here it is. Please don't break it." That was the deal. So this is on her as much as it's on you. And if it turns out that there is someone, somewhere, sitting up high and judging, then you'll have some company.

Funny thing is, Karah said she was never into guys with tattoos. Said you were the first one who really did it for her.

Though she teased you enough about it. Said, "Sure, they look good now. But what about when you're old, when they're all blue and faded and your skin's all wrinkly, what then?"

You told her you didn't live your life that way.

She called you a cliché. She laughed when she said it so you'd know she was kidding. Like when someone sends you an email, calling you a self-centered asshole but closes with a winky face at the end of it.

Maybe you are sensitive. Karah always said you couldn't take a joke. But it's easy for people like Karah to say things like that. Pretty girls with money and options. That's the part that really got to you, when it was over. You were a phase. The bad boy, the starving artist with the motorcycle and tattoos. Uptown girl slumming it with trailer trash. A mixed-race affair slotted just after a two-month, bi-sexual college relationship. Lesbian until graduation? Now who's the cliché?

She used to bust your balls about living in a trailer park, as you struggled to make your stamp on the art world, like everyone who lives in a mobile home fucks his sister, eats raccoon meat, has to reuse his cereal milk for coffee creamer. You dropped twenty grand, cash, your own hard-earned money, on that trailer. And that mobile home she mocked as so "Americana and kitsch?" That same one where she let you fuck her deep in the ass? You owned that shit. All yours, free and clear of any bank. No other choice. Mom and Dad weren't bailing you out. You've always seen the larger plan, the greater landscape, the grand picture. While the Karahs of the world were getting hocked up to their eyeballs, overextended with credit card debt, you were your own man. No landlord telling you what to do. No bank. No boss either.

Because you flipped that little trailer and lot, yes you did, doubled your profit, and you kept flipping, investing, until you had enough left over to start this little tattoo shop, far away in the city. Built it up from scratch, got a nice clientele, a good reputation. You didn't chintz on guns or color. Only the best for your customers. Now people pay good money to see you. Because you are a real artist. Earn a nice payday, too. A hundred and eighty an hour for your time. Some doctors don't make that.

Got a good little life, you do. Which is why, anyone ever found out, they might have a tough time understanding. Karah was, what, almost five, seven years ago? Shit, man, get over it, they'd say. You've dated a lot of girls since then, fucked even more. But that one always stung. She hit a sore spot. Brought up a lot of shit for you. Maybe if it had been anyone other than him.

You'd been losing out to the Bretts of this world your whole goddamn life. It wasn't the fancy cars or the more tangible, profitable future. When she picked him over you, she was saying, in effect, that you were expendable, a cast-off, a bum. You'd hustled for everything you'd gotten. He'd been handed his good fortune. So she was fucking him behind your back? Big deal. You could've lived with that. You didn't cry or slash his fucking tires like a bitch; you didn't take a crow bar to his knees like your old man might've done. You never confronted him; it was beneath you. You sucked it up. You drank. For a while. You wallowed, then you moved on. And look where you moved on to. Nice apartment in the good part of the city. Stopped the pills, the booze. No more partying. You were doing just fine.

Until that motherfucker made an appointment at *your* shop. Oh, it was the same Brett, you made sure of that. You checked. Even then, you stayed calm, swallowed ego when he didn't know who you were. You weren't upset when he mentioned the "surprise tat" for "his wife, Karah." A rose with barbed wire thorns, of all the cheesy bullshit. You grinned and nodded through the half hour consultation, as he showed you his shit, third grader outline; and you listened politely as he detailed the big ceremony at his big house up on the Ridge. (Like that's how people want to spend their afternoon, celebrating someone *else's* love and dropping a hundred bucks on an overpriced cheese plate. You gave it two years.) No, what finally got to you wasn't another pasty, day-trading whiteboy deciding to get "inked up" as a fashion statement—if you turned away all the whiteboys desperately searching for culture, you wouldn't have any customers—it was *this* doughy, pasty whiteboy trying to steal some of *your* hard-earned culture.

The rest was easy. Gina had always been crazy about you. A nurse at the clinic, Gina drew blood from sickos all day long. Looking for narcotics? Good luck. But tainted blood work? Fuck, nobody wanted to touch that shit. And it was practically untraceable. Hell, Brett was probably sticking it in half the office anyway. Guys like him treat pussy like currency.

It's not like you're a monster. Gave you a little pause. But you weren't killing the guy. Just sending him home with a nice, little communicable souvenir to share with his lovely new bride.

The night of, you almost got cold feet, considered avoiding Sanguine Red altogether. But it was late at the shop, just you two. He brought out the flask, said he could use a nip before you got started, if that was all right. Sure, you said. Then he offered you a taste, half an Oxy too, just to take off the edge. Why the hell not? It had been a while. You could handle it. Lightheaded and buzzed, you told Brett the red would contrast nicely against his fair, virgin skin.

Once you got to work, you stopped worrying so much. When the motherfucker left without tipping you, you didn't feel bad at all.

And you never would've thought about it again, wouldn't have wasted another minute of your time. Except you felt like celebrating. Raise a toast to closure. You were finally ready to cover up her name over your heart. You broke two cardinal rules of your profession: never tattoo drunk. And never tattoo on yourself.

Wasn't until you noticed the discharge a couple days later and felt the burn when you tried to piss that you made the connection. You played back the other night, rewound to the part where you tossed the corrupted cup. Couldn't get a clear picture.

So now you find yourself back at the clinic, slinking in your sweatshirt, hoping it's Gina's day off. You thumb the "STDs and You" pamphlets, waiting for the on-call, as you mentally brace for the needles and thin surgical rods they'll insert into tiny holes, the parts of a man's body that should never be invaded.

Watching through windows, you stare at the lonely cars on the highway, and you think you finally have an answer to Karah's question, the one about why the pretty things always cut the deepest. That's the only way the razor's edge can penetrate the scars.

THE BUSINESS OF DEATH
Eric Beetner

Times are tough in the death business.

That's what I thought to myself as I stood in the empty viewing room. No appointments at all for the rest of the day, and it was only ten a.m. As I looked more closely I could see the wallpaper peeling in sections. The stains on the carpet left over from Mrs. Needleman who spilled her wine last year. A clear violation of our no food or drink policy, but sometimes when a loved one has just died people need a damn drink. I wasn't about to get all hardass on her. Then she went on wailing about her dear departed and a full glass of merlot hits my carpet, which should have been changed during the Bush administration anyway. The *first* Bush administration.

It doesn't smell good either. What funeral home does? That weird mixture of death and flowers. And not even real death. The after effects of death. The chemicals of the trade. Real death smells much worse, like when they come to us. All the lilies in the world can't cover that stench.

The place doesn't even sound good. The front left speaker that pipes in the calming sounds of strings has something wrong with it and buzzes now like the harps are summoning both angels and a swarm of bees.

Like I said, times is tough. So when I got an offer, who was I to refuse?

* * *

The neighborhood has changed since my dad opened the place forty-six years ago. I wouldn't say we're overrun with crime now, but a few guys on the street would like to see it that way. They run around like extras in a traveling road show of *Goodfellas*. I won't call them the mob because the level of organization these guys display would be an insult to organized crime. But still, they do business in my neighborhood and unlike mine, their business is booming.

So one of the top guys, Bobby, came to me a few months back. He wants to talk, he said. He palms me an envelope before he even gets to what he's asking me to do. Smart move. Once I had that money in my hand it became real tough to hand it back. I feel like I might have been able to resist and not accept it once he started explaining what he wanted from me, but feeling the weight of that envelope... hoo, boy. Even if it was stuffed with singles, I'd have been doing okay.

Honest to God, I thought of the people on my payroll. I got an embalmer, ushers, a woman who comes in to play the organ, an assistant manager, a hearse driver. These are people who depend on me.

So I took the money.

Here's what he wanted: and let me say off the bat, it was a great plan and I was kinda pissed I had never thought of it. They had a body to dispose of. I didn't ask and didn't want to know how or why they had a dead body on their hands, but the body already existed so something was going to happen to it one way or another.

My part in it was to take the body and slip it into a coffin with someone else so when that person gets buried, the body they want to get rid of goes with it and it's like their body vanishes. Genius, right?

All I had to do was to remove the padding and little bed

cushion—which is all for appearances anyway—slip the new body under the old one, and they would piggyback ride into eternity together. The next day I had a woman who passed in her sleep at the ripe old age of ninety-two. She was already shriveled up like an apple left in the sun, so there was enough extra room in her coffin for a party of two.

After Hector, my embalmer, had gone home they brought the new body over. He was a male, probably mid-thirties. Since he wasn't for display I didn't have to do anything to him. He went in wearing the T-shirt he came in with, no lip glue, no makeup. Which was good. The makeup job to cover the deep red welts and abrasions across his neck, likely from a rope or heavy strap of some sort, would have taken hours and two tubes of makeup.

So out came the Eterna-Rest mattress and in went Mr. T-shirt.

The next day Edna Friedman's family had no idea and into the ground went a two-for-one special. And I got my carpets changed.

Over the next three months I had four more envelopes slapped into my hand. Bobby brought me a rather heavy guy who, luckily, went into a closed casket with Mr. Edington. Getting the lid shut on those two was like trying to close an overstuffed suitcase. It took me and Bobby and one of his guys all leaning on the lid before it clicked shut. Good news is a coffin is made to close forever, so once you hear that click, you're good.

After that I re-papered the walls.

I doubled up a skinny guy who came in wearing only his underpants with a middle-aged woman who lost her battle with cancer. Everyone was so distracted by the hideous wig her family put on her that nobody noticed the weird lumps in the mattress pad she made her eternal rest on top of.

After that I fixed the speakers.

It was all going so well...

Bobby brought me a body. Well, an envelope and a body. I'd given up worrying if I was doing the right thing or not. Obviously I wasn't, but the people he brought me were already dead so at least I wasn't contributing to that part of it. And my employees were getting paid, the lights were still on, the place was looking better.

I didn't have anything scheduled for another forty-eight hours; a body coming down from up north so the man could be buried in the family plot. So Bobby had to cool his heels, and his corpse, until then.

Then came a rush job. A hospital passing from an old lady who'd been clinging to her last breath far longer than the family expected. I can tell when I speak to family members if they are truly grieving or not. This lady was not. I don't know if there was a will involved or what, but the whole family wanted to wrap it up and get out of town and back to their lives as quick as they could. Everyone had already added days to their hotel stays waiting on the old lady to expire. They wanted her planted—and quick.

I called Bobby and told him. He wanted in. His corpse wasn't in a refrigerator. It was getting nasty. I told him to bring the guy by.

I did the drill, fit the guy in under the old lady and tried not to worry about the smell, which was more pungent than usual due to the stowaway's improper storage. Any way you cut it a corpse + time = unpleasantness.

So I turn up at the funeral the next day and discovered the old lady is the mother of some top cop in the department. The place is crawling with dress blues and captain's bars marking the shoulders of what seemed like every third guy in the room.

I stared to sweat. Fixing the A/C was next on the list with the newest envelope. I took one step into the room, saw all the uniforms, and the smell stood out to me as strong as if a skunk had wandered in. The flowers weren't covering it. The harp music wasn't either.

But people were in a rush, so I still felt okay. Just a tad nervous.

I made my rounds offering condolences to the family. They were, as I expected, going through the motions in double time in order to make escape flights later that afternoon. The cops, however, were intent on hanging their heads in silent prayer and engaging in copious backslapping and empathizing with their fellow officer.

Then they started to speak. You'd think this woman was Mother friggin' Teresa. The woman I'd spoken to on the phone, the daughter, implored me to help speed it up. When yet another spit-shined cadet went to the podium casket-side to say a few words, I slid up next to him and tried to give him the hook.

The closer I got to the casket I could really notice the smell. If anyone else did they didn't seem bothered by it. Maybe they just thought I was a really lousy mortician who can't preserve a body for eternal slumber. Didn't matter to me as long as they hurried the hell up and got out.

The longer the ceremony went, the more time the cops had a chance to nip over to the outer area where the bar was set up. I busted a few of them trying to cross into the viewing parlor with tumblers of scotch in their hands. I was gentle, but as long as I kept on my funeral director's hushed and reverent tone, no one would argue with me. Mostly they shot back the rest of their drinks like cowboys in a saloon and then left their glasses to soak sweat rings into the sideboard.

So when I tried to keep the last speaker from even starting

his homage to Margery, I encountered some resistance. The irony was not lost on me that it was a cop who was being the belligerent drunk and me who was trying to keep him calm and remind him of the proper tone of respect given where we were standing not two feet from the dead woman he was so intent on eulogizing.

A few emphatic raised-eyebrow looks from the daughter let me know she was going to miss her flight if Mom didn't get put six feet under real soon. And I was just as eager to get this latest body disposal over with and all these cops out of my funeral parlor.

So maybe I dropped my mask of funereal calm for a split second.

All I really remember was after a few rounds of, "Sir, could you please...?" I found myself pulling the guy's hands off my lapels. Or trying to anyway. We parried and waltzed, first knocking over a cascading arrangement of day lilies and sunflowers, then knocking knees-first into the casket and riser.

The shocked yelps from the crowd were in unison as the whole set-up tipped forward. The old lady rolled with her final resting place and when the casket came smashing down onto the new carpet, she pitched forward and slid most of the way out. To Hector's credit, her hair and makeup stayed impeccable.

I didn't know for sure if the gasp from the crowd was for seeing the old woman they loved being defiled on the floor of a funeral home, or if it was for the strange new body now peek-a-booing behind her, bringing his full three-day stench with him into the room. All I really know is that everyone out of uniform was locked in a stare at the disgraceful scene of an overturned coffin and a hitchhiker spooning their dead mother, while everyone in a uniform had eyes locked on me.

* * *

Nobody cared that the cuffs were hurting me. They took my statement, asked a lot of questions and got me to agree to testify against Bobby and whoever else they could snatch up for me to put the finger on.

I said yes to it all. But, I had a plan…

While they put out the dragnet, I got a few supplies ready. The body came in from up north. Closed casket, which is what I needed. The old buzzard had been dead a full week so nobody wanted to see that. Hector did his work embalming the body to keep it as fresh as possible. A closed lid meant no makeup so I sent him home with a "good job" then made the switch.

The old man went into one of our display models in the showroom. It was the most expensive one so I knew it was the least likely to be looked at too closely, let alone opened and the interior examined. I'd be long gone before anyone discovered the body.

Meanwhile, I'd be inside his ride. I'd taken out most of the padding like I'd done so many times before. This gave me room to be inside without my face being pressed against the silk pillows of the lid. My portable oxygen tank fit easily inside with me. My wallet was uncomfortable to lie on because it contained all the cash I had in the world and my passport was in my other pocket.

I arrived early the next morning before anyone else. I'd told them all I wouldn't make it in that day due to a doctor's appointment. Maybe they'd think I kicked the bucket myself when I never came to work again.

Being inside a coffin wasn't as bad as I thought. Back when I was studying to be a mortician we all took turns getting inside coffins. When your dad runs a funeral home, it's part of growing up, too. Everyone wants to take a turn inside to see what it's like. So I wasn't freaking out or panicked in any way.

When my assistant came down to wheel me upstairs I was

giddy with excitement, in fact. It was all working.

What most people don't know is that some models have interior releases. This is a leftover from the paranoid point in time when being buried alive was much more common than it is now since embalming. Partly out of superstition, partly out of the universal fear of premature burial, most caskets come with some method of easily freeing yourself from within.

And once we were on the way to the cemetery, that's exactly what I did. I'm sure more than a few people freaked out when a live man climbed out of the back of a hearse while stopped at a traffic light, but I was moving so fast at that point they probably all thought they were dreaming.

The money ran out pretty quick, but this island is nice. Bobby can't reach me here, at least. I used my skills to start a small taxidermy business. Mostly marlins and other big fish tourists pull out of the Caribbean. I love it. My little shack doesn't even have carpet. It's only reggae music over the speakers. And all my clients go on a wall somewhere, not in the ground.

Yeah, business is good.

RATCHETING
Ryan Sayles

It's when they kick your door in with you six inches inside it you finally realize that frantic call from Jennifer was real and not some sick joke.

There's nothing like noticing you're being followed home from the bar. No matter which left and right turns you make, those same two headlights stalk at your back, making no effort to conceal themselves. No trickery. You're not worth it. They know as well as you do if you called 911 or drove to a police station the cops would have you in handcuffs for the parole violation you've got hanging over your head. Nope. You're on your own.

You're on your own because you lied to, cheated on and stole from everyone else in your life. All those friends who liked having you around until they realized that when they turned their backs you turned your knives.

Then you made that left onto your street after figuring you'd make a stand at your house, your territory. That's when your phone lit up with Jennifer on the caller ID.

"Yeah?" you said, eyeballing the rearview mirror as those two headlights methodically make that same turn. A call from her only meant one thing: she needs money. Inopportune time.

"Dad! Dad! Stop! I'm in the car behind you—" she says in that voice she used back when she was a little girl and her doll's head came off and she'd come running over to you to put it back on. Panic with an expectation that Daddy would fix everything. Your life lesson to your fragile daughter? "Sometimes, honey, when it comes off it stays off."

But right now you look into that rearview with renewed interest and say, "What the hell are you doing following me, Jennifer? It looks like—"

"You owe them money, Dad! They want it—"

"Who?"

"They said you'd know. Dad..." her voice drifts off and you picture a thousand different snarling men—all your old friends who now want to taste your blood—sitting in the seat next to her while some other guy drives the car. Jennifer, her face weathering from the drugs she picked up after her mother died. Traded in her magician's kit for it; the tall hat and the fake rabbit. The wand. All the "ta-da's!" she'd sing as she showed you something magical. That dream gone. The dope rushed in to fill the void. Now her kit consists of a spoon and a rubber band. A dirty needle. You don't care; you only stayed with her mom because she got pregnant and even then when she contracted AIDS from the third or fourth dude after you left, you decided to stop pretending to care. Hell, you couldn't find a comforting word to say to your only daughter.

She was twelve.

"I need a name, Jennifer." You say as you pull into the driveway. And that's when they floor the gas and the engine roars as the car flies up into your yard. You run, your back to the threat, your back to your little girl all grown up, and even as you hear Jennifer screaming, being wrestled from the car and at least three sets of pounding feet charging after you, you just throw open your front door and slam it shut.

They mount the steps and you allow a surreal thought that maybe this is a doper prank. Jennifer's not above some bullshit shenanigans like this. She's got her mother's vengeful streak. Even when she was playing magician she got you with a gag every now and then. And after the way you left her in jail last month, you've got this coming. So maybe—

The running mule kick destroys your flimsy front door just as fast as it destroys your paper-thin delusion that this isn't going to end in blood.

You fall forward as the door caves in at your back. Go ahead and regret renting the house with hardwood. It hurts more as your face bounces off it. Sure, carpet would have stained, but you might have retained most of your consciousness after a hit like that.

Roll around for a second and take a deep swim through the black waters of your knock-out. Taste those pennies? Good. Your mouth is full of them. Your ears pick up every sound of them dragging Jennifer inside. She kicks and thrashes but they must have a good hold of her hair because for as feisty as she is, she ain't gettin' nowhere.

They grab you, whip you over on your back. A boot on your face pins you to the floor and the fresh scent of dirt and oil in his treads invade you. It's all you can smell. Jennifer's whimpers are all you can hear. The shadows of the men moving against the backdrop of their headlights streaming through the broken door are all you can see. Got a head count? Four, at least. How big was their car?

One man kneels down beside you and with him comes the looming presence you imagine Darth Vader had. Looming death. But first, whatever he wants from you, you're gonna give. Then death. This guy is like that. Oh, and he smells expensive too. That cuts through the soil stench.

"You live in a shitty neighborhood, Gil," he says and your mind races like a mouse in a maze when it realizes a cat had been let loose in there also.

"I'm not Gil," you say as best you can with two hundred pounds of goon leaning on your face. You've used fake names in the past. You're not really the long-con type of guy, but you've seen into the future far enough to know whoever it is you met today will want to kill you next week so it's better off just starting with a lie about who you are.

"Are you familiar with the word 'reckoning?'" he asks. His voice is even-keeled the way a man of gravity's can be, knowing that his power allows him to choose life or death for his enemies on a whim and not pay for the consequences. "Reckoning means to settle the accounts. It's simple. You owe me, and I have decided to cash in."

Jennifer tries to scream but whoever is wrangling her does too well a job. She squeaks and sobs lightly. Tired.

"Did I steal from you?" you do your best to ask.

"You owe me money," is all you're gonna get. This Gil name? Could be an honest mistake on their part, but they know Jennifer is your daughter and apparently you have an unpaid account. Even if it's all some insane mix-up, you can't argue with reality.

"How much?" you ask, deflated and wonder if the question made it to his ear or got lost in the size fourteen flattening your skull.

"Good, dog," he says. Leans in, says, "All of it."

A tear runs down your face. All of it means so much in your world. You've spent your life nickel and diming other people, taking what you can when you can, then moving on. Locust. Tucking it away. Some for now, some for later.

All of it means the some for later part. You have been doing this a long time, and that later part has gotten big.

"I hear," he says, "you got something like forty large in here."

"Twenty," you eek out around the rubber sole. How'd he hear?

"I smell bullshit," he says. He stares and you try and place his face. So many mugs over the years. This guy's jaw, the way his brow creases, you have no idea. And you want to so bad. He snarls. "Oh, it reeks, all right."

He stands up. "Do it," he says with a flick of his head to

the guy wrangling Jennifer. Without thinking about it, without hesitation, the guy grabs Jennifer's hand and his own mitts are so big you're startled at the way her little fist disappears into his. Just one little finger sticking out of his giant hand.

It's when the ratcheting clippers come up and her finger drops off like a dead tree limb that you feel piss warm your pants. Her screams immediately go in the background of your mind. You knew she was going to howl the instant you saw the flash of light dance along those metal pieces. Didn't need to hear it. Same sound Jennifer made back when she'd trip and skin a knee. Kid stuff, you blew off. Adult stuff, mutilation stuff, you lock onto.

"She's got nine more," he says. "And then you've got every digit on your body after that." You feel him punch your groin. Just a straight-up cock shot. You try and cough with the pain, but nothing comes out. "I start there on men, though," he says. "You'd be surprised how a man will let someone else suffer in front of them without cooperating, but when you cut off their dick they fall in line."

You openly cry. Try to talk. The boot eases up and your jaw throbs now that blood can flow through it again. "Bedroom closet. Shelf. Shoe box."

As soon as the last word comes out they hit you hard enough to leave a crater. Where it came from, who knows. You're on your back and just got thumped one for the record books. The air leaves your lungs and your guts wiggle the way a suspension bridge does in an earthquake. Like lightning: handcuffs. Leg shackles. Hog tied. They yank open your pants and your limp friend comes up for air. They snap those ratcheting clippers around him and with a couple of quick, well-practiced squeezes both the blades hold themselves onto your penis. Not cutting. Not yet. But they're like bulldogs with their jaws locked on to where they're biting. Make your next move carefully.

"I better count forty when I get that shoe box," the man says. "Or else we turn this up a notch." He kneels down and flicks the clippers. Sweat beads never ran so fast off your forehead.

You try to shout it's all there, but who cares. The way this guy rolls you know if there's a dollar short of forty grand you're singing falsetto for the rest of your days.

Somebody goes into the bedroom. Somebody comes back with the box. You think about how your life just lost any meaning as they pillage your retirement. You hear the bills flipping and flapping, rubber banded rolls being un-rubber banded. End it with this, please you beg to whoever you think listens to your thoughts.

"There ain't forty grand here, Gil," the man's voice says.

"Yes there is! Yes there is!" you shout, so nervous you don't hear how much like a child you sound.

A hand pats your forehead, mockingly reassuring. "Relax, Gil. There's almost forty-three."

"Who the fuck is Gil? I ain't Gil—" But a kick to the stomach cuts off that question.

The man walks into your line of vision and all you see is your daughter slumped into a heap, holding her hand in a bloody, white-knuckled embrace. They let her go; she's broken and she's been all the use she's gonna be now. She's sobbing quietly. Her stringy hair dangling over her face like curtains hiding a terrible show outside. She's shoeless. Her babydoll dress—something you thought died in the '90s—is dirty. Mangy. You think she looks like one of those stray dogs with the matted hair and burrs.

Pathetic, you think, even now. At your bottom, hog tied with your dick in a vice, you can't stop the vitriol for that precious girl you left to rot. Hell, she drug these people here. You were just at a bar, minding your own business.

"What goes around comes around, Gil," the man says as they gather by the door. "Thanks for making this easy."

And with that, they leave. Just like that. In like a lion, out like a lamb. Just you and Jennifer.

"Jenny, get me up," you say. "Stop blubbering and get these cuffs offa me."

Jennifer uses a sniff to stop her crying. She flips her head up, as if that motion would draw enough self-esteem to hit the reset button on tonight. She stands, shaky at first but determined. You see her mother right there. The way her mother would have her emotional roller coaster moments and the drama queen stuff you always hated. Her mother would use her broken heart to manipulate you. Remember always telling yourself that? The manipulation? The lies? How she'd always be crying or always be boiling over with energy. The way she pissed away your money, or the way she'd stay in bed for days.

But when Jennifer's mother got up, you remember that look. The shaky but determined look. Jennifer has that.

Jennifer rolls her head on her neck. Deep breaths. She walks over to the hallway. Steps inside the bathroom. Comes out with the old box of tampons you keep under the sink.

"Got a new woman here, Dad?" she asks, examining the box.

Trembling. You know what this means. "Show me your hand," you say, as indignant and furious as a man can be with his limp dick hanging out of his pants and hog-tied.

"You're asking a magician to reveal her trick, Dad."

"Show me your hand."

She does, and you see all ten fingers. "You fucking—"

"I told them you had the forty. Sorry. I owed them eight for a mule deal I fucked up." Jennifer smiles, digs around the tampon box. Pulls out your other seventy grand. "So I figure, they just want their cash. And I say, how about forty? I know a guy named Gil. He owes me, bigger than shit. Told them just to play along with some bullshit story I cooked up. Maybe cut off a finger."

You remember all that manipulation now? The lies? Mommy's little girl, all grown up. Jennifer smiles. "Thanks, Daddy."

You start to yell but she calmly walks over to you. You keep yelling as her rail-thin arm reaches down. You see those track marks. The shit-cheap tattoo on the inside of her forearm. You stop yelling when your own pulse is so full of adrenaline and anxiety that you can't do anything but watch as she grabs those ratcheting clippers. Grabs them hard.

"Love you, Daddy."

Squeezes.

No matter how loud you scream, she ignores it as she walks out of your life. And you won't stop screaming.

THE JUNGLES OF PEEKSKILL, NEW YORK

Angel Luis Colón

I got the call from my boss, Dorian Ramirez, while I was in the middle of a sale. The buyer: a nice widow by the name of Ethel Grainger. I got the lead from a shady estate lawyer Dorian works with. Ethel had come into some extra cash and was ripe to make a bad decision. I just had to nudge her the right way.

I raised a finger and smiled. "Misses Grainger, excuse me, this is the head of my company." I stood from her plastic-covered couch and walked into her kitchen. Becoming a widow seemed to suit Ethel. It was obvious the stove and the kitchen table hadn't been used in months. The ceiling was stained a dull orange from tobacco, but I didn't spot any ashtrays. Seemed those were buried along with her husband. Old pictures—almost all black and white—hung on the off-white walls. They were the same as the rest I'd seen. No kids. Just adults.

I connected the call. "Mister Ramirez? I'm here." I cupped my free hand over the phone to keep my voice from traveling.

"David," he barked more than stated, "is it Teeso?"

"No, sir, the tee is silent."

"So? Okay, whatever. Listen, I was going over my numbers—the big earners. Looks like you and I should have a talk about your future endeavors. You agree?"

My stomach flipped. "Absolutely. Do you want to work out a phone appointment? Maybe tomorrow morning?"

It sounded like he sucked on his teeth. "No. Dinner." That sucking sound again. "Tonight."

I didn't know how to respond. This wasn't a question. "Sure thing. Um..." I darted to Ethel's kitchen table and snatched a pen from the mouth of a ceramic fish. "Just give me the address."

"I'll have Ernie pick you up in an hour at your place." The phone disconnected.

"Mister Soo?" Ethel called from the living room. "Is everything okay?"

I took a breath. Put my phone into my pocket. "Yes, ma'am." Turned on my smile again and walked back into the room.

Ethel smiled. A frog wearing lipstick. She fingered the gaudy, gold necklace wrapped twice around her neck. "No trouble?"

"Not for me, no." I shook my head and sat back down. Collected my folders and papers detailing land ownership opportunities in North Carolina. "Seems there may be some problems with a few of our investors."

She leaned in.

I continued, "See, there seems to be issues with our tax assessor's documentation—nothing major—one of those annoying contrivances. Government out to get their cut and all." I winked. "Always the case, right?"

Ethel watched me put my papers into my briefcase. "Does this mean the offer is off of the table?"

"For now, I'm sure it'll pass over. I'll call you right back once we've gotten our ducks in a row."

"How long will that be?" Ethel asked. "Would you like something else to nibble on before you left?" She waved at a plate of sugar cookies I hadn't touched.

I half-wondered if she didn't want me to leave because

this house was so damn empty. Widows had a habit of keeping you around, but Ethel didn't seem to be the type to dangle the sale in front of me so she can have company. I frowned. "No idea. Sometimes it takes a day, sometimes a few weeks. We hold off because...well, I can't talk about that." I leaned in and winked. "Inside access and all."

"Now you're toying with me, Mister Soo." She cocked her head to the side and smiled—dried lipstick cracking on her thin lips.

I ignored the second flub on my name. "I apologize, Misses Grainger, it's...I guess I can trust you with this. See, in these cases the property values take a small dip and spikes once we've resolved the issue. My employers like to keep it quiet so we scrape in a little extra during closing."

Ethel's eyes lit up. "And what's to stop me from buying right now?"

I nod. Raise my eyebrows as if her suggestion was new to me. "Well, nothing really. Though, you'd have to sign off on the assessment and cover those fees. It's not necessarily illegal, more like one of those corporate white lies they're always talking about on the news."

She didn't have to say "yes" and coincidentally, the papers left for me to tuck away happened to be all five that she needed to sign to make this deal a reality. I placed them on her coffee table and held up the pen from the kitchen—her husband's name written in bold letters across its length.

"We act now and I assure you, Ethel, money will be made." I handed her the pen and watched her sign all the relevant spots.

When she was done, she gave me the pen back. I slipped it in my pocket.

The drive up to Peekskill was quiet. Ernie didn't like to play music while he was on the road. Add the lack of conversation, and I found myself captivated with my hands—cracked my knuckles, made fists. Examined old scars I forgot about. Anything to pass the time.

"Have you ever been up to Dorian's?" I asked.

He clenched the wheel of his S-Class so hard the peaks of his hairy knuckles were ivory. Ernie had a twitch. He always tried to cover it up by pretending to shrug, though there's only so much a man can actually shrug about. He had to be stressed because he was extra-unsure about the question I asked. "Once or twice," he finally mumbled.

That was a bummer. A little insight would have been nice. Dorian was a bit of an enigma. He was the kind of guy you couldn't get a read on and in my line of business, those were the types to worry about. That was also why he ran the show. I never personally met the man, but most folks who knew Dorian Ramirez couldn't tell me more than I already knew. Bronx-born, rags to riches story. On paper, he was a legitimate entrepreneur who gave Latino kids scholarships every year. In real life, he had his hands in a little of every-thing—money laundering, gambling, and the land sale scheme I was a part of.

My bit was pretty easy. Cozy up to old-timers with more cash than brain cells to burn. I'd convince them I had a lucra-tive opportunity—land investments, better than gold—and move on from there. In reality, we were selling worthless swampland and landfill. The buyer's dumped a sum on us and walked away with so many legal issues to come, it was a wonder their grandkids weren't going into bankruptcy. Do-rian's lawyers kept us all clean. Everything was on the up and up—so long as nobody dug too deep into the paper-work. The first few signatures brought with them plenty of guilt, but it's amazing what a sick mom, a sizable cocaine habit, and an affinity for a brand new Beemer will do to a guy's conscience.

Ernie was my boss in name only. He never told me what

to do or who to speak to. I got my leads by going back and forth with lawyers and paralegals that got a little action from Dorian. Ernie collected the paperwork, checks, and receipts and got them where they needed to get to. Those were the details I tried to avoid. This line of work was hazardous in more ways than one. Most times, if you kept yourself in your own tidy corner, when trouble came, you'd be lucky enough to know too little to be of any importance to the cops or the feds.

After another set of shrugs—I stopped counting—Ernie side-eyed me. Frowned. "When did he call you?"

The sudden conversation startled me. "Oh, well, probably like a half hour before you picked me up. I was finishing up a Carolina sale."

Ernie nodded. "I had as much prep time as you. That's how Dorian likes to do it—keep you on your toes." He rolled down his window. "Mind if I smoke?"

"Your car." I watched Ernie take a pull of his cigarette and shrug to himself. "You guys super close?"

Ernie snickered. "I see the man almost every day, but no." He pointed his cigarette behind us. "I know he rarely goes to his house. I saw him a few hours ago when he was picking up like, twelve pies at the pizzeria he owns over on Tremont."

"Twelve?" That amount seemed a little ridiculous, but it wasn't surprising to hear Dorian owned a pizzeria. The man owned one of everything.

Ernie scratched his nose. "He's staying home a few days. Sort of like a vacation for him. His wife and kids are gone for a while. When that happens he stays home all day...aw crap." He pulled the car out at the next exit. "I completely forgot the damn ice pops."

"Is that some kind of code?" If Ernie was working an angle here, it was working. Not only was I nervous, but his newfound chattiness threw me all sorts of off. I was nervous.

Last thing I needed was to get mixed up with two fellas I barely knew and whatever weird drugs they were into.

Ernie didn't answer my question. He floored it and pulled into a gas station with a mini-mart. "You need anything?"

I waved him off. "No thanks."

He opened his door and faltered. Turned to me. "You ain't Korean, are you?"

"No." I did my best not to come off pissed at that question.

By the look on Ernie's face, I was a terrible actor. "No offense, just checking. Dorian kinda has a thing about the Korean War."

"Okay..."

Ernie shrugged—good for him, it worked in this situation. "You'll understand when you meet him." He left the car. Jogged over to the mini-mart with the look of a man that needed something more important than popsicles.

Santa Claus. He looked exactly like Santa Claus by way of Gordon Gekko. It's the only way I can describe Dorian Ramirez. This was a Saint Nick birthed by the spirit of American capitalism—swaddled in the finest multi-figure Armani suit he could find.

He greeted us at the front of his three-story home with a yellow smile—a Cuban cigar clenched between thick, ringed fingers. He slipped the cigar between his teeth and offered me a paw. "Davey—is Dave okay? Pleasure to meet you." He had a thick Bronx accent—gruff and drenched with forced friendliness. The way he stood made you feel as if he was about to leave to do something better than speak to you. "Good drive up?" He turned away and shook Ernie's hand. "How are you, Ernie?" Dorian turned and walked into his house. "Come on in, gentlemen."

The house was huge, but sparsely decorated. I'd heard a few guys—Ernie included—joke about how cheap Dorian was. They weren't kidding. Nothing on the walls, only the bare minimum of furniture. No TVs, no fancy decorations on fancier pedestals. He led us into the kitchen—like the rest of the house, utilitarian. A fridge, oven, counter, and sink. Only what was necessary to call the room a kitchen.

"Are you guys hungry?" Dorian walked over to a table large enough to seat six but with ten chairs cramped around it. The table had two piles of pizza boxes on it—three empty.

I smiled and gave him a nod. "Sure."

Dorian motioned to the pile of boxes and walked to the sink. He grabbed a roll of paper towels and tossed it my way. "Don't dirty the floor. Ernie. How's business?"

Ernie did his shrug. "Same as it was yesterday."

Dorian unbuttoned his suit jacket with his free hand. Finished his slice in three bites. Wiped his mouth and beard clean, and then hooked his thumbs into the front pockets of his pants. He had a gut like Santa, but the rest of him was thinner. "You have Rico keeping track of sales?"

Rico was a pizza guy with a habit of sneaking a five or ten spot from the till of one of Dorian's bodegas. When Dorian found out, instead of firing the guy, he started forcing everyone that worked for him to handwrite each sale—what was sold and for how much—even if they had a computerized register. It was redundant and a waste of time, but nobody was going to tell Dorian that. They'd curse under their breath and continue on with their day. Why would they complain? Get in good with Dorian and you made money. We all knew that. As far as I knew only one of Dorian's employees ever went behind bars and he—if rumors are to be believed—didn't make it a week until the sharpened end of a toothbrush met the space between his ribs.

Ernie nodded. "We're keeping an eye on stuff. Rico's been behaving." He chuckled. "Though, the limp slowed him down a bit."

Dorian eyed him a minute and smirked. "Good." He

turned his attention back to me. "How's the side-business?"

The "side-business" Dorian's way of bringing up the more unscrupulous part of his life. The legit joints were chump change compared to what the land deals and other illegal activities brought in. I gave Dorian my winner smile. "It's been good. I actually closed off that one bid we had in North Carolina before I came out here."

Dorian smiled. "That's what I like to hear." He wandered over to me and patted my back.

I nearly choked on a bite of my pizza. 'Thank you, Mister Ramirez."

He laughed. "Good work is its own reward, Dave. See, unlike Ernie over here, you're a man with work ethic."

That came out of nowhere.

Dorian continued, "You're not the type who'd steal behind everyone's back, bullshit their way through the day, and come back to their boss with a smile on their face and a dagger behind them, right?"

I swallowed my pizza. "No, sir."

Dorian watched Ernie.

Ernie started shrugging something awful. "Dorian, what the hell are you talking about?"

Dorian turned his head. Stared out at his yard through glass sliding doors. The man had property that seemed to go for miles. The sun was setting. A few yards out, high grass grew. The stalks blew in the wind. "Why don't you step out-side for a little—get some air?" Dorian asked Ernie. He was still smiling, but there wasn't an ounce of joy in it. This was an animal act—baring of teeth—a threat.

Ernie stopped shrugging. Looked out at the reeds sway-ing. "I'm okay." His eyes widened. "Oh, man. I got your ice pops." Ernie rushed out of the kitchen.

I pulled a second slice of pizza from the box nearest me, folded it, and wrapped a paper towel under the edge of the fold. "You know, if you have business to discuss with Ernie,

I can head out." I was thirsty now, but couldn't muster the guts to even hint at it. Chewed my pizza and suffered through the hard swallow.

Dorian rested a hand on the back of a chair. "No, you stay here." He slid the glass door open and whistled between his fingers. In the distance, the high grass seemed to come alive. Dorian closed the door and turned to me. "How long have you been working for me?"

"Something like three years." It was probably longer than that, but it was the first answer that came out of my mouth.

Dorian pointed to me with his chin. "Are you content with where you are? Do you think you could be doing more?"

"Well, I..."

Ernie walked into the kitchen with a plastic bag. "Got the real fruit ones you like."

"Coconut?" Dorian clicked his tongue against his teeth.

"No, the pineapple." Ernie opened the freezer and slid the bag inside. "I know you weren't thrilled with the last batch."

Dorian nodded. "Great." He jabbed a thumb towards the sliding doors. "Grab a slice and take a walk outside."

Ernie stood by the fridge. "I'd rather not."

"Get outside," Dorian roared. Two short words, but it felt as if the whole room would cave in. As if the air were vibrating.

Ernie shrugged. Rubbed the back of his head. He took short, slow steps to the sliding glass doors and opened them. He turned to me, fished his car keys from his pocket, and tossed them over. Then he stepped outside and closed the door without a word. He lit a cigarette and sat down on a rusted folding chair.

The high grass danced violently not far from where Ernie sat. "What's out there?" I asked before I could stop myself.

Dorian walked to the fridge. Grabbed the entire bag Ernie had placed in the freezer. He walked out of the kitchen. "Come on. We need to discuss this business and where you stand." His voice echoed around me.

Outside, Ernie watched me leave. Behind him, the grass parted.

Dorian lay in an old-school cast iron tub filled to the brim with scalding hot water. Every time he shifted, water splashed onto the tiles beneath the tub and ran down the drains located at either side.

I sat on a closed toilet—hands gripping my knees and staring straight ahead. I had seen the rear of him when he undressed suddenly. Wasn't in a rush to see the rest of the show.

Dorian sucked on a pineapple ice pop. He pulled it out of his mouth and dunked his head under the water. Came back up and grunted. "I want you to take over for Ernie."

There was pounding coming from downstairs—Ernie's muffled pleas. I looked out the bathroom into the hallway that went on forever. Counted six bedrooms and another bathroom on our way here. "Should we let him back in?"

Dorian shook his head. "No. Jules will keep him company."

"Jules?" I looked to him. Kept my eyes locked on his.

Dorian straightened up and ran a hand over his wet hair. "Five years ago I was in Harlem at a special dinner." He reached behind him for a cigar and motioned to me to grab him matches that rested on the sink.

I grabbed the matches and passed them over. "Okay."

Dorian lit the cigar. Exhaled a thick plume of smoke over his head. "When I was leaving, a junkie ran up to me and offered me two kittens for a hundred bucks. I figured 'why the hell not' I'd take a look. Even if I didn't want them, I'd give the guy a fifty for his trouble." He pointed the lit end of the cigar at me. "Can you guess what this guy had to sell?"

I couldn't tell if this was a trick question. "Kittens?"

Dorian laughed. "To this junkie, maybe, but no—it was cubs. Later on I'd find out this guy stole two liger cubs from some weirdo out in Long Island that trained for circuses and shows."

"I'm sorry, liger?" I'd never heard of the animal before.

"Exactly what it sounds like. Part tiger, part lion."

"So I assume you bought them?"

Dorian chortled. "Of course I bought them. I'd have been crazy not to—they were beautiful."

"Why?"

Dorian watched me. He puffed at his cigar. "Who else was gonna take care of them?"

Ernie screamed again.

I turned my head towards the bay windows at the far end of the bathroom. It was a big bathroom. "Are they both out there?" I asked.

"Just Jules. His sister died last year."

"Is he going to kill Ernie?"

Dorian stood up from his bath. I diverted my eyes. Stared a hole into the marble floor.

"Hand me the towel by the door." His pruney hand appeared in my periphery.

I did as he instructed. Saw the plastic bag that had been filled with popsicles now filled with empty wrappers. "So you're punishing him. He stole from you."

Dorian toweled himself off. "He got complacent. There's no drive to do what he needs to do." He wrapped the towel around his waist. It threatened to fall off immediately. "I don't see the same problem with you."

I finally looked back to him. Felt my cheeks flush. "Why is that?"

Dorian walked out of the bathroom. "I know everything about my employees, Dave. You've got a lot on your plate and you like money as much as I do. Come on." He dragged his hand over his beard. "How's your mother?" He asked as we walked down the hall.

There seemed to be no need to lie. "Sick."

"I've heard. Last year I went to visit my mother and they were carting her into the back of an ambulance—heart attack. She was dead by the time they hit the first traffic light."

"I'm sorry to hear that."

"Don't patronize me. I was actually relieved." He turned to me at the head of the stairs back down to the living room. "I didn't have to look her in the eyes after a day of doing what I did." Dorian placed a hand on my shoulder. "You'll get there too. I know that."

I wanted to punch him right there. Wanted to watch him tumble down the stairs and land neck first on the granite below—to see that tiny towel unfurl and that gut wobble around longer than he took his final breaths. "I don't know where you get off…"

Dorian's grip strengthened. "We're born leaders, Dave. Guys like Ernie, they take orders. Us? We give orders under the illusion we have no control. Think about it. Every signature, all those commission checks." He poked me with a finger. "You made that happen and each person who handed you their cash did it with a free conscience because they had the belief it was their decision."

There was a knot in my stomach. I tasted acid at the back of my throat.

"That's why you're my man," Dorian said.

I looked down the stairs. "But Ernie. He didn't need…"

Dorian laughed. "Ernie's fine. I fed Jules before you got here." He descended the stairs. "Once he's fed he likes to sit around. Only gets riled up if he's hungry or threatened." Dorian stopped. Made a face like he was trying to remember something. "You Korean?"

"No. Chinese."

He seemed to mull that over. Nodded. "Good." He continued down the stairs and walked back to the kitchen.

I followed. It was dark out now. Ernie was pressed against the glass sliding doors, his eyes wet with tears, his mouth obscured by the growing fog from his breath. Behind him, the biggest cat I'd ever seen. It sat on its haunches—tongue hanging out and head drooped. It looked like a tiger with its stripes half erased. It had a gut that hung low and a short, bushy mane. It was Dorian in animal form. The man had his own living totem.

Dorian moved back to the pile of pizzas and scooped a slice into his hand. He chewed on it happily and wandered over to the sliding doors. Opened them and let Ernie tumble back inside. Dorian walked outside and embraced the big cat. The liger leaned into him and purred as loud as a muscle car. Nuzzled its head against his gut. Dorian patted its neck and gave it a soft kiss on the top of the head before coming back inside. As soon as the sliding doors shut, Jules the liger wandered back into the tall grass—slipping in like a ghost.

Ernie sat on the kitchen floor—speechless. He tucked his knees into his chest and sniffed. He was completely still. No shrugs.

Dorian ignored him. It was as if Ernie didn't exist anymore. A part of me wondered if Ernie was in on that too. Everything about him felt off.

I knelt beside Ernie and rested a hand on his shoulder. "Let me take you home." I tucked my arm under his and brought him to his feet. His knees buckled. Took a lot out of me to keep him up. Any slack and he would have fallen right down—prostrate before his former employer.

Dorian sat at the kitchen table. "Seven ay-em tomorrow?" he asked me. He looked at Ernie with tired eyes.

I nodded. "Yeah, I'll meet you at your insurance office in Parkchester." I helped Ernie to his feet and walked him out. It was nice outside. Not hot, not cold. The crickets chirped and the leaves of the trees rustled above. Any other time and I'd have called the night perfect.

Before I closed the front door I heard Dorian call out, "Don't be late."

I didn't answer—the conversation was done and Dorian struck me as the type to always have the last word.

I closed the front door behind me and got Ernie into the passenger seat of his car. Got myself into the driver's seat and turned on the car. I let it idle a few minutes before turning on the headlights. In front of the car, I saw two pin pricks of burning embers in the grass behind the fencing that cut off the front yard from the backyard—Jules. He was more impressive from a distance and in the lights of Ernie's car then he was when I saw him earlier.

It was then I realized why Dorian's house wasn't decorated to the gills. He didn't collect items—no—Dorian was past that. He collected us—Jules, Ernie, and I.

Jules moved forward and laid near the fence, staring at the car—at me. I met his stare. Did he pity me the way I did him? We were both trained animals on a leash, the business end held by a man we didn't necessarily have a grudge with. I laughed to myself when I questioned which one of us was really behind the bars of the gate. It was silly and I was overthinking this. I needed the money—that much Dorian was spot on about. Medical bills had a habit of stacking at the worst times.

I watched Jules for what felt like hours. He panted and licked his chops. It was only when he finally looked away did I feel comfortable enough to pull the car onto the main pathway and out of the property. As I drove, I picked up speed. Looked into the rearview and watched Jules' ember eyes fade away.

THE HAMMER PARTY
Kent Gowran

If bad news had a face, I'd bet my left nut it would bear more than a passing resemblance to Joe Ray Hammer. I wondered if he worked on getting his face to look the way it did, but he really didn't seem the sort to spend much time in front of the mirror, and so he probably came by his grim countenance naturally. I'd about given up waiting on him when he rounded the corner at the end of the block. His shoulders hunched against the cold, a fat cigar in his mouth, and muttering something at least bordering on obscene, judging by the looks the young women he passed gave him. I pushed myself away from the brick vestibule of a boarded up restaurant and out onto the sidewalk. He didn't acknowledge my presence until he'd stationed himself in the small wind-break and got his cigar going again.

"Natz."

No hello, no nothing, just my last name, like he didn't enjoy the taste of it.

I went for friendly, mostly to irk him. "How's the day treating you, Joe?"

"It's for shit," he said. He took the cigar from his mouth, looked at it a moment, and dropped it. "Probably already killed myself with those things."

"It's been awhile," I said. "Any word?"

He made a grunting sound like I had to be the dumbest fucker on the block. "I didn't call to catch up on the life and times of Carl Natz, now did I?" He rubbed his hands together, shoved them in his coat pockets, and said, "I hope you don't have any plans for tonight."

I did a quick mental rundown of my upcoming social calendar, and came up with nothing. "I can move things around," I said. "What's the word?"

"You, me, and Franco, we're—"

I held my hand up and interrupted him. "Which Franco?"

"How's that?"

"Paul or Richard?"

"Paul."

"Shit." I didn't like either of the Franco brothers much, but you could at least count on Richard to have your back if things got fucked up. "Too late to switch up?"

"Richard hung himself," Joe said. "Funeral was yesterday."

"Christ."

"Nice funeral, so far as that goes."

"I didn't hear anything about it," I said.

"I was stopping by to talk to him, see if he had any ideas, ran into Paul collecting his mail, and he told me the story."

"What's the story?"

"I think you'll like it."

"Yeah?"

"Richard tracked down the money." He let it sink in a moment, and said, "All of our money."

I got my head around it, and a big alarm went off almost immediately. "And he told his brother but not us," I said.

"Paul said they were planning on going after it. The two of them." He held up his hands, palms out, and squared his eyes with mine. "So, yeah, they were gonna cut us out, you and me, both." He snapped his fingers. "Just like that."

"And now it's the three of us?"

"He's the one who knows where it is."

I turned away, watched a bus rumble by, and something occurred to me. "Did he do it?"

"Do what?"

"Hang Richard."

"Ain't nothing impossible," Joe said. "But I don't think so. It was a turn of good luck for us that I came along. Can you imagine Paul even trying to track down either of us? Never would've happened."

"He's a weasel."

"Sure."

"We could get the location out of him," I said. "Like we used to."

Joe shook his head, and it was the first time I noticed how old he'd gotten. "No, not me. I don't have the stomach for it anymore." He gave me a look that said he could see I didn't either, but I wasn't so sure I wouldn't make an exception in this case.

"He's too chickenshit to lie."

"Probably."

It was only a word, but it carried a lot of weight. I looked out at the street, disgusted, and resigning myself to the fact I'd have to split the money three ways, a third going to a guy who'd never stuck his neck out. I let out a long sigh, made sure Joe noticed, and said, "He have any idea what happened to Romanski?"

"He's dead, too. That's how Richard found out where the money is. Guy was running scared, called him up in the middle of the night, and finally let it all out."

"What happened to him?"

"Didn't have anything to do with the money, I guess. Pissed off some people when he was inside. He gets cut loose, finds out he can't go home because these people are on top of his shit there, and he takes off."

It wasn't hard to imagine a guy like Doug Romanski pissing off the sort of people who would hunt a guy down from one end of the country to the other. Running probably only made it worse. If he'd made it back home before Richard took himself out, we'd have split the money four ways, which meant splitting into thirds was a better shake, even if I wasn't feeling good about where one portion would be going.

"Yeah, all right," I said. "What time are we meeting?"

Joe checked his watch. "I'll pick you up in front of Arturo's on Western tonight at eight. Get there early enough to pick us up some tacos for the drive out."

I should have been fucking elated at the prospect of the money finally being in my hands, but something about it didn't sit right in my gut. I thought it was probably Richard's death. He never seemed the type to me, but I guess that's nothing more than a thing people tend to say whenever someone decides to exercise their prerogative. Could be splitting the money three ways had me in knots. Paul was, to my mind, coming along for the ride and collecting without having done any of the work. Goddamn leeches. Always someone who thinks they should get something for nothing, maybe by virtue of the family they were born into, or hey, I'm a good guy, give me a boatload of cash, and it's all horseshit, but it's the world we live in.

My train of thought was threatening to start sounding like the punk rock records I used to listen to, and, almost reluctantly, I changed tracks. By the time the sun came up again, I'd have a quarter of a million to my name, in cash, and maybe that's strictly small time, but I started stacking the cash in my head, and I liked the look of it there. Yeah, I liked it a lot.

By the time Joe's car rolled to a stop at the curb on the other side of Western from Arturo's, the tacos in the bag were far past cold. I hustled across the streets, drew a few honking horns, and went around to the passenger side of the car. Paul was in the front seat, looking out at me, and nearly dropped out of the car when I yanked open the door.

"Get in the back, Franco."

Paul looked like he wanted to protest, but Joe said, "Go on, get in the back. Let the grownups ride in the front."

Paul mumbled something as he climbed out and I took his place in the front. I dropped the bag of tacos on the seat and slammed the door. "Freezing my ass off."

"I had to stop for a few things," Joe said as he dropped the car into gear and pulled away from the curb.

"Jesus," Paul said from the backseat. "I barely had time to get the door closed."

Joe grabbed the bag of tacos and tossed it over his shoulder. "Shut up and eat something."

"They're cold now," I said.

Paul ripped into the bag. "I'm starving."

Joe looked at me. "How's your back doing?"

"Fine. Why do you ask?"

"Long night ahead." He looked to the backseat. "You want to tell it?"

"Nah," Paul said around a mouthful of food. "You can."

Joe reached out, turned down the sports talk radio, and jerked his thumb toward the back. "Got shovels, a lantern, and some good work gloves in the trunk."

"Gotta dig up the money, huh?"

Paul giggled. He actually giggled, and I wanted to reach back and knock his teeth out. Maybe I needed to set aside some of the cash for a bit of therapy.

"You remember the car Romanski drove off in the last time we saw him?"

Oh, I remembered it. "Yeah, a fucking Maverick."

"He buried it."

"Buried what?"

"The car."

"Why the hell would he do that?"

"Doug was kinda..." Joe trailed off as he took the entrance to the expressway and pointed us toward the suburbs. "I don't know. Funny, maybe? Might be he had a reason, could just as well be he wanted to be a pain in the ass."

"Good thing you've got me along," Paul said as he hung his chin on the seat between us. "Digging will go a lot faster with the three of us."

He wasn't wrong, but his breath stank, and I pushed his face back. "You smell like death, Franco."

Paul got quiet, maybe sulking, and I said, "Hey, sorry about your brother. Richard was a good guy."

"Thanks." Sullen as fuck, just like a kid.

"So, here we are," I said. "Three guys traveling to the 'burbs on a winter night to dig up a pea green Maverick."

"A Maverick with three quarters of a million inside it," Joe said.

Paul perked up. "It's like being explorers. Or treasure hunters. Like the Donner Party."

"They were pioneers," Joe said.

He wasn't deterred. "We can be the Hammer Party. Tell our grandkids about it and shit."

I couldn't look back at him. "Paul?"

"Yeah?"

"You know the Donner Party?"

"What about them?"

"They ate each other. Things got tough, and they went cannibal."

Joe stifled a laugh, and said, "True fucking story, right there."

"First sign of trouble," I said, "I'm digging in."

"Assholes." Paul leaned over the seats and turned up the radio.

The idea of digging the Maverick, or any other car, out of the frozen ground wasn't thrilling me. Still, by the time we'd spent more than an hour on the expressway, and then another forty-five minutes or so getting ourselves deep into the god-damn suburbs, I was more than ready to be out of Joe's car. The smell of tacos, bad breath, body odor, and who the fuck knows how many years of cigar smoke lurking in the uphol-stery, had me craving fresh air, no matter how cold.

Paul read the directions to Joe from a piece of crumpled up notebook paper, and when he finally announced the last turn was coming up, I almost said a silent prayer of thanks to a God I don't even believe in.

We came to a stop in front of an old barn leaning so far to one side it looked like a mild breeze could flatten it. I looked around, didn't see any other buildings, and said, "Doesn't seem to be particularly inhabited around here."

"My brother told me Doug's family owns the land."

Joe and I looked at each other, and maybe he suddenly turned into a mind reader, because he shook his head, his frown got a little deeper, and he said, "Let's get out of the goddamn car before I have to kill someone."

The trunk opened to reveal the lantern, a trio of shovels, and a few pairs of good leather work gloves. The money for this stuff, and probably for gas, too, would have to come off the top. A small price to pay, and I was fine with it. I kinda hope Paul would make some noise, mostly so I could give the leeching little shit a piece of my mind. Like Joe said, we needed him to get to the location, and I had to concede the point even more after the route we took looked like we were going to end up chasing our tails for a while. I wasn't any less suspicious, but I was resigned to the facts of the situation.

We each pulled on gloves, grabbed a shovel, and filed around to the dark side of the barn where not even the light from the moon could reach. Joe stuck his shovel into the ground, and got the lantern going. The light wasn't great, though it would let us see well enough to get the job done.

Joe rammed his shovel blade into the frozen ground. A

small chunk of earth broke loose, and we all looked at each other.

"Long night ahead of us," I said.

No one bothered to disagree.

It had been nearly seventeen years since we pulled the job together. Except for Joe, we'd all been young back then, and dumb enough to think the money could really be a way out. I couldn't even remember exactly what I thought I was going to do with myself, though if anyone had told me I'd still be freezing my balls off every winter in Chicago, I'd have told them they were fucking crazy.

"What if it's not here?"

Joe and I stopped digging, and turned to look at Paul who all of a sudden had a worried look on his face. We'd managed to dig down a foot over a decent size area over what I imagined to be a very long period of time.

"Keep digging," I said. "It's all we can do."

"Yeah, but what if it's not there?" Paul looked from me to Joe. "What if we get to the car and there's no money?"

"Jesus." Joe rammed his shovel into the earth and leaned on it. "If there's no money?" He smiled, his teeth glowing yellow in the lantern's light. "I'll bury you with the goddamn Maverick, Paul."

Paul swallowed hard, and Joe let out a big laugh.

"Come on," I said. "We have to keep digging."

Joe pulled his shovel loose, gave Paul one more look, and went back to it. I stood, waiting for Paul to dig in again, and after a few moments, he did.

My shovel hit something, it wasn't more dirt, and my heart skipped a beat. I wanted to shout out, but instead I started digging faster. Joe and Paul picked up on it, all three of us going at the hole with a renewed vigor. Shovelful after shovelful of dirt, and we began to define the outline of the long buried automobile. My hands hurt, my back ached, and I was as excited as a kid on Christmas morning.

From what we could see, it looked like Doug made the original hole at a descending angle, and put the Maverick in face first. As we cleared away the last of the earth from around the back end of the car, I hoped he'd put the cash in the rear. With the first light of the sun starting to show off to the east, the three of us sat on the edge of our little excavation and looked down at the car. I felt a stiffness creeping into me, and stood up. I walked around a bit, watched my two cohorts go on staring, and finally said, "Let's pop it open."

"Right." Joe got to his feet and grabbed his shovel again. He looked back to me, leaned his head toward the car, and said, "You want to do the honors?"

"You go on ahead," I said. "I'm too nervous." I hadn't planned on saying so, but it was the truth. I guess what Paul said earlier, about the money not being there, had wormed its way into my thinking.

Joe got the shovel under the lip of the trunk, but it didn't budge. I hopped down, tapped Paul on the arm, and all three of us put our weight on the wooden handle. The metal groaned, started to give, and then popped open. In the trunk there was something wrapped up in a packing blanket, and the three of us stood there, all hands still on the shovel, looking at it.

"All right," Joe said as he pulled away from us and set the shovel so he could lean on it. "Get it out of there."

I started to move toward the open trunk, but Paul rushed in and started clawing at the blanket. "It's all taped up," he said. "Give me a minute."

I stood there, watching him, and my hand went around the handle of my shovel. One good crack across the back of the head, I thought.

Paul backed up, turned to face us, holding a steel brief-case Joe and I both recognized. The grin on his face almost made me feel bad about what I'd been thinking.

Joe swung his shovel at Paul's head, and the sound it made when it connected echoed through the still air. He stood there a moment, looking at me, and the case fell from his hands.

"What..." He couldn't find the words he wanted to say.

"It's not your money," Joe said.

Paul's mouth moved in silence some more, and his eyes went wide with shock as I rammed the blade of my shovel into his gut. He rocked back onto his heels, arms suddenly thrust out reaching for a hold that's wasn't there, and then he toppled backwards, landing partially inside the Maver-ick's trunk, the shovel still sticking out of him.

Joe dumped a shovelful of dirt back to the hole. "Money splits better two ways."

He wasn't going to get any argument out of me. I grabbed the other shovel and started throwing dirt.

IOKI AND THE FAT JAP
How I was recruited by the F.B.I.
Tom Pitts

Wham. In an instant I was being propelled over the hood of a brand new Toyota; arching in mid-air, and for one brief second suspended, before smacking down onto the car. I rolled over the hood as though I had practiced it a million times. My heavy Schwinn one-speed bicycle didn't make it as far. After impact, it too had arced high in the air, then, in an incomplete somersault, crashed down onto the hood of the car.

It happened at the intersection of Market and Kearny, a huge, congested big city artery where Third, Market, Geary, and Kearny Streets all met. With momentum pushing me, I thought for sure I had enough time to make it to the other side. I was wrong.

Immediately, traffic around us halted. My acrobatics had stunned onlookers. I heard several people shout, *"Are you all right?"* and a couple of cries of, *"Oh, my God."* I was all right. I was worried about being delayed and not making it to City Hall in time for my filing. I pulled my bike off of the hood of the car with exaggerated care. Cars trying to navigate their way around our mishap began to honk and bleat. The driver's door swung open.

"You can't leave. You can't leave." The voice came from inside the car and was high and abrasive. It was a shrill command.

The driver struggled to get out of the Toyota. He pushed

and squeezed his way onto the street and stood with one hand on his hip and the other held up as if to say, *halt.*

I hadn't moved.

In front of me stood a soft, fat Asian man. His lips were large and puffy, his skin smooth and his forehead high and shiny. His shirt collar was clean and white, so tight it seemed to strangle his air supply. His face turned red as he barked at me. "Give me your driver's license. You're not going any-where."

I wasn't going anywhere. With a fabricated limp for sym-pathy, I guided my bike off Kearny Street and onto the side-walk to exchange information. The angry man got back into the driver seat and honked his Toyota over to the curb. It gave him time to deliberate with his passenger, then, when he climbed back out of his car, he promptly declared me guilty.

"You ran the red light," he said. It was a statement, not just for me, but for everyone within earshot of his stage voice.

He didn't ask if I was okay; he didn't look at the damage to his car; he only stood with his hands on his hips wonder-ing why everyone wasn't stopping and joining him in con-demnation.

The passenger in the front seat sat silent through the whole incident, waiting for the big man to take care of business, keeping his head down.

"Give me your insurance. Give me your license," the man demanded.

I tried to explain. "I'm on a *bicycle*—I don't have insur-ance."

His fat face turned red again. "Maybe we should call the police?"

It was a threat, an effective one.

"No. No police." I was scared of the police; I always had drugs in my pockets. I was in a hurry to get to City Hall. I was scared of losing my job, and, at the moment, I was scared of this angry Asian man shooting tiny, white pellets of spittle at my face. I just wanted my day to go on as it had before this asshole derailed it. With a sigh of resignation, I handed him my California driver's license.

He snatched the ID from my hand, glaring at me suspiciously while jotting down my address, making sure my face was the same as the picture. I looked at his registration. The car was rented. I didn't write down a thing.

"This is your fault," he said, finger wagging.

It wasn't. The details didn't matter.

Weeks went by. The accident had been pushed to the back of my mind. I was eighteen years old. My life was constantly bubbling and reconstituting itself with new drama. The incident had been just another notch on my belt as a bike messenger, along with flat tires in the rain and road rash.

That day was the furthest thing from my mind as I sat in my tiny bedroom on Pierce Street, drinking my sixteen-ounce Budweisers and watching my twelve-inch black-and-white TV. The doorbell rang. Desperate for company, I was quick to answer it.

"I got it," I called out to my roommates and pulled open the door. There was the fat Japanese businessman.

"Tim Potts?" he said. He was looking right at me, but announced it like a formality, like I was about to be served a summons. I said nothing. With a great flourish he produced a yellow carbon-copy receipt and waved it under my nose.

"Tim Potts," he said, "you hit our car. These are the damages. You must pay us this amount." When he said "us" he stepped aside just a little and I saw a frail young man behind him. The young man looked only at his own feet.

"This is my brother, Ioki. He was in the car. He is also my witness to your crime."

Ioki looked sad and didn't say anything. He glanced at me through the greasy bangs that hung over his eyes.

The fat man went on with his speech, but I'd tuned him out. I held the yellow piece of paper in my hand, staring at the figure in the bottom right hand corner. The total was hundreds of dollars. No way I'd ever be able to pay this guy. He was dreaming.

"No," was all I said. It was all I could say. I was in shock. The fat man looked at me as though he didn't understand. "*No way,*" I added, just to make myself clear.

"What do you mean, no? You don't have a choice, Tim Potts. You have no witnesses, you have no evidence, and you have no money." He made a big swooping gesture with his hand meant to take in the scope of my miserable and impotent life. "You must pay us, or we'll sue you. We will take you to court. I have money; you have none. This is America, and in America...*the rich win.*" With this last comment he held his fist high in the air, pointing his finger toward God as though he'd just received this additional commandment right there on my front stoop.

He had me. He'd touched on one of my worst fears. Fighting a broken system, running in a fixed race, being locked in a losing battle, outgunned, out financed. His theatrics were drawing the attention of my roommates. My nosey landlord lived in the flat upstairs. I wanted him to be gone. I needed to buy some time to think about this. Finally, I agreed to pay him twenty dollars a week. I handed him a twenty, and, hoping to never see him again, was already formulating excuses for why I wouldn't be able make the next payment.

He snatched the twenty out of my hand with great satisfaction and, as though he'd read my mind, said, "We *will* be back."

One week went by and they didn't show. I was ready to call their bluff, I was ready for a screaming match, I was ready for anything but to give them another twenty dollars. Another week went by and another no-show. After a few more weeks, I thought, once more, that I'd never see the fat Japanese businessman again.

Winter rains gave way to summer and my life moved on. When you're young, time is so full that the few months since the accident seemed like years. I guessed that *the rich* decided this battle wasn't worth winning. Twenty dollars was not enough to chase me down for, no matter how badly they wanted to teach me a lesson.

In June, my doorbell rang. A long, impatient, annoying ring. I peeked out the window to see who was on the front stoop. There, again, was the fat Japanese businessman. After all this time? For twenty bucks? That greedy, vindictive son of a bitch. I'd been waiting for this moment, still smarting from my naiveté; I wanted to show him my backbone. With my teeth clamped together and my jaw set firm, I swung open the door.

"I don't have your money." That was my greeting, all he would get, but as soon as I said it, I saw he was not the same man at all. His eyes were red and puffy and I saw tear tracks streaking his fat cheeks. He was still dressed in a suit, but he looked disheveled and broken.

"I'm not here for your money, Tim Potts. I'm sorry." His tone was softer, more effeminate. "It's my brother, Ioki..." His voice trailed off while he choked back several sobs. "...He's missing."

I was confused. I didn't know what this man wanted. Was it all part of some elaborate ruse? Was he trying to draw me out for some other kind of extortion?

"I don't want your money," he repeated and plucked a twenty dollar bill from his breast pocket as an offering. "Look, here is your money back, okay? I just want to ask you a question. May I come inside?"

"No," I responded without pause. His tears had emboldened me.

"Ioki is my brother. He is lost here in America. I must find him. You must help me find him." He was pleading with me and commanding me at the same time.

"Why the fuck would I know where your brother is?" I couldn't even remember Ioki's face. I couldn't have picked him out of a lineup.

"Because he knows where you are. Did he come by here to pick up our payments?"

I didn't want to remind him I was only twenty dollars in. I thought about lying and telling him that I paid his brother the remaining balance, but his concern was not for my debt, it was for Ioki.

"No, I haven't seen him."

"Please," pleaded the fat man as he plucked another twenty from his pocket, "can I come back next week and see if he has come for the money? Just give him this."

I thought about it, debating whether I wanted to get further involved. The fat man took my hesitation to be haggling and promptly produced another twenty.

I relented. "What do I tell him if I see him?"

The fat man's eyes lit up. "Don't tell him anything, just give him the twenty and tell him to come back Friday for the next payment."

I held the three twenties in my hand and watched the businessman climb back into his double-parked rent-a-car and drive away.

It was three more Fridays before the fat man returned. This time he rang my doorbell and immediately retreated into a black town car. When I reached the sidewalk, I could only see his chubby hand beckoning from the rear window. I climbed into the seat beside him and he signaled for the driver to pull off.

"Have you seen him?" I could tell by his tone, he expected

no response. I shook my head, but he wasn't watching. He continued, "I need you to make a phone call, can you do that for me? I will pay you twenty dollars."

When I hesitated, he rolled his eyes and said, "Okay, forty. Here's twenty now and I'll give you the other twenty after the call." He believed that all people below a certain income level would do *anything* for a twenty. He folded the bill around a card. On the card was a name and phone number. The number was local, the name was Japanese. Not Ioki's name. "When they pick up, just ask for this man. Listen to what they say, and then hang up."

Like the saying goes, it was his dime. I called, let it ring endlessly, reported back, and collected the other twenty. That was it. Easy money. The disappointed-looking fat man thanked me and instructed the driver to return to my home.

It was a pattern he kept for several weeks. The fat man would show up at my house on Friday, we'd take a short drive, I'd make a phone call, hang up, and collect twenty dollars. Soon he expanded my duties. He had me go into a newsstand in Japantown to fetch Japanese newspapers. It hardly seemed worth twenty dollars to have me walk a few short feet into a store to purchase a one dollar paper, but once more, it was his dime.

I got used to the Friday night errands, enjoying the extra pay. Then, they stopped all together. I once again pushed Ioki and the fat Japanese businessman to the back of my mind.

"Mr. Potts? This is Special Agent Reilkoff from the F.B.I."

I thought maybe it was a prank, but the voice on the phone had an officious tone. I could hear typing, coughing, and the echo of leather shoes slapping linoleum.

"Have you had any contact with Haru Nakamura?"

I'd never heard the name. "No," I answered without confidence.

"Are you sure?"

It sounded like a test.

"No."

"No, you have not had contact, or no you're not sure?" He knew exactly what I meant. "Mr. Potts, Haru Nakamura is a dangerous criminal and an international fugitive."

There was a long and pregnant pause. I could still hear the echoes of phones ringing and other office sounds being bounced off the high walls and ceilings of the room he was in.

Reilkoff began to tell me what the F.B.I. knew—what I already knew: I'd been in an accident with Mr. Nakamura and a payment schedule was set up. How he knew these things, he didn't say. The debriefing was one-way and Special Agent Reilkoff didn't pause to allow any questions. He told me how this Nakamura had made a career of embezzling partners and defrauding travel businesses. He didn't say how Nakamura had done this, he only gave me astronomical totals from his crimes.

When he concluded, he said, "Mr. Potts, we need your help in catching this criminal."

"How can I help? He stopped showing up here weeks ago."

"Oh, he'll be back. We *know* he'll be back."

"Why would he come back to me?"

"Because..." The agent sounded annoyed that I hadn't been able to follow the breadcrumbs he'd laid down for me. "Because of Ioki. He has to find Ioki."

"His brother?"

I heard Agent Reilkoff snicker. "Ioki isn't his brother—he's his *lover.*"

Suddenly things made more sense. It seemed the subservient young man had broken his bonds. On the run from Japan, he had grown tired of the tyrannical Nakamura and escaped here in California. Ioki wasn't missing—*he was hiding.* Hiding from the fat, sweating, lecherous, desperate Nakamura.

Images lighted my imagination: a terrified Ioki submitting to the clumsy fondling of Nakamura; shutting his mind off; letting his body be used until the day fate would allow him a chance to flee.

Nakamura was in love. He was like a truck stuck in the mud, spinning his wheels in desperation. The man who had made his living by slipping away with other people's money was exposed, unable to flee with a broken heart. His obsessive, controlling love was going to be his downfall.

I was drawn into the intrigue, pulled by my inflated civic duty and the duty to do what's right. I put aside my nihilist punk-ethos and tried to think of what my father would do. I told the agent I'd help.

"Good," he said, welcoming me aboard. He gave me the number of a travel agent who'd fallen victim to Nakamura and told me that the travel agent would call to help set up a sting.

"The travel agent is gonna set up the sting?"

"Look, these guys have been hurt by this asshole more than anybody. They have the initiative and the desire. This guy I'm tellin' you about has lost more than three hundred thousand dollars and he's got a vested interest in bringing this fat prick to justice. Now if you can help us, Tim, there might be a sizable reward in it for you."

That was it. The scales had been tipped.

"But you want *me* to contact the travel agent?"

"This guy has our complete backing, just follow his lead. When Nakamura calls, just call that number and tell him what Nakamura has instructed you to do. He'll let you know what to do next."

He gave me his own number, repeated the contact information of the travel agent, and told me they'd be "in touch."

I hung up the phone feeling inflated. Had the F.B.I. just asked me for help? They needed me to close a case. After my being in this country less than a year, the U.S. Government had solicited me to help solve a problem. The excitement overrode the facts. I was being sucked further into a mystery, an adventure. I sat staring at the phone, waiting for it to ring. I was ready to kick down doors, exchange envelopes, and play both sides against the middle. All the phone had to do was ring.

It didn't. It didn't ring for another two weeks. Finally, on a Wednesday, I got the call. Haru Nakamura's voice came over the phone with its familiar, heavily accented, feminine gate and told me he wanted to meet at the Cathedral Hill Hotel in two days. He'd never asked me to meet him before. He'd always picked me up at home. He'd never called me in advance before, preferring to show up unannounced in his town car on Friday evenings. His voice sounded different. There was apprehension coiled in his words. Did he know that I'd been contacted by the F.B.I.?

"Tim, you will be there?" He wanted it to sound like a command, but it was a question, a plea.

"Yes, I told you, I'll be there." I felt like Judas accepting a dinner invitation to the last supper. I wanted to get off the phone.

Before he hung up, he asked, "Tim...have you seen him?"

He knew the answer, but had to ask. I felt sorry for him.

As soon as I hung up the phone, I called the number the F.B.I. agent had given me. The voice on the other end sounded like the agent's. Was it the agent? I felt my heart sink. Had I been duped a second time? Was a con man using me to set up another con man?

"We'll be there. You just do what you are supposed to do. We'll take care of the rest."

"Who? The F.B.I.? Who's gonna be there if things get weird?"

"Nothing's going to get weird. Just show up and we'll

take care of you."

It occurred to me that I was being reassured by a travel agent, helping him take his vengeance. I didn't know who was who anymore. I didn't care. I was going through with it just to see what would happen next.

I showed up at the Cathedral Hill Hotel at the appointed time, locked my bicycle to a parking meter outside, and walked up to the revolving doors. Entering the huge, expansive lobby, I looked for signs of my protectors. I saw none. I took a seat on a large, white couch and waited. I watched for Nakamura, I watched for agents. I wasn't sure anymore if they'd be F.B.I. agents or travel agents. Minutes crawled by. Should I be wearing a wire, I wondered, or perhaps a bulletproof vest? I imagined Nakamura wandering in and being tackled by a team of agents. I saw guns drawn, badges flash, a glint of steel glancing off the handcuffs as they came clamping down on the fat man's wrists. I thought about how much the reward might be. I calculated percentages from the astronomical totals from Nakamura's crimes.

After half an hour, I imagined what else I'd be doing right then, where I'd go afterward, what I would eat. I yawned. The traffic in the lobby was constant. A steady stream of new faces let me know that none of them were the slightest bit interested in my intrigue. I yawned again. The couch felt comfortable.

After forty-five minutes, I decided that Haru Nakamura was a no-show. He'd been spooked. Perhaps he had a sixth sense that tipped him off, or maybe he'd found Ioki and no longer needed me.

I headed to the bank of pay phones across from the elevators and dialed the travel agent's number.

"He's not here."

"No shit, Sherlock," said an angry voice on the other end.

I thought it was a little harsh considering I'd done my part, cast my web. Something had tipped Nakamura off. The fat man had slipped away again. An image of his greased, naked body flashed in my mind.

"What do you want me to do?"

The voice seemed resigned to failure. "Just go home," it said.

Months later, letters began to arrive at my apartment, forwarded from address after address. Osaka, Tokyo, Daly City, Redwood City. All of them in Japanese. A gentle calligraphy adorned the expensive parchment. The paper was transparent and fibers frayed from the edges. It felt expensive, important. There were exotic postage marks, colorful, indecipherable. Some envelopes were small like wedding invitations; some were wide and serious like wills and deeds. A few had different surnames, but they all ended with:

Ioki Yoshida c/o Tim Potts
137 Pierce
San Francisco, California
USA

There it was. Ioki and I were inextricably tied. I knew it; the senders of these letters knew it. The thread of my life had been knotted forever with this wayward son, this sad, abused soul; running from that greasy monster, that fish-lipped Napoleon, the clown sadist. I looked down at the letters in my hand and wondered if they were from his family, desperately trying to recover their lost boy; messages of forgiveness, the all-clear to return home.

There was a grocery bag on my floor brimming with empty aluminum cans, sixteen-ounce Budweisers. I gave each envelope one clean rip before sticking it between the cans.

THE TIP
Tim O'Mara

Even before Joe took a seat, he knew something didn't feel right.

Most times he was greeted by a "Hey, sweetie" within five seconds of entering the place. Tonight he slid into his usual booth—"usual" in the sense that he sat there three or four times a month on his way down to take care of some business in the lower part of Florida—and the dinner menu was in his hand before he even got settled.

It took a good half-minute before he saw Stephanie coming out of the kitchen holding a tray with at least a half dozen tall glasses. She didn't notice him as she brought the drinks over to the table ten feet away.

He detected a slight limp when she walked and she was wearing long sleeves. He'd never seen that before: she had the most beautiful tattoos on her upper arms and loved showing them off. And what was up with the jeans? This time of year Stephanie liked to show off her tanned, almost flawless legs. Not tattoos down there, but the beauty mark two inches above her left knee did draw one's eye.

"This one's my baby girl, Jessica," she said the first time he'd eaten there three years ago. The way she turned to show him the artwork you'd have thought she was a supermodel. And with that face, she could have been. Maybe a few years ago, anyway, before the little cracks of hardness showed up. "And this one's Jesus Christ, of course."

As soon as she saw him, her face brightened. She came over to the booth.

"Hey, sweetie," but there was a fatigue in her voice, not like she was tired, more like she'd had enough. *Of what?* And then he knew.

Joe looked her up and down—not in that creepy customer/waitress way, more like a friend or a concerned older brother—and said, "Hurt yourself?"

She forced a smile. "Bumped into the knife drawer in the kitchen a few days ago," she said. "Too damned spacy to keep my eyes in front of me."

The way her eyes checked out the ceiling tiles when she explained that told him she was lying. And the sleeves?

"Got a little summer cold. Been feeling chilly the last few days." She accented that with a bad imitation of an exaggerated shiver, selling it too hard.

Her boyfriend's back in the world.

She'd hinted a few times in the past that he was quick with the temper and even quicker with his hands. Never to the face, though. Always the arms and the legs. Probably like his father had taught him.

She shrugged whenever Joe asked why she stayed with him, and said he was the father of her baby and was hoping they'd get married someday.

Those two tattoos.

Joe had heard that answer in so many varieties from so many women over the years. Why does every asshole out there seem to have a woman who loves him, and just knows she can change him if just given a little more time?

"When did Terry get out?" he asked, himself just a little too tired to do the dance tonight. He kept his eyes on her as he reached down and scratched his leg just above the ankle. It was going to take some time getting used to that area being vacant.

She smiled the kind of smile people do when caught in a

lie. He could tell she was surprised he remembered the guy's name. Part of *his* job.

"Two weeks ago. Came right home and was back at work the next day." She took a quick look around the dining room—nobody seemed to need anything at the moment— and slipped into the seat across the way from him. That was a first. "He was real good the first eleven days. Went to the garage early, came home for dinner, watched Jessica when I had the night shift."

Eleven days. Like the answer to how many days have you been sober.

"And then…?

She grabbed the saltshaker and started making circles with it on the table. It was then he noticed the small bruises around both of her wrists. He knew from experience what caused those particular types of bruises, and it wasn't be- cause Terry was buying his baby's mama the wrong size bracelets.

"Then…he wasn't so good. Wasn't Terry's fault, not real- ly. His boss got on his case about showing up late and one of the engines he worked on had to be redone which cost the boss an extra three hundred dollars and it's just a lot of pres- sure for somebody trying to make a life for himself…and his family after being away for a couple of years."

He had no answer for that. "Being away" one of many euphemisms for what happens when you get caught with enough black tar heroin to get charged with intent to dis- tribute and the state decides to pay your rent for thirty months. That's another problem with these assholes: they never seem to get in enough trouble to do real time. The kind of time it takes for the women in their lives to smarten up and move on. Six months here, a year here. Too little time to give up the hope. He'd thought maybe two and half years would've been enough to do trick this time, but Stephanie here was a true believer.

"He still at the garage?" Joe asked.

"Yeah," she said. "The boss said one more screw up and he's gone—he's a good worker, Terry is, he'll be fine—but he's still there."

"No." He put the menu down. "I mean right now. Is he at the garage *right now?*"

"Oh," she said, now realizing she was confused by the question. "No. He's actually out back." She motioned with her head towards the kitchen where Joe knew the back exit was. Joe never ate anywhere without knowing where the back exit was. She put her hair behind her ear, briefly exposing a small, black-and-blue circle behind the ear before the hair fell back. "My boss needed some work done on his pickup, so he asked Terry to take a look at it. My mom said she'd watch Jessica tonight so Terry could make a few extra bucks."

He shook his head and tapped the menu. What he wanted wasn't on it. "Chef still making those meatloaf burritos?"

"You're the only one who still asks for 'em." She stood. "You got twenty minutes to wait? Off-the-menu items take a little longer."

Joe smiled. "I have a rare evening with no plans." *Except maybe one now.* "I need to step outside and make a phone call. Grab a quick smoke."

"I didn't know you smoked," she said.

He took the pack of cigarettes out of his jacket pocket that had been there for almost a year now. He only pulled it out when he needed an excuse to step outside on occasion. This was one of those occasions.

"I quit," he said, showing her the pack. "Mostly." He faked an embarrassed shrug. "Just do one or two a week now. Helps take the edge off a long drive."

Stephanie smiled that smile. "Good for you. I'll go put that it for you."

As she made her way back to the kitchen, he looked at his

watch. Twenty minutes was plenty of time. She'd come back with some water before that but would probably assume his phone call had taken longer than expected. Maybe she'd think he was getting in a good stretch. He'd told her more than once that he drove a lot for his job. Of course, he never told her what he did for a living and Stephanie was not the type not to ask too many questions.

The boyfriend, Terry, knew that, didn't he?

Joe went outside and put the pack of smokes back in his pocket. After he made the phone call—that part of his excuse was true—it took him less than a minute to locate Terry. He was the only asshole behind the diner with his head inside the mouth of a pickup truck. There was a work light hanging from the hood of the truck and it cast a glow on Terry that made him look as if he were being interrogated in a bad 1950s movie. Even from ten yards away, he could tell that Terry was frustrated over something and talking to the engine as if it were an unruly step-kid.

"Trouble?" Joe said as he approached.

Terry looked over and grinned. His smile did not match Stephanie's. There was no joy in it, just a big old toothy smile that pretty much said the same thing he had just told the engine.

"No," he said. "I just like looking at engines on nice nights like this evening."

Joe laughed. Lots of guys he knew who went in and out of prison had good senses of humor. They needed them.

"Maybe I can give you a hand," he said.

Terry turned back to the engine. "Got two of mine own," he said. "I'm good."

As Terry raised his right hand to prove his point, Joe pulled out a pair of handcuffs from behind him and grabbed Terry's arm. With the dexterity of a magician, he slipped one cuff around the wrist and the other he attached to the latch in the hood.

"Motherfucker," Terry said, and tried to jerk himself out of the handcuff. "Fuck."

"Now you've got *one* good hand," Joe pointed out. "And if you keep pulling on that, you're gonna end up with some nasty bruises around the wrist. The kind Stephanie's wearing tonight."

Terry stopped pulling. "That what this is about?" he grimaced. "You one of the guys she's been with since I been away?"

Joe reached out and slapped Terry in the face. After the shock wore off, Terry raised his uncuffed hand in an effort to lash back. Joe grabbed the hand and squeezed it between the thumb and the wrist. Terry let out something that with a little more volume might have passed for a scream.

"That's your scaphoid bone," Joe explained as he squeezed a little harder. "If I twist it a bit more, it'll break. That'll sound very much like a stepping on a twig, and probably put you in a cast for a good four weeks." He slapped Terry again, this time on the other cheek so both sides of his face would sting. Joe liked balance. "You don't strike me as the kind of guy who has decent health insurance, so that would be quite a burden on you as you wouldn't be able to work during the recovery time. Unless your boss doesn't mind having a mechanic who's only got one good hand."

Terry took a couple of deep breaths and shook his head a few times in an attempt to get rid of the ringing in his face.

"The hell do you want, man?" he asked. "That bitch tell you—"

Joe slapped him again before he could finish the sentence.

"There's the first thing I want," Joe said. "You're not supposed to refer to the mother of your child as a bitch, Terry. Unkind language leads to unkind behavior. Now," he squeezed the bone in Terry's hand a little harder, "the only reason I'm not breaking your scaphoid bone is because of that little girl of yours. I know you're a crappy boyfriend—

and I'm sure you're not a great dad—but you have a marketable skill, which does require use of both hands. It's the same reason you never seem to hit Stephanie in the face. You're smart enough to know it might cut into the tips she gets from guys who like the way her face lights up when she smiles."

"I knew it," Terry said. "You are one of those guys she's been with."

This time, Joe flattened his hand and drove it into Terry's left side. Again, not having the proper oxygen supply to make an intelligent statement, Terry just grunted.

"Now that rib I just broke?" Joe said. "You don't need that to do your job. You'll find yourself being real careful leaning into an engine for a month or so, but you can still do your job. Speaking of which..." He reached over and grabbed Terry's cell phone from his back pocket. He punched in some numbers. "This is your new boss' number."

"I already got a job," Terry said.

"You're moving on to bigger and better things, Terry." Joe showed the phone's screen to Terry. "Turns out my friend Gabe is in need of a new mechanic. He's got a shop up north, about two hundred and fifty miles from here. I just got off the phone with him and you start in two days."

Terry thought about that for a few seconds and said, "I can't just up and leave, mister. I got—"

"There's nothing for you down here anymore. Gabe's expecting you by tomorrow night. He's got a place behind the garage you can stay in. If you're not there by tomorrow night, Gabe's going to call me and I will find you and then I *will* break your scaphoid. For starters. All that's going to do is delay the start of your employment with Gabe by a month or so. That's not going to help anybody."

Terry tried to straighten up. With the busted rib, he could only do so much.

"You can't make me move, man. My life's down here."

Joe shook his head and smiled. Then he did the same thing to Terry's right side that he'd just done to his left. Again, balance. Joe waited until Terry was back in a listening mode before speaking again.

"Past tense, Terry. Your life *was* down here. What does your boss pay you, by the way? A few hundred a week?"

Joe took another painful breath. "Three," he managed to say.

"See there?" Joe said. "Life is getting better. Gabe's going to pay you five hundred a week and give you a place to stay. Now, half of that's going to Stephanie, and just to make sure you don't forget that, Gabe will take care of sending it for you."

He could see Terry's mind working on that. Hard to think with two broken ribs and one hand cuffed to the hood of a pickup truck, but he was giving it his best.

"That," Terry said, "only leaves me with two-fifty a week. How's that—"

Joe slapped his face again. "Because that extra money goes to Stephanie and your daughter and reduces the need for Stephanie to pick up extra shifts. She spends more time at home and that's good for your daughter. And think about all the money you'll be saving on your commute to work every day."

The thought of that must have somehow amused Terry because a small smirk crossed his face. Joe couldn't help but be a little impressed: handcuffed with two broken ribs and this guy could do some basic math and find a bit humor in the situation.

"Anything else?" Terry asked. "I mean, since you got my attention and all."

"Oh, yeah," Joe said. "That gun you got at home? My guess is a Glock semi, and you keep it loaded next to the bed. You're gonna give that to Gabe, too."

The smirk left Terry's face. "How do you know 'bout my

gun? Stephanie running her mouth again. I got a right to—"

Joe grabbed the hand again and squeezed. "The bruise behind her ear, asshole. Ask your parole officer what having a firearm in your possession is worth. If I wanted to, I could jam you up big time right now, but that's not in your family's best interest. You're still worth more out of jail than in. So tomorrow night, when you're unpacking at Gabe's, you're going to hand over your gun and forget all about any Second Amendment rights you think you have coming to you."

Terry did his best to straighten up. When he got as far he was going to get, he asked, "How'd you know it was a Glock?"

Joe allowed himself a smile and lifted his pant leg, right where he had scratched a few moments ago. He could see a wave of fear cross Terry's face. But there was nothing there.

"Carried one myself for a while."

"And?"

"And I found it did a little too much of my thinking for me," Joe said. "Guns make you feel bigger than you are. Like the kid whose lunch money you used to take in high school who now realizes he can afford a Hummer. Trust me, Terry. As soon as you give it to Gabe, you'll feel better about yourself."

"I ain't feeling too good right now."

"This, too, shall pass." He was about to head inside, when he turned back, realizing he'd left Terry cuffed to the truck. As he let his wrist free, Joe said, "And no goodbyes. You finish up with this job, get what's due you from the boss inside, go home and gather your stuff, and leave."

Terry rubbed his wrist. "I can't see my little girl? What's Stephanie gonna think?"

"That you're one more asshole who found something better and hit the road. If you really cared what she thought, we wouldn't be having this conversation. You can call your daughter from Gabe's. Tomorrow. Do I have to mention that I'll be checking up on you, Terry?"

Terry fingered his ribs and winced. "No."

"Good."

Back inside, Joe had just sat back down as Stephanie was coming out of the kitchen with his burrito plate. He took a long sip of water.

"Perfect timing," she said, sliding his meal in front of him. Her smile seemed a bit brighter than before, but he knew that was probably just his imagination. "You get that phone call made? Smoke that cancer stick? All good?"

He reached down and scratched above his ankle again. A cop friend of his told him a while ago that he'd be doing that for a few months. Kind of like when you lose a leg or something. "Far as I can tell."

"Good." She looked down at the table. "Anything else I can get you?"

He gave that some thought and said, "How about some hot sauce?"

"Oooh," she teased. "Deciding to live a little dangerously?"

"Not this guy." Joe laughed. "Just looking for a little change."

THE FINAL ENCORE OF MOODY JOE SHAW
A Denny the Dent Tale
Thomas Pluck

Early in the morning, before the people come out, sometimes I'm happy. The black car's tail lights look like the eyes of a dragon in the fog, or something big and old and evil. I'd kill a monster like that with my two hands, if it would make people stop staring with their cruel little eyes.

I used to hate them for it. Put some mean ones in the ground. But now I just stay out their way. They don't mess with me, I don't mess with them. Before dawn, hunting scrap metal in my truck, they can't see who's inside.

The car pulls away, and I get out. The fog rolls around my work boots. They're so worn I walk bowlegged, but my size is hard to find.

There's a water heater out by the curb, the old kind. I heave it over my shoulder, then lay it down easy in the bed of my old green Ford with hardly a sound.

Up the street, someone pulls a curtain aside.

I know better than to smile. Learned that the hard way.

I'm north of six and a half feet tall. Near four hundred pounds. Got hands that can bend rebar like a clown does balloons. Did that once, for the kids walking past a construction site, before their parents took them away.

I squeeze into my truck. The springs creak. Remy, my pit

bull, butts her head against me and disappears into my hand as I scruff her ears.

The kids called me Denny the Dent. Beneath my do-rag, my head's got a cut, like you took a scoop of peanut butter out the jar with your finger. Been there since I was born, when the doctor pulled me out. Mama said it's 'cause a sweet peach bruises easy.

I ain't been sweet for a long time.

It's a good morning. I get a couple old air conditioners, some black pipe. I strike gold behind a Dumpster at an apartment building and find the rusty exhaust from some tuner's car. I take it all to Newark Salvage, a scrap yard down by Port Newark. Matos pays me fair. He's a good man, and his little girl smiles at me from behind the counter. People are afraid of a big man, but they like to cheat a slow one. I ain't slow, though. Not really. I'm not smart, but I listen good. And I ain't never laid a hand on no woman, or hurt no one who didn't have it coming. Anyone who says I did will answer to these two hands.

I like kids before they learn to be mean. To be afraid. The young ones don't whisper nasty things like I can't hear, or I'm too dumb to understand.

Simple. Slow. Retard.

I park by the lake, where Ike sits watching the fishermen and the ducks. He's on the good bench sucking a bag of wine, holding two takeaway bags from Sandy. She's got a shack off the highway, covered in white siding, where all the truckers go.

I give Ike a ten dollar bill, and dig in with my plastic fork. There's a tin plate of big rib bones and greens for Remy, and I set it down for her. I shovel in red beans and rice and chicken and her country meatloaf too.

"What's the good word, Big Man?" Ike's real old. He won't say how old. Got leathery skin over long bones, still got some muscle, but not like me. We watch the sun drop over the lake and turn it into a big mirror.

I ask him how Sandy's doing.

"Just fine. She asked for you. Says the police still coming round."

There was some trouble at her place. And the probation man, back when I used to see him, said one more strike and I go away for good. I sure miss Sandy, though.

"Deacon's got a job for you, you want it." He knows I do. Ike can hold a conversation all by himself, and that suits me fine. "Old lady in Forest Hills, big old mansion, other side this park? She got a wrought iron fence needs scrapping. Deacon Bennett says some joyriders crashed right through her yard, tore it all up." He scratches the gray fuzz on his chin. "She can't pay, but that iron's got to be worth your while."

I nod, and scrape my plate clean. Say it's gonna be cold tonight.

"Thanks, Big Man, but I need the sky over my head. When it gets too cold, I got a church lady lets me sleep in the basement." Ike sleeps under the stone bridges in the park in the summer. I told him he can stay with me and the dogs at the junkyard, but he's like me, he likes being alone most of the time. He pets Remy's ears, plays with her.

I get up, stretch. Some boys riding in a low-sitting car hoot and yell "Frankenstein!"

I glare and they show fingers and drive away. I let them go. Won't be the first car I put in that lake.

But Mama says I can't think like that. She talks to me, when I'm quiet, and let the world go by. Telling me to be good. To let evil be.

I killed the man who hurt her. Horace, her boyfriend. He was lifting weights, showing me how, and I stomped his thing.

Weights fell on him and crushed his head. But his boys, they took it out on Mama. Burned her up. Nearly got me too.

I hear her voice when I look at the scars on my arms. Sometimes I listen, sometimes I don't.

After Mama died, I lived with lots of different people. Some good, some bad.

There was this good couple I remember well. They fed us good and never raised a hand. I remember their names but if I think on them too hard I'll get angry that I was taken away from them. So I just call them The Good Ones. They taught me never to lay a hand on a girl in anger. Even if she hits you, or calls you retard. This big mean girl was trying to hit my dent with a stick to see if she could knock it back out and I pushed her away. She fell down and told on me.

They made me sit in the corner and told me why it was wrong. That I was gonna be big, real big, and that meant I had to watch my temper, and protect the little ones from the big ones.

Girl was big as me, but that didn't matter. They said I didn't know better then, but that I do now.

They saw I was upset so they hugged me and I've tried to know better ever since.

"I hope that junkyard ain't getting to you," Ike says. "Once a man owns land, he changes."

I don't own the junkyard. Not really. Anyone owns it, it's the dogs.

The dogs are all fighters, or used to be. Some missing a leg, or an eye, or both. Faces scarred like melted candles. Man who used to fight them died here. All they left was the soles of his boots.

After I feed the dogs from a barrel of food, I get in my van. It's got a clean mattress and thick wool blankets taped over the windows. It's just a shell, but when the city shut off the electricity and padlocked the front gate, I moved out the front office, to back here.

I lay awake thinking what this old lady will be like. Some old people are mean.

The old lady's house is surrounded by trees that are old and twisted, like hands coming out the ground to feed some giant living down deep. The paint's all peeling, unlike the neighbors. Theirs stand straight and clean. Got new cars in front. Her driveway's empty. I back in, park in the shade. Music comes out her open windows. Horn music with no words, with some sadness to it, but some jump, too.

I leash Remy in the truck, windows down. She's the friendliest thing in the world, but she scares people. Just like her daddy.

The iron fence is rusted and twisted. Some car hit it hard enough to tear one post out the ground, big chunk of concrete and all. Some sections are too long to fit in the truck, but I figure I can bend them in half easy enough, and take one piece at a time.

My knock sends paint flakes off her door like dandruff. I wait a long time, knock louder. The curtain moves on the house next door, and I'm about to leave before they call the police, when I hear a ragged voice over the music.

"Help!"

One sound I know is fear.

The door jamb cracks apart with one shove. The house is big and dusty, black cobwebs in the corners, and smells like Ike does up close. The rug's so thin it might be painted on the floor. The walls are covered in shelves, lined with books and little things I know better than to touch.

But no old lady.

"Did you hock your saxophone?" a voice says. I look up and see a blush red ghost. She's bent over the staircase, got her leg caught in the railings. I climb up the stairs and they creak like the whole house is gonna come down.

"Be gentle, bear. I've been up here a while." Her voice makes me want to do what she says. Like a kind school-teacher.

I pick her up by her bony hips and lift her over the rail-ing, slow. She leans into me with a gasp. "Oh, you're not..." She looks me up and down, squinting like I'm a ghost. "My, you're the size of Mount Fuji."

She's tiny and hunched, white as a fish's belly, spotted all over with marks of age. Her skin hangs like the crepe paper we used to make things in kindergarten. But her eyes are clear and sharp, two cups of black coffee.

I carry her down the stairs, set her on the landing. "All the blood rushed to my head," she says. "You must be from the church. What's your name?"

I tell her.

"Denny, I'm Mrs. Kolb." She rubs her ankle. Spreads her wrinkled old toes. "Thank you. I twisted it, nearly went over the bannister."

The carpet at the top of the stairs is peeled away. She must have tripped over it. I tell her the deacon said she needs her fence scrapped.

"Yes, someone stole my car and crashed it. I'm afraid I can't pay you much," she says. "You can have whatever scrap value the metal brings."

I help her to her feet, and she limps to the kitchen like a ballerina on twisted toes, steadying herself against the wall. I get a hammer and tools from the truck to put her door jamb back together.

"I'll make lunch," she calls from the kitchen "Do you like tunafish?"

Before I can answer, two police cars roll up.

* * *

The cellar is cool and dark. The windows have bars. They remind me where I'll go, if the police see me.

Bang bang bang. Only police knock like that.

"Hello?"

"Ma'am, we received report of a break-in on the premises. If you'll come outside we'd like to have a look around."

I squeeze the hammer in my hand. Hope I don't have to use it.

"They were mistaken," she says. "The church sent a man to work on my fence, and my front door sticks in this weather."

"Can we speak to this man?"

I duck my head under the rafters, and slip behind the old boiler.

"Well, he said he needed some tools," she says. "He won't be back for a while. You're welcome to wait if you'd like. I'm making tunafish."

"We're gonna look around if you don't mind."

"No, you're not," she says. "I haven't tidied up and I don't want anyone going through my house. Everything is all right, except for my neighbors and their overactive imaginations."

"Ma'am—"

"I may be old, but I still have my marbles," she says. "Thank you for coming so quickly. You can wait for him on the porch if you like."

Teacher voice works on police, too. They don't wait.

When I come up the stairs, she's on the porch glaring at the house next door. Where I saw the curtains move.

"You're not the first fellow I've known who needed to keep a low profile," she says, pleased with herself. She folds her little hands like a frightened dove in her lap.

The curtains move in the window next door, as I go back to work.

* * *

I tack down the rug for her, and fix the cracked door jamb with some scrap wood from my truck. I dig up a big section of fence, and break a good sweat bending it so it'll fit in the truck bed. I collect the concrete too, fill in the post holes and pack them down. Even string up some orange tape where the piece was. I take Remy for a walk, clean up her mess, and feed her dog chow in a hubcap, and wet it down with the hose. She wags her uncut tail so hard it whips my leg. She whines when I put her back in the truck, even with the windows down.

When I'm mopping my face and packing away my tools, a black German car pulls into the driveway next door. Bald man gets out, wearing a suit, carrying a white hard hat. He narrows his eyes and walks to the edge of his property, looking from my truck to the fence and back.

"She finally getting that thing replaced? I offered to do it, but you can't tell her anything."

I keep loading my truck.

"You know what they say," he says. "Good fences make good neighbors."

I shrug to him.

He frowns as I head inside.

Mrs. Kolb has a plate piled high with little tunafish sandwiches on white bread, all cut into triangles. Horn music wails from her record player.

She sits on a wicker chair. Pours yellow tea into fancy cups. She offers me a seat, but if I took it, it would end up a bunch of toothpicks.

"My new neighbors started a homeowner's association," she says. "They're all against me. My house is a little dilapidated, but I've lived here since I was born. And I'm not going anywhere until I drop dead." She breathes in the steam from her tea.

I smell mine, too. Toasty.

"It's green tea," she says.

I take a sip. It tastes like old paper. I tell her.

She laughs. "Yes, it does."

Her tunafish is good. It's got pickles in it, and celery, and spices. Makes up for the weird tea. When I'm half through the plate, a skinny little woman opens the front door without knocking.

"Mrs. Kolb?" She's got her hair tied back and her elbows look sharp enough to draw blood. She runs to the table on pointy little shoes. "Mrs. Kolb! I came as soon as I heard. The police?"

"Yes, someone mistook my handyman for a burglar," Mrs. Kolb says. "Denny. This is Carmela."

"Denny," Carmela says. She offers me her hand and I hold it gentle. Her skin feels soft as a rich man's wallet. Her shirt's cut real low. I don't look at it.

"That must've been the Entwhistles, they're such pains in the patoot," Carmela says.

"You mean ass," Mrs. Kolb says. "Pains right in the ass."

"Oh, Mrs. Kolb." Carmela covers her mouth like she's embarrassed but she ain't. I can tell people. I watch them all the time, and they treat me like I'm a rock or a tree. Or at least as dumb as one.

"Denny saved my life," Mrs. Kolb says. "I tripped over my rug like a fool, and nearly broke my neck on the stairs."

"I told you not to go up there, you can always call me."

"But my best books are up there. I won't ring you every time I want to read a passage from James Baldwin or Willa Cather."

"I'm going to fix that rug right now," Carmela says.

"Denny did already."

Carmela squeezes my arm and her nails poke my biceps. Leave little crescents. "Look at you, I bet you can lift the whole house! Well, let me check. You can't be too careful.

My mother lived to be ninety-nine, and I took care of her every day."

Carmela stretches her face into a smile and bends to put an arm around Mrs. Kolb's shoulder. "She's such a sweetheart, isn't she, Denny?"

Talking to people makes me more tired than any kind of work. I nod, when I remember this is one of the questions they expect you to answer. She shifts her hips as she walks up the stairs. Pauses halfway to see if I'm looking.

I'm happy to get back to my junkyard that night. Mr. Matos pays good for the section of fence. I buy big bags of dog food to fill up the bins. Then I meet Ike for dinner at the park. This time Sandy gives us fried fish and remembers to give me lots of little containers of hot sauce.

"How's that old lady?" Ike says, smearing a slab of catfish with tartar sauce.

I tell him she's nice and makes good sandwiches.

"Come on, Big Man. I know you don't like talking, but tell me about her."

I tell him about the music playing, how her hands are soft and kind, like a grandma's.

"What kind of music?"

Shrug.

"Well, ask her what it is next time. For me."

I tell him I'll try to remember.

As I sit with the dogs and watch them play and tussle in the moonlight, I'm just happy Mrs. Kolb's not mean like old Miss Stacey. The Good Ones had her babysit me, when they went out some nights. That was when the mean came out.

Quit being so *rambunctious*. Fetch me the remote, Retard.

If I didn't, she knew just where to pinch and twist. Her

yellow fingernails sharp as claws.

I knew not to hit back. She was big and old and mean, but she was still a girl.

When the Good Ones came to pick me up, Miss Stacey grabbed me by the ear. Said if I snitched, she'd tell the police I hit her, and they'd take me away.

I should've told on her. They took me away anyway.

The next morning I show up early, and try to give Mrs. Kolb twenty dollars from the salvage yard.

"Oh no you don't," she says. "That's yours. You earned it."

She takes slices of white bread and cuts a hole in the middle with a glass, then fries it in a pan with butter and cracks an egg right in the middle. "Egg in a nest," she calls it, and sprinkles salt and pepper on them from shakers shaped like little Chinese cats. She keeps the yolks runny and when we dunk our little circles of bread in it, the yellow spills out thick as paint.

When it's late enough for me to make noise, I start digging up the rest of the tangled fence. It's good hard work. I get another section in the truck, one of the small ones that don't need bending. The metal's shaped into leaves and acorns, and it's a shame it went to rust.

"I hope you don't mind tunafish again," she says. She's got the music loud, horns again. Her eyes look grayed over. "The church only takes me grocery shopping once a week. I buy cans because who knows when they'll abandon me. They want to take my house and stick me in a loony bin."

I listen to the record, and eat the sandwiches. Ask her who's playing.

"Oh, you like it? When I was younger, I went to jazz clubs. Newark was known for jazz, you know. My love for the music scandalized my family, I have quite a collection."

She stretches out her arm to point at her shelves, like she's wearing a fancy dress instead of an old housecoat. "I could renovate the house if I could bear to part with them, but as you can see, I never toss away a book or a record, even the ones I didn't much care for."

She asks what music I like, and I don't really know. I like what she's playing, even though it's got no words. I like what Sandy plays, and that's almost all words. And I like the old songs Ike sings to himself in the park.

"I'll play you my favorite." She shuffles to the record player. Lifts the needle and removes the black disc real careful, then replaces it with another one.

A smiling bald man is on the cover, holding a gold trumpet. Big glasses, big beard. "Moody Joe Shaw," she says, and her eyes light up. "He was the best to come out of Newark. Still is. I went to all his gigs. He was hot stuff."

Horns flutter like birds out of the speakers. It's real pretty, and she closes her eyes and smiles, holding the record cover close, dancing with it slow.

"This is his best, in my opinion. 'They Call Me the Jive Bomber.' I've got every record he ever played on." She's got a whole wall of records. The shelves are bowed under their weight. "Joe got around," she says. "Played solo, as sideman, and also a studio musician."

We listen to them until she falls asleep in her chair, and I go back to work.

A city truck pulls up an hour or so later. Older fella with a belly on him gets out, puts a hardhat on, starts talking about permits. I say I don't have one, and he tells me I have to stop working. But I'm almost done with that section, so I just keep at it. The curtains next door open a crack.

I look right at them as I bend a section in two and toss it in my truck.

* * *

I tell Ike about the inspectors, and he says he'll pass it along to the deacon.

"So, what the lady say about music?"

Shrug. I tell him about Moody Joe Shaw, and all her records.

"He was the best, Big Man. The king of hot jazz, decades before his time. Had a photographic memory. I knew it," Ike says, smiling at the ducks circling in the lake. "I knew it. She have any children?"

Shrug again.

"Well, ask her."

Saturday I show up later. I like her eggs, but people like to sleep in, and I don't want more complaints. I drive by the intersection up the block to see if that city truck's there. It's clear, so I pull into her driveway.

I don't hear her music, and it sets me on edge. The windows are closed, but it was chilly last night. I rap on the door. Then I smell it.

The stink of gas.

I bust her door open again and get a face full of it. I leave the door open wide. Five steps in, I feel like I fought twelve rounds. Can't breathe.

I yank the windows open and call her name. I don't know where she sleeps. I check every room. The house shakes as I hit the stairs three at a time. A picture rattles off the wall. The smell's worse up here.

Upstairs I find her in bed with her mouth open. I shake the bed hard but she don't wake. The window's open a crack. I slam it open and the pane cracks like lightning.

My heart hammers at my ears. I try to think how they make someone breathe on TV. I carry her downstairs into fresh air. Cradling her like a baby, my hand trembles. Then I slap her. Light as I can.

She wakes with a snort. Stares at me, confused.

"Joe? You came back."

She reaches up to stroke my face. Her fingers are cold like raindrops, tracing my cheek, then up, circling in my dent, like Mama used to do.

"Don't leave me," she says.

I hold her a while, like that. Until she gets some good air in.

"Denny," she says. "How'd you get here?" Her eyes are wet with tears. I hold her until she stops shaking.

Inside, I turn off the stove. Mrs. Kolb looks around like someone switched the world around on her. I'm glad when Carmela knocks on the door.

"I must've left the oven on, but I don't remember using it," Mrs. Kolb says. She's drinking tea with honey for her throat.

"Maybe you brushed it."

"For supper, I ate matzo crackers with butter and jelly, I had no reason to even be near the stove."

"I'm sorry to say it, Myra, but maybe you ought to consider what the deacon talked about," Carmela says.

"I want to die in my own home," Mrs. Kolb says. Her eyes go hard.

"Oh don't talk like that." Carmela waves a hand. "You're spry!"

"I've watched too many friends go, hooked up to some machine. That's not living."

"Have you...have you heard the voices again?" Carmela puts a hand on her shoulder. Her nails flash red.

Mrs. Kolb looks at the spots on her knuckles. The papery skin. "I know they're not real."

"But you hear them?"

"As long as I don't *listen* to them, I'm not a loony bird!" Mrs. Kolb's teacup rattles in the saucer.

***

I get two sections of fence in the truck this time, tying them down with straps. The deacon pulls up in his old Buick, comes out with a sack of groceries. He smiles as I sweat, buckling the straps tight. His suit's loose on him, and he favors his right leg.

"Heard the neighbors caused trouble." He glares at the house where the bald man lives. "Some people just have no charity. Mrs. Kolb's a good woman. When she passes, this land goes to the church. Long as we put a school on it. That doesn't sit too well with her neighbors. I'll go down and talk to the inspectors tomorrow morning."

The scrap money burns in my pocket. I take some of it, not all of it, and hand it to the deacon.

The deacon takes a twenty, and closes my hand. "You're a good man, Denny. I'll put this in the poor box for you." He walks toward the house.

I ask him if Mrs. Kolb has any family.

"Just us, Denny. Keep an eye on her, won't you?"

I tell him I will.

The longest section of fence is caught up with tree roots, and the scrap yard's closed by the time I'm done. Mrs. Kolb asks me to stay for dinner. The sun's gone down and I know I missed Ike, so I stay.

The deacon brought ham steak and she fries it up with a can of white potatoes and green beans. She makes me watch her turn off the gas, then check the pilot lights.

We eat at the empty dining room table and it makes her happy. She puts her favorite record on again. "Do you want to dance?"

I tell her I don't know how, and she says that don't matter. She puts my hands on her waist. It's not really dancing, we're just stepping in a circle, but she smiles like a young girl. I pick her up by the waist and spin her around, and she laughs, and I wonder if Sandy will get jealous of me slow dancing with an old white woman. When the song's over I set her down in her chair.

"Denny, I want to ask you a favor," she says. "I feel silly asking this, but…would you stay after dinner a while? It's those voices. I swear, if you tell me you don't hear them, I'll check *myself* into the loony bin."

I take the dog leash out of my pocket.

"Yes, go walk that sweet little dog of yours. You can bring her inside, you know."

I tell her I don't want Remy to get rambunctious.

"Oh, I'm sure she'll behave."

I bring some ham to Remy, and give her a good long walk around the neighborhood by the park, away from the houses, so I don't cause trouble. The leaves are falling, and Remy plows through the piles, chasing them.

Miss Stacey's in my head again. I couldn't lay a hand on her. Couldn't snitch. But I had to get away. My legs ache behind my knee, where her nails used to pinch me. Pain usually don't bother me. I just go somewhere else, talk to Mama. But Miss Stacey's meanness made Mama's face fade away.

You're so stupid your mama killed herself to be done with you.

I knew I was gonna do something bad, like I'd done before.

Miss Stacey had a dog mean as she was. A fat barrel of white curly fur, all yellow around its black teddy bear eyes. Caesar would snap when anyone but her got close. Miss Stacey would throw a stinky wet tennis ball for him to chase. Dog didn't even play fetch. Anyone but Miss Stacey tried to take that ball, he'd bite down hard on the tender meat between finger and thumb.

But like I said, pain don't hurt me. Not like other people say it does. You get enough pain, and it's like the heat or the rain. Something you can't do nothing about, so you just work through it.

He got fed the dinner the Good Folks left for me.
That kind of hurt's hard to work through.

A police car rolls through the park, sweeping its spotlight. It turns my way like one white eye. Remy perks up her tail.

I bolt for the trees.

The engine roars. Remy matches my stride like it's a game. Cutting across the roads, around the bridges. Blue lights flash through the trees. I know this park, but the lake in the middle makes it tough to cross. And there's never just one police.

I go places cars can't go. Get them going in circles until they stop and shine their lights through the trees. Parole officer once told me I had low cunning. Ike says that's the best kind.

We make it up a dirt trail to the bridge over Bloomfield Avenue. Other side of the street, there's people lined up at a hotdog truck. Woman's got a shark gray pitbull on a leash.

Her dog perks and smiles across the street.

So does Remy. She bolts for him, through traffic.

Then I'm running. Tires squeal as stomp their brakes, horns blare as they dodge me. I hunker low to grab Remy's leash. Blue lights blind me and something hard crunches against my arm. Cop car's in front of me, mirror dangling.

Remy's gone.

The pain's far away like the stars. I punch through the window and close my hand round his neck. Drag him out by the scruff like a kitten. His partner's out the door.

My boots crush the hood as I go over. Get him by the neck too. My fingers touch my thumbs. Smack them together like one man, and their feet kick above the ground.

People swim through life never knowing it's there. Then they suck air wide-eyed like big fat carp dragged from the water. Like Mama's eyes when the smoke cleared. Crying even though she's gone.

Her tears splash my face and I wake up. "Your girl's all right, *huevón.*" The pretty lady with the gray pit bull is holding Remy up to lick my cheek.

I drop the police by the car, still breathing.

"Thank you." I take Remy in my arms.

I run back into the park. One cop stares and the other spits up.

Two fish thrown back today.

I wake up cold everywhere except where Remy is curled beside me. After I found Ike beneath his trestle, he led me to a cave in the trees where he keeps some blankets, cans, and a spare jug of wine. It's more like a cubbyhole cut into the side of some rocks with a dead oak stump for a roof.

In the morning, we eat one of Sandy's cold plates together. My arm aches under the cloth where Ike tied it. But it's stopped bleeding, and it ain't broken.

I tell him what the deacon said, that Mrs. Kolb has no children.

"Said to ask *her,*" Ike says.

I leave Remy with him and head back to my truck. Long way around the park. A police car eases through Mrs. Kolb's neighborhood. I see a landscaper's truck, men blowing leaves around, with headphones on. I take a garbage bag and bag leaves with them until the police car goes by. The men look at me weird as I walk away.

Mrs. Kolb is sitting on the porch in her housedress.

"There you are. The voices were bad last night." She looks bad as me, and I slept in a cave.

I drop to one knee beside her porch swing. Tell her I hear voices, too. She can tell I ain't lying. I ask her what they tell her.

"Terrible things," she says. "Let's go inside."

She fixes two cups of yellow tea.

"When I was young, I made a terrible mistake. That's why these voices torment me."

I sip and listen.

"These houses all around us, the people might look happy, but most of them live in fear of one kind or another. You know how they look at you," she says, pointing with her teacup. "When I was young, I thought I was different. But when it came down to it, I was just as afraid as the rest of the people sheltered away in this little enclave. I made the wrong choice, and I've regretted it ever since."

I've done things I can't take back too. I tell her with a slow nod.

I ask if she has any children.

"No, Denny. I do not." She looks into her cup a long time. When she looks up, her watery eyes turn hard as marble. "I can't tell if you're being cruel, or if you just have rocks in your head. You should go."

There's still one section of fence left in the yard. So small I could tear it out with my truck. I feel bad leaving it.

I stare at those curtains across the way before I leave. Don't know if those neighbors are looking. His big black car isn't home.

I go home to the junkyard to wash up and get a change of clothes. Keep thinking about those cops, and how Mrs. Kolb turned mean, and bad thoughts cloud my head. I hit the weight pile to get my mind right. But that's not enough. I get under the back of a truck with no front wheels and lift it high, over and over, until I can't no more. I wash up again, trade my black do-rag for a white one, lose the uniform for an old pair of overalls. In disguise, I drive to the park.

Ike's got plates from Sandy, and we eat on the other side

of the lake with the sun to our backs, far away from the roads. The lake glows as the sun goes down and I think of the carp down there, and the cars and the bodies down with them.

"People talking about what you did last night. Some folks court trouble, but you got its nose wide open."

I say I thought they killed Remy.

"Well, she's right here, ain't she?" He kneads her neck as she eats. "You talk to that old lady, or you just terrorize the city?"

I tell him she said she had no kids.

"Really now." He bends a plastic fork against his chin.

He slips a pint bottle from his pocket, offers. I wave it away. Don't like the taste, and it would take a couple of those to get me high.

"I never knew my real folks. They didn't have foster homes back then, like you had. Just the orphanage. The nuns, man, they could be mean. But the good ones, they were good as gold. You know the good ones."

He drinks some.

"Sister Kathleen, she was one of the good ones. I liked to sing choir. Was real good, before my balls dropped." He laughs, takes another drink. "She took me aside one time, told me my father was a great jazz trumpeter. I didn't believe her. Music's sure not in my blood. She gave me a recorder, you know those? They're like a flute. Well, I might as well have used it to shoot spitballs, for how good I played. So for a long time I thought she just told me that stuff about my father to make me feel good. But the more I asked around, more I heard that Moody Joe Shaw got a rich girl in trouble, around the time I was born.

"Her family hushed it up, got him sent away. Just a nickel marijuana beef, but he got beat pretty bad in there. He kept playing, but they say he wasn't the same after that. Angry. Got killed in an argument over money down South. He threw a fist and the singer pulled a knife."

Ike wrings his hands. They're dry and cracked, but the way he folds them. Like two doves shivering, close together for warmth.

"Need you to do this for me, Denny. Tell her who I think I am. And if, and if she wants to see me, you come get me in your truck. Will you do that?"

He knows I will, but I tell him anyway.

Miss Stacey had a step stool she used to get things off high shelves in her kitchen. Like her instant coffee. She needed a cup when she stayed up late to watch me. I got a lot of bruises on my legs and little crescent scars under my arms, while I waited for her to need something off a high shelf.

When she got on that ladder, I grabbed Caesar's tennis ball. He growled and bit down hard on my leg. I threw that ball, he ran and knocked the step ladder clean over.

Miss Stace's hip cracked like a dead tree branch.

"Dial nine-one-one, Denny!"

I gave her the phone. It was the old kind, numbers all around like a clock. I looked at the numbers on the dial like I didn't know what they said. Asked her which one was nine. Which was one. I dialed a lot of wrong numbers before the ambulance came.

She went to the old folks' home and I went back to juvie.

When I get to Mrs. Kolb's I start working without calling on her, so she can't tell me to go away. Figure with the fence done, she might be in a better mood. It comes out easy.

I knock on her door. No answer. I hear the *Jive Bomber* album playing. I knock harder, then try the knob. It opens. I look around, then go in.

No smell of gas. I call her name over the music, walking slow, so I don't give her a fright. She ain't hanging upside down from the staircase, either.

The trumpet fades and I look at the shelf of records, thinking of Ike listening to them with her, eating tunafish sandwiches. Feels almost as good as me seeing my mama again. The record spins down and the needle lifts.

I call her name.

"Up here," she cries.

I trip over the carpet at the top of the stairs. It's come undone again. I find her in the hallway beneath the attic steps, all twisted. She clutches a little black box in her waxy white hands. I help her up and she hangs like a doll. Her legs dangle wrong. She cries and the box drops from her hands. Batteries spill out when it hits the floor.

Down below, the record starts up again. Low trumpet, creeping like the sun through the trees in the morning.

"Told you I've still got my marbles," she says, her voice cracking. I sit down and cradle her, careful. She winces and shakes. "The voices kept me up all night. They said terrible things. That you were here to steal my house. That Deacon Bennett and I were having relations. In the crudest of ways." She nods toward the box. "It's a radio of some kind. I found it in the attic. I got so piping mad that I slipped and fell."

Her head lolls to my chest. I think she's gone, but she gathers breath and starts again.

"Wish I could dance to Moody Joe one last time."

I pick her up by the waist, and turn to the music. Her forehead is cold against my shoulder.

"Had a boy like you, once," she says. "Let him go. I was afraid, angry. Afraid of my father, angry at myself, and the stupid...cruel...hateful world."

I tell her I know her boy. And that he's a good man.

There are tears on my shoulder before the music ends.

In my eyes, too.

I set her down gently. Thinking how I'm gonna smash the window next door, tear open those curtains, and close my hands around the neck of the hardhat man and his wife. I'm about to go downstairs and get the record to leave on her chest like flowers when I hear a voice over the music.

"Mrs. Kolb?"

Carmela. I step back in the bedroom, quiet.

She walks up the stairs. Stops when she sees the body, and sighs.

"Oh, honey."

She kneels to pick up the batteries. They clatter across the floor. "If you'd only listened and moved out, you'd be yakking it up and boring their heads off in the senior center, where you belonged. You'd have had to sell the place to pay for it. Maybe they would've let you play your damn jazz records." Another long sigh. "Now we'll have to fight the church over that school."

I step out.

She gasps. "Oh, it's you. You scared the shit out of me."

I hold out the last battery.

"You ought to leave." She tucks the black box in her purse. "You don't want to be here when the police show up. I called them."

She snatches the battery and runs for the stairs. I don't even chase her. She trips over the rug and hits the landing with a crack and a scream.

I stomp down the steps. She crawls for the door, shrieking.

"No! You don't understand! She wouldn't listen!"

She drags herself across the floor. I bring my boot down on her bad ankle. Moody Joe's trumpet wails from the dusty speakers. I turn the volume up so Carmela don't ruin it. When the song's over, I tip the shelf on top of her.

The floor bounces with the weight of all those records crashing down. The needle jumps off the record. I take the disc and slide it into the sleeve, then hold it up. Moody Joe smiles at me.

I take him to the park to see his boy.

PEEP SHOW
Holly West

Jimmy Price hates the sound of sirens. They remind him of the night Mama died, eight years ago.

Tonight, they wake him up. He doesn't glance at the digital clock sitting on the upturned milk crate he uses as a bedside table, but it reads 4:53 a.m. It's still dark out; the sun won't begin to rise for at least another hour. The wailing is distant but getting louder. He puts his hands over his ears and squeezes his eyes shut.

His little dog, Trixie, yaps. She doesn't like the sirens either. "Hush," he whispers, uncovering one of his ears long enough to shove her under his blanket. The apartment manager, Mrs. Hosharian, had given him a stern warning when she discovered the furry fugitive he'd been hiding: "She can stay, but keep her quiet. If someone complains to the landlord, she has to go."

The threat of losing Trixie has loomed since he found her, a fuzzy white mutt tied to the parking meter outside of a coffee shop on Santa Monica Boulevard. The day after he took her home, someone stapled "STOLEN DOG" posters on several telephone poles in the neighborhood. That dog, named Bella, looked a lot like Trixie, which concerned Jimmy. What if someone mistook her for the lost animal? He tore all the posters down, stuffed them into his pockets and ran home as fast as he could.

Tonight's racket taunts her and she wriggles to free herself, nosing his arm. He pins her down too tightly and she lets out a squeal. He's a big man, six-foot-five and over three hundred pounds, and Mama always said he didn't know his own strength. He tries to be gentle with Trixie but sometimes he forgets. He forgets a lot of things.

The sirens are so loud now that he can hardly stand it. His heart thumps and he ignores Trixie, who's barking with abandon. Most of the time, he doesn't mind living alone but the neighborhood isn't as good as the one he lived in with Mama and sometimes he gets scared.

To soothe himself, he thinks about Regina, the pretty Oriental lady who lives upstairs. She's kind to him, always taking a moment to say hello when they meet at the mailbox. He keeps an eye out for her through the peephole in his door to make sure he catches her when she gets her mail.

Once, on his way home from walking Trixie, he saw her standing on the street, smoking a cigarette, all dressed up in a short skirt and high heels. Mama didn't like girls who smoked; she said it make them look trashy. But he'd never seen a girl as beautiful as Regina and decided he could over-look the smoking.

"Your dog, so cute," Regina said, bending at the knees and resting gracefully on her haunches to pet Trixie. Her accent was thick and exotic. She'd told him where she'd come from once, but he could never remember where it was.

"You can walk her with me if you want," Jimmy said.

Regina shook her head and stood up. "I go to work now." She finished the cigarette, dropped it, and extinguished it with a pointed toe. "I wait for ride."

It was getting dark and he didn't like the idea of her being out alone. "You be careful. It's getting late and I don't think it's too safe around here."

She giggled. "I be fine, Jimmy. You big strong guy. I got you to protect me." She raised herself on tiptoes and kissed him on the cheek, which made his stomach flutter. After she was gone he picked up the cigarette stub, marked pink with her lipstick, and put it in his pocket.

Bertie, his friend from the community center, once asked him if Regina was a tranny. Jimmy didn't know what he meant. "A *transsexual*," Bertie said, wriggling his index finger in front of his pants, pretending it was a ding-a-ling. "Everyone knows the tranny hookers hang out on Santa Monica Boulevard near your apartment."

Jimmy didn't know whether to believe Bertie about the hookers, but he knew Regina wasn't one of them. He stopped talking to Bertie after that.

He's calmer now with the vision of Regina fresh in his mind and he scrambles after Trixie. She's stopped barking but her ears stand at attention, her throat vibrating with the effort of a low growl. He presses her ears down against her head so that she can't hear, then realizes that the sirens have stopped.

Flickering red lights show through the slats in the vertical blinds, blinking on-off, on-off. He carries Trixie to the window, moving the hard plastic strips out of the way to look outside. There's not much to see; his only window is perpendicular to the street and all that's visible is the stucco surface of the apartment building next door, illuminated red by the flashing lights.

There's a loud bump just outside Jimmy's front door and Trixie barks in response. His heart jumps and he curls his fingers around her tiny mouth. She shakes her head in violent protest but he keeps a firm hold.

He moves toward the door and stubs his toe against the metal bed frame. Seized with pain, he drops Trixie and she hops away from him, yapping with excitement. He limps after her and scoops her up, quieting her in the process. He continues to the door and puts one eye against the peephole.

The fluorescent lights in the building's small entry way

brighten the stairs leading up to the second floor. There are people moving around, but it's hard to see what they're doing. Someone passes in front of his door, blocking his view. He backs away, nervous that somebody might guess that he's watching from inside. He waits a few beats then looks out again. Two men carry a long black bag down the stairs, one on each end of it. Jimmy doesn't know what might be in it, but nevertheless, his stomach lurches.

A second later, there's a knock on the door. With all Trixie's barking tonight, he's certain that whoever it is wants to take her away. He has to hide her. He snatches the blanket from the bed and wraps her up, fighting against her indignant squirming. He hurries to the bathroom and closes her inside the cabinet under the sink and turns on the faucet to mask any noises she might make.

He opens his front door and finds Mrs. Hosharian standing there in her dingy pink bathrobe. Her face is free of the heavy makeup she usually wears and her eyes are puffy. She looks as old and tired as Mama did before she died.

"Trixie is barking," she says. "The police are here and the owner is on his way over. You know I'll get in trouble if he finds out about her."

Jimmy is relieved—no one's after Trixie—yet. He just needs to keep her quiet. But why are the police here? And what was in that bag he saw being carried out?

"Is something wrong, Mrs. H?" he asks.

Mrs. Hosharian raises her hand to mouth and shakes her head sadly. "Regina is dead, Jimmy. Someone killed her last night."

His legs turn rubbery and he leans against the doorframe to steady himself. This must be a joke.

"That's not funny, Mrs. H."

"I'm sorry, I know she was your friend."

The blood rushes to his head, blinding him. He grabs Mrs. Hosharian by the shoulders.

"What happened to her? What did you do to her?"

Startled by his fury, she sobs, "You're hurting me! Let go!"

Her apparent fear jolts him to his senses. He recalls his Mama, slumped over in her favorite chair in the living room.

The television was tuned to a program he knew she didn't like. He ambled over, thinking she lost the remote again and he clicked his tongue. When she was younger, Mama had been smart as a whip, but age had messed with her mind and now she needed reminding sometimes. But when he got closer he saw that the remote was right there where it always was, balanced on the arm of her chair so she could reach it easily.

"Mama?"

She didn't react. Her eyes stared ahead blankly and she sat perfectly still.

"Mama?" he repeated, shaking her gently. He'd gotten in trouble plenty of times for being too rough as a kid, even if the damage he inflicted was accidental. But when she didn't respond, he shoved her a bit harder and she fell forward.

"Mama! No! I didn't mean to hurt you! Wake up!"

Everyone says Jimmy didn't kill his mama—that she had a heart attack and died right there in her chair. He doesn't believe them.

Now he drops his arms to his sides, horrified at what he's done to Mrs. Hosharian. "I didn't mean to do it, Mrs. H., honest I didn't."

She steps away from him, adjusting the collar of her robe. "It's all right, Jimmy," she says. "We're all upset. Just keep Trixie inside your apartment and don't let her bark. And if the police want to talk to you, you be sure to cooperate."

The idea of talking to the police unsettles him. Will they take him to jail? That's how it went on the cop shows he and

Mama used to watch together. He doesn't want to go to jail.

He hears the running water in the bathroom and remembers that he left Trixie under the sink. He frees her from her confines but doesn't turn off the faucet. She's managed to untangle herself from the blanket and as soon as he opens the cabinet she leaps out. She zips around the bathroom, a happy dog enjoying in her newfound freedom. Jimmy laughs until she squats to take a pee, then he swats her. She stares up at him with her big black eyes and continues doing her business.

Jimmy rests his back against the bathroom wall and sits down on the floor. It's a small space and he has to fold his legs under him to fit, but it's safe in here and the sound of the running water pacifies him. He thinks about what Mrs. H said about Regina.

She can't be dead. He'd talked to her just last night, hadn't he?

He can't remember.

Since the night she kissed him out on the street, his habit of looking for her out his peephole has become an all-day affair. He's stopped going out except to walk Trixie and he set up a stool beside the door so he'd be more comfortable while he watched out for her. Last night he'd sat there for hours, as he usually did, waiting for her to come home from work. He never did find out what she actually did for a living, but sometimes she'd come home with men. When he asked her about it she told him they were her cousins. Regina had lots of them.

"You must have a big family," he'd said.

She laughed at that. He liked it when she laughed. "I do, my family very large," she replied.

At some point during last night's watch, Jimmy dozed off. He woke up abruptly, his back stiff from being hunched over on the stool. The digital clock read 3:13 a.m. and he stood up to squint into the peephole, concerned that he'd missed her.

Should he go up to her apartment to check if she was all right?

The thought excited him. He'd only ever seen her outdoors and he wondered what her apartment looked like inside. He decided that as her protector, it was his duty to make sure she was okay. He told Trixie to stay put and he went upstairs to the second floor, hesitating just before he got to her door. He raised his hand to knock but stopped when he heard noises coming from inside. He stepped closer and put his ear against the door. Was that Regina moaning?

She's hurt, he thought. He pummeled the door franticly. "Regina! Are you okay? Open up!"

His fist was poised mid-knock when she finally opened the door. She was wearing a sheet around herself and her hair was undone and messy.

"Jimmy, what you doing here?"

"I—I—I heard noises. I was afraid you were hurt."

A gruff male voice spoke from inside. "Who's that?"

Regina turned away from the door and addressed her companion in a soft voice. Jimmy couldn't hear exactly what she said but one of the words sounded like "retard" and he knew she was talking about him. His face got hot. He hated that word.

Regina faced him, her head down. "Go to bed, Jimmy. I see you in morning."

She shut the door in his face.

Trixie nudges Jimmy's hand, letting him know she's still there. She's added a couple of little poos next to her puddle of pee. He straightens his legs some and lets her climb onto his lap, stroking her absentmindedly.

After Regina closed the door, Jimmy didn't know what to do. He knew for sure now that she had a man in there. Was he another one of her cousins? What was he doing there so late? He knew that sometimes women had boyfriends—Mama always called them her "special friends"—but he didn't like the idea of Regina having one besides him. He was the only special friend she needed.

The moaning and grunts started up again. That was it—Regina had to be in trouble. He rapped on the door again and as soon as it opened, he barreled in.

The room's only light came from candles burning on a nightstand. There was a heavy scent in the air, so dense that it nearly choked him. Regina was on the bed, pulling up the bed sheet to cover herself. Jimmy didn't see her companion until was almost too late—the man grabbed a table lamp and swung it, nearly making contact with Jimmy's head. Jimmy raised his forearm to block it and tore it out of his hands.

"Get out, Jimmy, I call police!" Regina screamed.

Her naked companion scrambled for his clothes. He held them in a bundle in front of himself and raced out the door without bothering to dress.

"You wait," Regina shouted after him. "You give me money! Stop him, Jimmy!"

Jimmy responded like a robot, chasing after the man. But while he might've been big, he was slow and clumsy—he stumbled on the lamp on the way to the door and by the time he got outside, the man was gone. Jimmy returned to Regina's apartment, ashamed.

"I'm sorry, Regina," he said sadly, "I couldn't get him."

Regina had put on a loose robe made of shiny material patterned with flowers. She walked over to him and placed her hand on his arm. "That's okay, Jimmy, I know you just worried about me."

Warmed by her touch, Jimmy smiled down at her. He'd never seen such a beautiful girl and he thought that maybe she wouldn't mind if he kissed her. But the front of the robe was open and he saw that she was flat-chested, like a boy. At first, he didn't understand but then he saw it: a ding-a-ling hung between her legs, just as Bertie had demonstrated. The blood rushed to his head, blinding him.

Someone is banging on his apartment door again. The running water mutes the sound, but he knows they've finally come for Trixie.

"Open up, Mr. Price!"

Jimmy climbs into the bathtub holding the dog against himself. He sinks into the cold porcelain. Why won't they just leave them alone?

"I won't let them take you," he sobs into Trixie's fur, rocking back and forth.

Their knocking continues and Jimmy hugs Trixie closer until she squeals. He doesn't seem to hear it. He just keeps rocking, squeezing her against him. Back and forth, back and forth. Tighter and tighter. Harder and harder.

"I won't let them take you, I won't let them take you..."

"We're coming in, Mr. Price!"

Trixie nips Jimmy's hand and he pushes her down between his thighs, closing them around her to keep her still. She wriggles and squirms and he presses them together until she submits. Finally, her body goes limp.

He's startled by the clatter as the police bust his apartment door open. His legs part and Trixie jumps to life, out of the tub and out of the bathroom.

"Trixie!"

All at once, two police officers appear at the bathroom door. "Get out of the bathtub with your hands up, Mr. Price," one of them says. "A neighbor saw you leaving Regina Mookjai's apartment a couple of hours ago and we need to ask you some questions."

* * *

Jimmy's room at the Atascadero State Hospital is not as large as his apartment had been, but that doesn't bother him. It reminds him of his room at Mama's house.

A nurse has just administered his medication. She was the pretty nurse, the one he liked best. Calm now, he sits on his bed with his back against the wall, rocking back and forth. He's holding Trixie, the stuffed dog Mrs. Hosharian had given him, against his chest.

"I won't let them take you," he whispers.

BLOOD EYES
Trey R. Barker

I wasn't asleep, but it was late in the day. So when she came in, a fragile body built on fried food curves, and slammed the door? Woke me right the fuck up. I stumbled up from my desk, tried to straighten my clothes.

"Barefield's best detective." She said it with disappointment.

"Barefield's *only* detective."

"Even better. John Blood?"

"That's what the door tells me. What can I do for you?"

She glanced at my office but there wasn't much to see. Couple of books, a few CDs, old newspapers getting older by the minute. No pix of me with famous people or nabbing the bad guy or whatever real detectives hung on their walls.

She licked her lips, a piece of paper wadded up in her right hand. "Can you find my son?"

She said so starkly, almost pleading. "Ma'am, I can damn sure try. How long has he been missing?"

"Couple of days."

"Name? Age?"

"I call him Yo-Yo. He's twenty-seven."

I'd expected someone younger. "Uh...did he maybe take off with a girlfriend?"

She took a deep breath. "No. He's got some...other... problems."

"Drugs."

"Not a user. More of a...distributer."

"Dealing."

"Just weed."

"Uh-huh. Did he—sorry—does he owe his contacts money?"

A tear slipped from her already-swollen eyes and the anger drained from her face, replaced by melancholy. This job handed me sadness constantly, mostly from spouses who'd been certain of fidelity, but what I saw here was worse. What rocked across her face, through her soul, was a hurt endlessly deep and torturous.

"I think a cop is looking for him."

"Arrested?"

"No, but they have a history."

"Him and the cop?"

Through my window, she looked into the Barefield afternoon haze. "He killed a girl. The cop, I mean. Arrested her and she got beat to death in the jail. Jenny." She wiped a tear away. "Jenny was Yo-Yo's friend. Mine, too. We've known her...knew her...for years. I miss her."

Silence slipped into my office like clouds into a funeral, regardless of the sunshine.

"I just need to know he's safe. Good or bad. As long as I know my baby's safe."

By seven a.m., the next day, the sun was already scorching.

As I headed toward the address she'd given me, I called Jesse. He answered immediately. "The fuck do you want?"

"I sent you some info last night."

"I got it."

"Yeah? 'Cause I never heard from you."

"No, Blood, I had a date."

Jesse was a computer genius but women were not on his list of accomplishments. "So now you're date's over and—"

"You don't know, I could be getting blown right now."

"Okay...well, whatever. What'd you find on Yo-Yo?"

He sighed, which let me know fantasy versus reality. "Some social media. Not a whole lot on the guy. Couple of arrests for possession, though."

"Address?"

He read off a place in Hurricane, a small town about fifty miles from Barefield.

"But I found Jenny. Arrested four months ago. Cannabis. Popped in Balmorhea. Got attacked by an inmate in the Reeves County Jail. Slipped in some water or pushed or whatever, smashed her head against a toilet."

"Who was the arresting officer?"

"Nada. Sealed file."

Getting a file sealed took some doing. Not impossible, but tough. "Sealed because of the wrongful death lawsuit, I'd guess?"

"Sealed *before* she was arrested." He smacked his lips, which he always did when he had good information. Like it was the most delicious thing he'd eaten in months. "Rumors swirling all over Hurricane, too. Going big on dealers. Hired some hotshot undercover drug guy."

"Name?"

"Sealed."

Again, odd but not uncommon. Undercover cops had to protect themselves.

"So I'm wondering," Jesse said. "If Yo-Yo is dealing and Cantrell's hired this guy?"

I saw it, too. The Hurricane chief was named Cantrell and he had forty stripes in a Hurricane uniform, thirty as chief. I didn't know him but had heard he was a decent guy. Wanted a quiet town and a quiet career. I couldn't see him hiring a drug *wunderkind* on his own, but if Hurricane was cracking down, Yo-Yo had probably gotten rolled up.

"They haven't started hooking people up yet."

That surprised me. "Isn't that interesting."

"It's coming quick, though."

Hurricane was my starting point. Yo-Yo might not be there but chances were good the neighbors would have a line on him.

Especially if they'd bought his smoke.

I'd say it the lesser side of town, except Hurricane—population 987—didn't really have a lesser side of town.

It was all lesser.

I drove, mildly surprised at how empty the streets were. I turned here, turned there, made my way toward the address Jesse gave me. But when I turned a corner, the last one, I nearly shit myself.

Cops were everywhere.

Hurricane only had four or five part-time officers. Yet as I parked a half-block from the crime scene tape, I could have swum in the sea of cops I saw. A two-block stretch was locked down tight with cops everywhere and squad cars at each end.

This was the hooking up. This was a mass arrest and it had only started a while before. I saw ten or twelve people, hands zip-tied, surprised and angry. They sat on the curb, guarded by fifteen or twenty cops, none of whom looked like an undercover drug officer. Everyone I saw had crew cuts, creased uniform pants, dark shirts with badges and name badges, duty belts crammed with gear.

At either end of the two blocks, people stood anxiously behind the crime scene tape. Some cried, some pounded the air, others looked numb. Beyond them, a few cars—high mileage, low vintage, primer gray the paint scheme—were haphazardly pulled into the grass and on the sidewalks. One, a shit brown mid-'80s Camaro, had just turned around and was leaving.

A Hurricane officer stopped me. "No access, need to know only. Official police operation."

I nodded deferentially. "I probably need to know...I live here."

His eyed me hard. "Name?"

"Uh...Johnny. Johnny Bongiovi." I pointed vaguely to a house. "I just started renting a few days ago." I leaned in close. "Is this it? The big arrest?"

"How'd you know about that?"

"I called. Gave some information." I put a finger in front of my lips. "Shhhhh."

"You called Officer Steiger?"

Bingo. Score one for the detective.

"I did. Didn't think the arrest would be this big."

He got all chest-puffy and official. "Tip of the iceberg. We're cleaning house and we're not the only ones. All of west Texas going to be clean soon enough."

"Better have enough handcuffs."

He pulled a couple of zip-ties from his pocket. "This what modern policing uses, sir. The sworn officers and us reserve officers."

"Ah. Didn't know that." I took one and played with it idly while we both watched the arrests.

Eventually, he gave me a stern look. "Get on inside, Mr. Bongiovi, and don't open your door for anyone but the police."

"Yes, sir," I said, palming the zip-tie and hoping he didn't remember it.

"The fuck're you?"

This tough broad didn't bother with screaming or running. She smashed the beer bottle she'd been drinking from and jacked it straight at my face.

I stepped back. "That was...totally hot. Wanna go out?"

Stony, pissed-off silence.

"Sorry, inappropriate. I'm not the cops."

"'Cause a cop who'd illegally enter my house would tell me he's a cop."

"I apologize. Let me start over. I'm not here to rape or plunder or whatever."

An amused smirk rolled across her thin face and it was somehow familiar. "Think you could get that done? That whole rape and plunder thing?"

Tough and prepared. I could dig this chick. I lowered my hands, trying to make her see I wasn't a threat. "Mrs. Dennis hired me to find Yo-Yo."

"Linda?" The woman looked away and, again, she looked familiar. Crack detective that I am, I had no idea why.

I nodded toward the street. "What's going on around here?"

"You blind?" The bottle still under my chin, she craned her head toward her front window. The curtains, dirty but intact, were wide open. "They're arresting everybody."

"All the dealers, I hear. Didn't realize there were that many."

"Hurricane ain't no South Dallas, but we got peeps doing their dirt." She shook her head. "Dammit. They're taking *everybody*."

"Hurricane PD cleaning up, huh?"

She snorted. "How some old men gonna clean? They tell people to cut their lawns and cross the kids after school. Heavy lifting is the county boys. Or maybe DPS...who you don't see."

"Don't see Yo-Yo, either."

"'Cause Yo-Yo's not missing."

Crack detective that I am, I knew that was a clue.

"He split."

In the street, real and reserve cops brought more and more arrestees out of the houses and sat them on the curb.

Was there anyone left on these two blocks?

She lowered the bottle. "Cantrell hired himself a drug Messiah. Goes to all the small towns and smacks the drug-gies."

"Steiger."

She looked surprised. "Yeah." She pulled a picture from the stack of chaos on her coffee table. The man in the picture definitely looked undercover; ears and lips covered in ear rings and studs, arms covered in tattoos. His clothes screamed, "Don't look at me but if you do, see how cool I am?" Standard bullshit drug cop uniform: badass and hip-ster all in one.

The heat was already up and her air conditioner, an evap like everyone else on the downside of middle class, worked feverishly but it wasn't kicking out much cool. She stared out the window, humming a Rolling Stones song. "Yo-Yo knows him. They go back."

"Back to Jenny?"

"Linda tell you that?"

Her eyes flashed, angry and scared all rolled into a deep green and suddenly I knew the face. "You're Linda's sister. Or cousin or something."

"Yo-Yo is my nephew."

"You should have told me that."

Her anger was fierce and instant. "Fuck you. You come storming into my house? Maybe you ain't the police but maybe you are. Maybe you work for Steiger, trying to put Yo-Yo away."

"I didn't storm into your house." I'd actually just walked in the front door. "And I'm just trying to help."

"Same fucking thing Steiger said. He sat right there." She pointed to where I had planted my ass. "Wanted to get Yo-Yo back on the straight. Productive member of society and all that bullshit that all the cops always say. He didn't care about that. All he wanted was Yo-Yo's customers."

Before I could say anything, Cantrell pounded on the door, shaking the entire house. "Bongiovi? We know you're in there."

She looked at me. "Bongiovi? Seriously?"

It wasn't my greatest made up name. "First name I thought of when I saw the Camaro."

Cantrell and his reserve boys escalated.

From yelling to pounding, from pounding to kicking. The door shook, the frame threatened to snap. Their voices banged through the open windows.

The woman, fear on her face like heat on a summer day, pointed me toward the back door. "Find Yo-Yo, he can tell you. Steiger as dirty as the day is hot."

"What?"

"Go, dammit."

"Shari, open this fucking door. Now."

Someone kicked the door and through the window, I saw Cantrell and at least four reserve officers. Getting cranked up, handcuffs and OC spray out, adrenaline dumping into their systems.

Her voice was a terrified whisper. "He's been talking about Lakeview."

"Where?"

The glass in the door, old and brittle, cracked.

Her face went white, all the Texas tan gone. "The trailer park. South past Industrial Drive. Five or six miles outta town. Yo-Yo probably hiding with a girlfriend."

I was halfway through the kitchen when the front door crashed. Four or five men piled in immediately, hammered Shari to the ground, pretzeled her arms up behind her. She was zip-tied and crying before I'd even gotten out the door.

"Where is he?" Cantrell spoke slowly, redneck and Texas thick.

"There's no one here."

She said it as I dashed down the back steps and slipped into the crevice between the house and the bushes.

Lakeview Estates.

What the fuck ever.

It had about twenty weed-strewn slots for trailers, half those filled and maybe half of that half lived in. Two trailers were burned out shells, black fingers wrapped around stained skins. Another had a collapsed roof and weeds growing from the inside. Most of the occupied trailers were rusted, some with windows of plastic sheeting or cardboard. There were a couple of decent trailers, but they were definitely in the minority.

No lake either so whoever named the place had a twisted sense of humor.

Parking, I wondered exactly where I was going to start. I had no interest in randomly knocking on doors until I found Yo-Yo or a girlfriend but I had no other information.

I started walking and as I came around a corner, I saw an old pit bull. The hair around his muzzle and eyes was gray, and he moved stiffly and with great effort. More than old, though, he was worn out. Scarred with clumps of fur gone down to the skin. He was chained and the chain disappeared around the corner to the front of the trailer. Near him was a bowl half filled with dirty water. There was shade but only because the sun was behind the trailer. As the day slipped into the heat of the afternoon, that shade would disappear and there was nothing else; no doghouse or awning, not even a bush.

It pissed me off.

He barked, a weak and tattered thing, but his beautiful brown eyes held no malice.

"You okay, buddy?" I squatted so that he could get a

smell of me. His back end, long since clipped of a tail, wagged lethargically and after a few minutes, he strained forward at the chain. His nose twitched and eventually he licked the top of my hand.

"See? I'm not as bad as they say."

His eyes brightened at the sound of my voice and he let me scratch behind his ears. Then he coughed and wandered back to the shade. I realized then that he was probably not long for this world.

A thick, hard hand grabbed the back of my neck. Pain shot through my head and spine. "About time, Steiger. Now we'll deal."

He spun me and Yo-Yo and I stared at each other.

"You ain't Steiger. Who the fuck are you? Another cop?"

"Whoa...hang on. Fists down. Your mother hired me. Your aunt said you might have a girlfriend here."

He laughed and the sound chilled me. "Yeah, here for a little pussy. Just not between no legs." He squeezed hard. "Get the fuck out. I talked to Shari and I called my mom. They know I'm alive so they don't need you anymore."

His hand slipped around to the front of my throat and he backed me up, squeezing my airway just enough to make me nervous.

"Come on now, I'm not a threat."

He moved me around the corner of the trailer and toward the street and from the corner of my eye, I saw a shit-brown stain. At first I thought I was seeing stars from lack of oxygen.

But stars didn't look like a shit brown Camaro.

I pushed back against Yo-Yo and we stopped. "Son of a bitch. Steiger lives here. That's what your aunt meant by Lakeview."

He had a predator's face. "Time to take care of some business."

"No, not business...Jenny."

His hand was still on my throat. "The fuck did you say?"

I kneed his balls. When he doubled over, I bashed his nose with a downward right cross. Blood exploded as he hit the ground.

I stepped back but not far enough. He came up quick and hard. His first punch went mostly wide but still caught enough of my temple to rock me. I staggered but got my hands up just before he started swinging. "What the hell? Stop it."

Connecting on every third punch or so, he drove me back. Pain flared, hotter by the second. My stomach lurched, nerves and fear and pain, and as my back went up against the trailer, I threw up.

"You asshole." He held his next punch and stared at my breakfast down his front.

I heaved again. "Your fault." I spat, wiped my mouth with my hand, and spat again. "You don't hit me, I don't throw up."

We stood toe to toe for the rest of forever. The anger in his eyes was as depthless as the hurt and loneliness I'd seen in the dog's eyes and in that silence, broken only by the whistle through his broken nose, I heard the Stones' song again. Not the entire song, just the part Shari wanted me to remember.

Just as every cop is a criminal...

"He wanted your customers. That's what Shari said."

"Getting the picture now, PI?"

"You're telling me he's not a cop?"

"Was once. Took a nickel behind a distribution charge. Came out a heavy for Texas Syndicate.

I shook my head. "Can't get hired if you're a felon."

"Hurricane, Tulia, Ransom Canyon, Balmorhea, all those little towns hired him."

"I'm telling you, they can't hire a convict."

"You got no imagination, do you? His name ain't on any felony conviction."

I was confused.

"Felony conviction got overturned by local court on some bullshit technicality. The DA didn't fight it because his office got a pile of money donated. *Boom*, charges never got refiled. Record's already been expunged."

"Bullshit."

"Money can do anything it wants. Shove it up the ass of a small county and Steiger gets cleaned up. Hires to little towns that can't afford specialty poh-leece, cleans up all the drugs. No records to check because Steiger gets everything sealed up nice and tight. Undercover work."

"Balmorhea? That's where he arrested Jenny."

Yo-Yo spat. "Where he murdered Jenny."

I shook my head. "No, you're looking to hang him because of Jenny. Jenny got arrested, bitches in the jail did what they did. That is not Steiger's fault, not the judge's fault, not anyone's fault except those women. There is no grand conspiracy."

He stepped up, anger in his eyes like hellfire and damnation. "Mention her one more time and I'll kill you."

I softened my voice. I could hear the hurt in his voice, see it in his eyes. "Yo-Yo, there's nothing here except a drug cop and you're on the shitty end of it this time. That's all."

"Then who's paying for the lawyers?"

"What lawyers?" With just a few words, he'd made me feel stupid.

"The ones that show up and post bail for all of Steiger arrests? Those lawyers that pay whatever fine the town demands before everyone walks away?"

The trailer door opened suddenly and Steiger stormed out, his face a potent mix of surprise and anger. "The hell is this?"

He made a made a dash for the car and clambered in, locking the doors just as Yo-Yo got to him. Yelling, threatening, Yo-Yo banged his fist against the glass.

Steiger cranked the engine, gunned it, and slammed the

thing in reverse, twisting the front end around toward Yo-Yo.

Yo-Yo tried to jump out of the way but the car caught the toes of his right foot. Steiger threw the car into drive and let it slash forward to catch Yo-Yo's entire right foot. Even over the engine screech, I heard bones snapping.

Yo-Yo howled as the car fishtailed and knocked him off his feet. Then it straightened out and headed for us. I shoved Yo-Yo toward the trailer's steps and ran the opposite direction.

Between me and the burned trailer was a fire hydrant—

Laugh at the irony later...

—and I tried to keep myself visually between it and Steiger.

Yo-Yo was near the trailer, his foot bloody, his face a rictus of pain, the dog looking scared but as though he wanted to help. I ran hard, my legs and lungs already on fire. I could feel the heat from the car, smoking the air behind me, calling and taunting.

I juked at the last second and the Camaro slammed into the hydrant. I expected a gush of water, an explosion of twisting metal and pipes, of the undercarriage being ripped to shreds.

I got a muffled thud, some smoke and dust, and squat else.

The car had gotten hung up on the hydrant and was slowly tipping onto its side. Steiger was furiously trying to get free of the seatbelt before the car finally came to rest on its top with a desolate crunch.

Yo-Yo and I went to the car and Steiger was suspended by the seatbelt, staring at us upside down. "Do it."

"Do what?" I asked.

"Just do it." Steiger closed his eyes.

"You want me to kill you? I gots no problem with that." Yo-Yo said

I lost control of Yo-Yo at that point. He dove into the car and started punching Steiger, battering the man's face, knocking out teeth, reveling in the blood.

I let him get a minute or so in, for Jenny, before I pulled him away. He whirled on me, fists bloody and ready. "Going to beat me, too?"

"If I have to."

"And then who? The dog? I bet you could take him. He's old and about ready to die. That's a good plan, Yo-Yo. Go down for drugs *and* murder, 'cause they love murderous drug dealers in Texas. Hell, you'll even go straight to the head of the lethal injection line...Steiger being a cop."

"He's a dirty cop."

I said nothing.

"Dammit." Yo-Yo punched the car two or three times.

"Get outta here," I said. "I'll take care of this."

Yo-Yo stared at me. "You'll kill him?"

"I'm not a killer."

"Everybody's a killer."

I shook my head. "Get out or you'll have to kill us both."

He jammed a finger at Steiger. "You stay the fuck outta my way or I *will* kill you."

"Eat shit. Kill me already."

Yo-Yo stormed off. A few seconds later, I heard a car start and blast into the afternoon, kicking up dust.

Steiger got the seatbelt undone and fell to the roof of the car. When he finally crawled out, I made sure he stayed on the ground, a well-placed boot to his bloody face, pressing him into the dirt.

He grimaced. "You have any idea who you're screwing with?"

I took a guess. "Well, a former cop now fronting for TS. You show up, put people in the jackpot, TS pays to get them out and viola...new guaranteed customers, new guaranteed dealers, a whole new town in TS's back pocket."

He looked surprised. "You ain't as stupid as you look."

I dragged him toward the trailer and he fought until I bashed the open cuts on his face. "A lot of work, doing things this way, but it does give you some measure of legal coverage, doesn't it? Anyone asks, you've got chiefs up and down the line willing to vouch for you but all the records sealed up."

When we got to the trailer, I called the dog over.

He refused, his anger at Steiger hotter than the afternoon. His rear end was tucked down, his body language hunched and scared. "Don't think your dog likes you."

"Fuck him and fuck you."

Keeping watch on Steiger, I went—carefully—to the dog, took him off the chain, and gently undid his collar. When I was done, he scooted to the far end of the trailer, watched us warily. I slapped the collar on Steiger and hooked him to the chain.

"The second you walk away, I'll be gone to Mexico."

From my pocket, I pulled the zip-tie. After jerking Steiger's hands behind his back, I zipped him tight.

"This gonna teach me a lesson? Listen, pissant: you got no play. TS's light days are beyond your worst nightmare. Leave me here? In the sun?"

"Just like you left your dog."

"Who gives a shit? Maybe I die, maybe I keep doing my thing."

I shook my head. "No. I'll call the Attorney General's office, maybe the Texas Rangers."

"TS has my family, you think I give a shit about the Rangers? I been down once, I can do it again. Long as TS has my family, they got my help and you got dick."

"They have your family?"

"Parents and little sister. Snatched them right outta the house in Fort Stockton."

Did they? Or was he yanking my own dog chain? I wanted to be sympathetic but I just wasn't sure I believed him.

With a yell, he charged. I punched him but he came again. Another punch and he hit the ground. "I'm so fucking tired of all of this."

"Then maybe I'll call TS, tell them you've been stealing."

I'd expected fear. I got relief. "I'm asking. Hell, I'm begging."

Surprised and disturbed by his request, I left him zipped and chained, gathered the dog up and took him to my car.

Ten minutes later, we were on the highway, the dog and me, headed to Barefield. I'd made three calls: the Attorney General, the *Barefield Industrial Times* newspaper, and a friend who knew how to get a message to TS. I had no idea who'd show up first.

The dog had his head out the window, flying like dogs do, the grin on his face somehow larger than his face. His butt waggled fiercely. I could almost imagine him screaming "Rock and rooooollllllllll, baaabyyyy."

I drove him around for the better part of forty-five minutes and not once did he come back inside. As we rolled into Barefield, though, he looked at me, age creaking through his now shiny and wet eyes. He settled quietly into the passenger seat. Even sleeping, his face was a grin.

By the time I got home, he was dead, the grin still there.

I sat with him for a while, then took him to my garden to bury him in the shade.

A FEAST FOR HOGS
Jeffery Hess

The bitter taste in Allen Kinsey's mouth convinced him this would be the longest helicopter ride of his life. He didn't want Maria sitting next to him—not now, not ever. She ruined everything.

The morning sun beamed through the windshield and over the pilot's shoulder. He adjusted his aviator sunglasses. Liftoff felt like riding an elevator of a skyscraper, but today it failed to give Kinsey that sense of immortality it usually did.

Bile behind the bitterness roiled into his throat. He tugged to loosen his tie an inch or so and unbuttoned the white shirt he wore beneath a tan cardigan his wife Christine had knitted him. He'd had every right to leave Maria behind, but only one reason not to. He'd promised to take her up the next time he had occasion to fly and he always kept his word, unlike some people, namely this cheating bitch sitting next to him in the back of his helicopter.

She called the helicopter rides *viajes magia* and anytime an opportunity for "magic travel" presented itself, she lit up, bounced on her toes, and stretched her arms overhead as she clapped her hands. The way she wiggled her hips as she did that always made it hard to concentrate. And he always loved that she wasn't afraid of heights like his wife.

Maria stared out the window, looking down at the ground with her forehead on the glass and a smile he recognized even from behind. It was impossible to keep her fully in her seat and he never wanted to seem like a father figure to her, so she never wore a seatbelt. In his mind, no better reason existed to ignore safety procedures.

The love he felt for her overtook his hate as the hem of her green dress rode high, revealing the tanned thighs that had clamped his torso and his head, on various occasions. Kinsey adjusted his sunglasses over his eyes because he and Maria were through. She just didn't know it yet.

Maria's excitement pissed him off today because of her oblivion to his pain. It made his pulse throb into his throat. She didn't love him, *really* love him, or else she hadn't been wholly satisfied by him. Either way meant the end of their relationship, the past year a waste.

He bit his tongue to keep the peace because he couldn't resist her anytime she got angry. The passion in her expression always proved too much to bear without caving. No. He just had to suck it up long enough to fly her around town and then back to her car. After that, it was *Adios, perra*— good-bye, bitch—and he'd never think of her again.

As her green dress rode up higher, he touched his shirt pocket. A folded piece of paper crinkled against his fingers. The sensation comforted him. He needed some sort of reminder to keep him strong, so earlier that day, he'd written a single word on the piece of paper that anytime he thought he might cave in to his desires, he could pull out the piece of paper and be reminded of why he decided to cut ties with her after this flight, this *viejes magia.*

He hadn't broken his vows in eighteen years of marriage, until Maria. Her beauty was eye catching, but he'd been around lots of beautiful women in his life. Maria had a way of looking at him that invigorated him physically and emotionally. Drawn to and aroused more strongly than by anyone else, ever, but it was more than that. She made work and home and the daily problems fall to the background. When he was with her, no one else existed except the two of them.

They had a year of passionate afternoons a couple times a week and an evening every month or so in her apartment, but it was on the first overnight business trip he'd snuck her on that he realized just how deeply he was in love with her.

After all this time, the last thing he wanted was a confrontation, or drama. He was just fulfilling a promise until the immanent termination of their relationship, where he'd turn his back on her—cut her out of his life completely. She always impressed him as stubborn enough to try getting through his secretaries, but if she did, she'd have to deal with the two thousand pounds of security guards he called assistant managers.

The headphones almost blocked out the high-hertz hum of the engine and thwacking of the blade rotating overhead, a noise perceptible most vividly in his ribs. Through the windshield and windows along the side door, Tampa unfolded beneath them. It was impossible to focus on any single thing for long. They flew from Davis Island over the downtown skyline, across Dale Mabry Highway, and passed right over the Buccaneers' stadium, which looked small from up there, but still bigger than everything else except the mall across the street. He recognized other buildings and neighborhoods, knew who owned which stretches of land beneath the green treetops, and could identify every road running through the muck of his state like tributaries to the Hillsborough River.

The eastward ride was bumpy in unpredictable patterns. Some bumps jostled them as if he were driving his Mercedes in a cypress swamp. Others dropped his stomach as if gravity switched on and off. There were moments where Maria bounced around, bumped her knee or her head and cursed in Spanish. After a few moments he looked over at her sitting sideways in her seat, breathing shallow as if whispering a song. Her head pressed to the window in the center of the door.

"My apologies for the bumps," the pilot said over his microphone. "The air should smooth out when we get further east."

Maria's color faded from tan to pale to green. Kinsey hated her. Could barely stand to look at her. He raised his voice into the microphone built into his headset, "My petite-flower is wilting back here," he said. "Maybe we should do this some other time." He sat back as a surge of resentment flooded his torso.

"It's your call, Mr. Kinsey," the pilot said. "But I can't guarantee when the air currents will be any better in the next few weeks."

That was unacceptable to Kinsey's time line for this pending project. "I need to see Loughton Groves before then," Kinsey said to Maria. "My decision is due in three days."

"This may be your best bet," the pilot said.

Kinsey looked to Maria. He wanted to spite her, but she looked too green and pathetic. Before he could tell the pilot to turn around, Maria smiled until her green cheeks dimpled and she nodded. Their hands squeezed each other's.

"How long that take?" she asked, her head hung low, her eyes upward and expectant.

The pilot looked at his watch, "I can have us over there in twenty minutes if you don't mind a few more bumps."

Kinsey looked to Maria again. He wanted to cradle her in his arms.

"I'll be fine," she said.

Kinsey nodded and gave the pilot a thumbs-up. "Do it, but find smoother air, will you?" He patted Maria's knee. "Hold on, my flower. This will be quick." If she heard him, she didn't acknowledge.

The air got even choppier for a few silent moments. The helicopter bounced around and Kinsey tightened his seatbelt across his lap to prevent gaps that would jar him in this turbulence. He looked at Maria. Sweat visible on her forehead, gone was the Maria-ness that made her beautiful.

Blood surged to his temples and heat radiated across his brow and over his ears as he thought about his security chief, a man he called Platinum, leaving Maria's apartment one anguished morning. His team had assembled audiotape recordings of his phone conversations with Maria; photos of them in the bed. Evidence that would hold up in any court-room. He didn't want to think about the two of them in bed, sweaty, and her sighing from the ecstasy provided by another man.

The land they were going to see was deep into the unin-corporated county, completely undeveloped. It had the po-tential of being his biggest residential development project to date and that kind of money might settle his mind.

As they approached the property, vast areas of green and brown land without an inch of concrete opened up before him. Unspoiled land. The land as he imagined it was in the time of his childhood, thirty years ago when he was a third-grader shooting rabbits in the woods with the .22 rifle his father had given him. As pristine as it had been in the days of the Seminoles and the dinosaurs before them. The air smoothed out. The ride was calm. The pilot let out a loud sigh.

Kinsey adjusted his sunglasses. The headphones blocked out everything except the sound of his thumping heartbeat. They hovered over the parcel of land he was planning to buy. Land Kinsey knew well. It looked different from the air, but the expanse of cypress knees, palmettos, and scrub pines was where he'd spent weekends and hours after school play-ing Cowboys and Indians or Army.

This was the terrain of feral hogs and a pack of them ran through the underbrush off to the helicopter's left. Kinsey stared as their movement reminded of the time he crossed paths with them at nine years old out in the cabbage palms and Cyprus knees between his house and State Road 60. He was a grown man of forty now, but that terrifying day out hunting rabbits plays on loop behind his eyes.

He and Bobby Little had their .22s and pillowcases full of bologna sandwiches and half-pint orange juice cartons when they stumbled upon a lone piglet digging its nose into the ground. Young Kinsey leveled his .22 at the piglet's shoulder, but did not take the shot. Instead, the piglet looked up, squealed, and ran into the brush. Moments later, a chorus of rustling and snorting caused him and Bobby Little to drop their pillowcases as they scrambled to run from a pack of the wild, snorting beasts. The thick-skulled hog that chased him was twice as wide, three hundred pounds if it was an ounce. Its brown hide slicked black with mud or blood, especially around its mouth that had tusks as long as Kinsey's arm and sharp as razor blades.

Any direction he went, a pig was hot on his heels. It was a pack of them. His legs pumped like pistons and he grunted with each step. The fear of them feasting on his flesh, stripping his bones clean with their tusks and teeth, propelled him faster than he'd ever run before, or since.

Years later, he'd study zoology and even ethology at the University of Florida, where he'd learned about a hog's habits and behaviors, all of which made him hate them even more.

They always travel in groups of two to thirty or more, with some groups reaching a hundred, at least temporarily. As big and aggressive as the boars are, a sow protecting her piglets is even more dangerous. He didn't know it as a nine-year-old, but he must've stumbled upon a piglet nest.

Aggressive enough to charge with their tusks. All of them screeching their high-pitched alarm, that was like ice picks in his ears.

Little Allen Kinsey was the first kid in Brandon to grow up wearing sunglasses. His parents weren't strict about much, but they insisted he not spend time outdoors without his sunglasses. They were child-sized versions of the kind they never left the house without. He grew to believe in their power. During the chase, his glasses fogged up, which made being chased in the woods all the more dangerous.

He didn't know then that the hogs were sure footed and rapid runners up to thirty miles per hour and able to jump three-foot high obstacles. If he did, he would've tried to shimmy up a tree.

During the chase, little Allen Kinsey tripped over a cypress knee and lost his sunglasses as he crashed to the ground. He got whipped ten times that evening when he showed up without them.

He hated the hogs so much, he'd never eat pork, but they are what ultimately got him out of the woods and into town toward pavement, where everything was smooth and the only things to occupy his energies had wheels. Skateboards, bikes, motorcycles, cars. There was a time he raced all of them, and he rarely lost.

Now he was in a helicopter and he seethed inside. Still, he couldn't help admiring the green space he would convert from dangerous regions into subdivisions, golf courses, and manicured parks so his grandchildren could thrive in the safe environment he never had. He wanted to know children would be able to run and play without fear of being gored by tusks or trampled or otherwise ripped to shreds.

Maria glanced up and swallowed hard, seemingly grateful for the smoother air. She picked at a chipped fingernail long enough to glance out the window. She smoothed her finger over the jagged paint on her nail as if embarrassed by the imperfection.

This ride, this relationship, would be over soon enough, but what he feared most was having too much to drink at a business dinner some night and showing up at her door, drunk and love struck. Or going crazy if he saw her in town one day. He was certain he wouldn't bear the pain with any semblance of dignity. This thought, this fear, caused sweat to pour down his neck.

Kinsey leaned over. He felt the seatbelt cut into his lap, but struggled against it. He ran his hand long the side of her neck and under the fall of her dark hair. That always put her in the mood. He loved her most when she was in the mood. He could barely call what he did with his wife as intercourse. If he had to, he'd describe that as her tolerating his carnal desires adequately. But he and Maria weren't just on the same page, they could've actually written an instruction book for passionate sex. He'd been with women who faked the enthusiasm, but he'd never met a woman who so consistently displayed the exhaustion or appreciation as Maria. She smiled at him now, tender and pleased. He took a moment to inhale the coconut fragrance there and tightened his grip as he used his other hand to slide open the door.

Wind rushed into the cabin and blew Maria's long, dark hair into his face.

The pilot contorted in his seat and hollered, "What the hell? Close that door!"

His sunglasses were identical to Kinsey's. Kinsey held the door open with one hand and squinted against the wind blowing into his face. The altitude seemed higher suddenly and wind made him conscious of the helicopter's speed. So high. So fast. He fought to hold the door open with one hand. With his other hand, he grabbed Maria's head and pushed it into the opening. She struggled against him, but he bore down with his left hand and summoned the strength necessary to push her head, neck, and shoulders through the opening.

His skin chilled from the cool December air, made cooler by the altitude. He pushed harder on her head. Yelled, "You broke my heart, you fucking whore." The rotor wash and the headphones kept the sound of his voice from reaching his own ears, but he felt the words strain his throat. He had no way to know if she heard him. "Fuck!" he yelled.

She'd come off her seat a little. Her hair whipped at him now and strands caught in Kinsey's mouth. The idea of closing her head in the door surged through him like whiskey.

"Shut that door immediately!" the pilot yelled. The helicopter ascended as he fidgeted his attention between Kinsey and the air on the other side of the windshield.

The guy had worked for Kinsey for more than ten years, but Kinsey had no confidence the pilot would keep his mouth shut. Kinsey's arms struggled to hold Maria and the door, but anger raged through him instead of muscle fatigue. He looked away from the pilot and at Maria's flailing arms as they slapped at the bulkhead in an attempt to gain purchase and push herself back into the cabin. Kinsey grunted from the frustration. He changed his grip from her neck to her shoulder and pulled Maria back in. Fastened the door closed. His ears popped with the pressure of altitude.

Maria yelled in Spanish. Screamed, at Kinsey. A solitary string of words that she rattled off like automatic gunfire.

Kinsey leaned toward the pilot. Yanked the seatback. "Don't you ever question me again. You understand? I thought she was going to vomit." Kinsey sat all the way back into his own seat. "I really did," he said more to the pilot than to Maria. After a few minutes, he tapped her knee. "We're almost there," he said.

Maria didn't speak for the rest of the flight. Kinsey knew it was killing her to keep her mouth shut. That wasn't her style. She was vocal, mouthy. Unable to hold her tongue or keep her temper from flaring. Hers was a head full of opinions. Enthusiasm. Kinsey usually loved when she argued with him. He kind of wished she would now. But it was too late for arguments. Reconciliation. Makeup sex.

The helicopter pitched forward. "Mr. K., I'll have us down in a minute."

Kinsey turned his attention to the window and marveled

at the stretches of land beneath them. Pins on a map were never as impressive as seeing his land from the highest possible vantage point.

They descended into a clearing of pines and palmetto scrub near a pond on the undeveloped Loughton family property that Kinsey was interested in buying. This parcel was twenty thousand acres tucked away in the northeastern part of Hillsborough County, a couple miles from the nearest paved road. The pond beside their landing spot was black and weeded over with tall grasses and cattails.

On the ground, Maria opened the door beside her even faster than Kinsey had done mid-flight. She took no time or caution in jumping to the ground, where she landed with her high heels stabbing into the sandy earth like tent stakes. With the door open, the cool December air filled the cabin. After a hint of struggle, Maria stepped her muddy shoes free and stormed off toward the edge of the palmetto scrub.

Kinsey sat back—felt the overhead rotor blade turning to a gradual stop. There was no way to know if the pilot bought the airsickness excuse.

"Sorry, Mr. K.," the pilot said. "I thought…"

"You thought what?"

"I didn't realize you were trying to help her. I couldn't tell from up here."

Kinsey watched Maria. It took her many steps with those high heels to traverse the clearing. She halted at the edge of the scrub—palmetto and pines sprawled out in every direction, all the way to the horizon. She stood cast in full sunlight. Pine needles provided little shade. She was yelling. Probably in Spanish though Kinsey couldn't tell.

"Look at her," Kinsey said. "She's more out of place than a pearl in an outhouse."

"She is striking, sir."

"What's striking is the potential of this fucking land."

The pilot didn't respond.

"You don't think it has potential?"

The pilot turned sideways to face Kinsey. Their matching sunglasses staring into each other's. "I understand development and progress and all, but it's still a shame that stretches of nature like this are disappearing."

Kinsey pointed out at the scrub land around them. "Progress makes the wetlands go away. DDT makes the mosquitoes go away. Air conditioning makes the heat go away. But I make homes for the complainers to live in. Guys like us are the last generation that really remembers nature. You know what I mean, son?"

"I know. It's just a shame, is all."

"Do you know who we're building these communities for?"

The pilot looked out at the land before him. "People with money?"

"We're building houses for people looking for a better life. And where better than the Sunshine State to start that better life? What's not to like? It's year-round golfing with beaches nearby. Like being on vacation every day for the rest of your life. People have been blazing a trail down I-95 for the past fifty years. Well guess what? Miami is crowded. And expensive, to boot. And don't get me started on what the boatlift did to the area. No, sir. What these good people want is a nice, clean place that's affordable. A place for working stiffs to raise their families. No projects. No traffic. No snow. They'll be so happy to be away from the morass of the great North, because these aren't just houses, they're trophies to these people. We're making trophies here, son. This parcel happens to be for much bigger trophies, granted, but it's all the same. And we're presenting them to the fine people flocking to our fair peninsula. And in the meantime, just remember that everything we do for them here will feed your family. Your family likes to eat, don't they?"

"More than you can imagine."

"So keep that in mind the next time you question bullshit details like the size and shape of some fucking swamp land. Or what your boss is doing in his own fucking helicopter."

"Point taken, sir."

"Sometimes you have to chop off toes to save the foot, and then chop off the foot to save the leg." Kinsey sat back. It was the first time he'd ever said that aloud. He'd have to trust people to get where he's going which was as much a leap of faith as flying in a contraption like this. He laughed as he scratched his head where the wind had blown his hair out of place.

The pilot checked his watch. "The weather is only going to get rougher the longer we stay here, Mr. Kinsey."

"Yes." Kinsey slapped the back of the pilot's seat. "Right. Okay then. Take off."

"We'll have to wait for your lady friend."

"No we won't."

Kinsey couldn't see the pilot's eyes behind his sunglasses, but the man shook his head and asked, "Sir?"

"I want you to get this bird in the air now."

He shook his head faster. "You can't just leave her out here? It's twelve miles to the nearest road."

"That's her problem."

"There're no smooth paths, sir. Not to mention wild boar and snakes."

To hell with her, Kinsey thought. But he wasn't prepared for Maria to sprint the distance back to the helicopter once the rotor blade got spinning again. She banged on the door, but Kinsey held the handle.

"Don't be a child, Allan," Maria yelled as she tugged on the door.

Kinsey held firm and shook his head.

Maria pounded on the door, ducking as the propeller

reached maximum speed above her head. She pounded and seemed to be pleading or even begging. Kinsey didn't know if she begged for forgiveness or simply not to be left out there.

Maria's strong fists thudded like distant gun fire, but the anguish on her face was all too close. Tears puddled in her eyes. Kinsey read that as panic more than regret for what she had done and that meant little to him. She continued to pound and cry harder.

Kinsey touched the piece of paper in his shirt pocket and then pulled it out. With one hand on the door handle he used the other to hold the paper to the window.

Maria stopped pounding on the glass to read the single word, Loyalty. She looked into his eyes then.

"Up," Kinsey shouted into his microphone.

"Sir, are you sure you want to do this?"

Kinsey put the piece of paper back in his pocket, leaned forward, and grabbed the pilot by the throat, pulling him across his seat until his torso and head were in the backseat area. He heard gurgling in his headphones. Kinsey said, "If you question me again, I will have your eyes poked out and the only thing you'll ever fly again is a fucking kite you won't even be able to see. Is that perfectly clear?"

"All right. Jesus," the pilot said. "Don't get all excited. I'm on your side, remember?"

Kinsey wanted to leave her there, but no one deserves to face the doom he feared most in the world when he was a child. He opened the door and pulled her in.

Anger and fear beamed from her eyes as she climbed to her seat and hugged her knees, rocked a little. Her pulse throbbed inside the vein along her throat. She blinked a hundred miles per hour, but held her breath for a few moments as if she'd forgotten how the process worked. She gasped upon remembering.

Kinsey sat back and listened to the thrush of the propeller. "Now," he said. "Let's go."

The pilot worked his levers and lifted them off the ground. Maria didn't press her face to the window. Instead, she sobbed through a cold stare at her own feet as they ascended.

With his hands in his lap, Kinsey watched the ground shrink beneath them and the tree tops become a sea of green down below and thought about all the good times he'd had with Maria over the past year and a half. She was so lovely to look at. So sweet to spend time with. Sexy in lurid ways that left him exhausted.

Then he thought about the pictures of her with Platinum.

Kinsey touched the piece of paper in his shirt pocket again, leaned across her, and paused his face in front of hers. She opened her mouth as if desperate for a kiss. The thing Kinsey feared most in this moment was the inability to keep his cool. Her lips were slick and full and it took everything in him to reach across her and slide open the door. Maria slapped and beat on Kinsey's arm until he felt bruises bubble from his bones. He focused on holding the door open and used his other hand to shove her sideways in her seat. She gripped onto the doorframe like an X with her hands and muddy shoes. He pounded her splayed fingers with his fist.

She hollered curses in Spanish and turned enough to claw at his face, knocking off his sunglasses.

He squinted through the sunlight as the glasses flew out the door, almost in slow motion despite the wind pushing against their faces. He wiped at the spot on his face where her fingernails gouged him deeply enough to smear blood onto the back of his hand.

She hollered curses in Spanish again until he reared back and placed his foot in her middle-back. "I was always good to you," he said as he straightened his leg and forced her out of the helicopter. Her decent as the aircraft climbed to cruising altitude seemed in slow motion. She grew smaller like a doll falling to the ground, and then smaller and finally out of view as the pilot took them southwest.

Kinsey swallowed the clot of emotion in his throat and pulled closed the helicopter door. His life was simpler in this one way, but it was exponentially more complicated as sadness would overrun him like new residents flocking to his state.

It wasn't the first time he'd killed somebody, but this was the first woman. No pleasure came with the physical act. Instead, only an ability to get a deeper breath, as if his lungs re-inflated for the first time in weeks. He'd never be reminded of the woman he just turned into hog chow. The thought made him laugh. He left his microphone in position and let it run its course. Laughter couldn't be any worse than what the pilot might have heard during the struggle. After a moment, Kinsey adjusted his posture in his seat. He squared his shoulders and tightened his tie before smoothing hair with his hands. This trip had cost him his sunglasses, but there'd be no ass-whipping when he got home. He squinted into the sun as the pilot headed in that direction.

ITCHY FEET
S. W. Lauden

The first wave of strangers descended on the yard sale like vultures in the pre-dawn gloom. Hordes had been arriving in the hours since, paying Joe for the privilege to haul his unwanted memories away. He was judging the rabble from a perch on the porch when one of them walked up.

"How much for this seltzer bottle?"

The man was tall and lanky, with dark eyes and a bright red nose. A tiny bowler cap teetered on his smooth, white head. Joe wasn't sure if he should laugh or run.

"The circus in town?"

"Oh, man, you're still hilarious."

The clown's make up cracked and flaked as he lisped. Joe couldn't look away.

"I'm sorry. Do I know you from somewhere?"

"Never mind. I'll give you a couple of bucks for the bottle."

"Fine."

He dropped two crumpled bills into Joe's hand and shuffled away. Joe's wife walked up a few moments later.

"Did you see that freak, Helen?"

Joe spun around to point at the clown, but he was already gone. His wife frowned.

"Christ, Joe. Are you drunk already?"

She fixed him with a glare and turned to leave. Joe tried to grab her arm. Helen quickly spun away and hissed.

"Keep your hands off of me. You're pathetic."

She stormed off with a flip of her blonde hair. Joe was about to chase after her when their teenaged son stopped him.

"Out of my way, runt."

Joe knew it was a mistake the minute the word left his lips. There was a time when "runt" was just a funny nickname. Now it was more like a declaration of war.

"I told you to stop calling me that."

The boy stepped forward, his chest puffed out. Joe studied the acne-scarred face that looked so much like his own. It was impossible to know where he had gone wrong.

"Jesus. Take it easy."

Joe reached into his pocket and produced a twenty dollar bill. Only one more week until college started and then they could file the divorce papers. Eighteen years of misery was finally coming to an end—but not until their son was off at school. Helen insisted.

"Go see a movie or something, why don't you."

His son grabbed the money, muttered "asshole" and headed for his car. Joe could still remember the day that he left for college. The sense of freedom he'd felt standing outside his dorm as his parents drove away. He hoped it would feel the same when he was on his own again. If nothing else, he'd have lots of time to kill.

Joe glanced over to where the clown had reappeared on the other side of the yard. He was shaking his head and flashing a mischievous grin. Joe dismissed him with a flick of his wrist.

The hours seemed to stretch as the day went on. Joe was thankful that Helen was keeping her distance. It allowed him to sneak a cocktail or two. He stood up to get a third when the clown strolled by. Joe shook his head and snorted.

"If you're looking for a whipped cream pie, you're out of luck."

"Still can't hold your liquor, huh?"

"Stop pretending like we know each other."

"I know you better than anybody ever will. Better than that bitch you call a wife, that's for sure."

Joe took a step forward on instinct. The clown might be right, but he was still in for a beating. Sweat rolled down Joe's face as he clenched his fists. That's when the first spray of liquid hit him in the eye. The clown adjusted the plastic flower pinned to his lapel and burst out laughing.

"Bull's eye! Man, that never gets old."

Joe was wiping his face when Helen walked by. She wore that same disgusted look, the one she reserved for him alone. He motioned to the clown, but she wouldn't take her eyes off of Joe's cocktail. He gave her a defiant toast and swallowed the last gulp.

Helen went over to help a couple of neighborhood dads. Joe watched as they rifled through a pile of his old golf clubs. They were flirting with her while gripping the shafts. He was sure Helen was sleeping with at least one of them. Probably both.

"Who the hell wears high heels at their own yard sale?"

Joe was talking to himself, but the clown joined in.

"It's not your fault. You gave her all of this and she still isn't satisfied."

The clown motioned to the impressive two-story house. Joe didn't even bother looking up.

"Sometimes it feels like this place is crushing the life out of me."

"It doesn't have to be this way."

Joe rattled the ice cubes in his glass and thought it over. He decided his new friend had a point.

"Come on. I need a refill."

A bottle of bourbon and a can of diet soda were still on the counter. Joe filled his glass with fresh ice and mixed a stiff drink. His lips were already on the rim of the glass when he remembered his guest. He eyed the clown with a sideways glance.

"Thirsty?"

"You know I can't drink."

"Right...Where did we meet again?"

"Elementary school, when they still called you Joey. We got back in touch your freshman year of college."

"San Francisco, huh? That makes sense, judging by the looks of you."

Joe gave a nervous laugh. He still couldn't visit that city without having panic attacks. Not since the night that somebody dropped something into his drink at an end-of-semester party. He liked it so much that he started dropping it into his own drinks after that.

Those next three months were still a total blank. An epic, summer-long blackout when he started wearing tie-dyes and grew a beard. That was before he snapped out of his hippie trance and transferred to a school back east. Joe was clean-cut and wearing a suit from the moment he arrived on his new campus. He didn't come home to California until he had an Ivy League MBA to hang on his office wall.

"To the good old days."

Joe raised his glass. His face was pink from alcohol and sun. The clown's lip curled into a sneer.

"We had some real fun together that summer."

"I honestly don't remember."

It was a lie. The memories were bubbling up even as he said it. They were choppy and silent at first, like watching a horror movie through somebody else's bedroom window. The clown went on in a whisper.

"You're not trying hard enough, Joey. Picture their faces when you woke them up in the middle of the night. Pure fear is a beautiful thing."

"Shut up!"

Joe collapsed to the tile floor. A flood of images raced

through his mind—strange apartments, couples in their beds, a kitchen knife in his hand. He was shaking when the clown knelt down beside him.

"I'm amazed that the cops never figured out it was you."

He slid the kitchen drawer open and handed Joe a familiar weapon.

"What the hell is this for?!"

"It's time you came out of retirement. Don't pretend like you haven't thought about it. Let's start with your wife."

Joe stood up and inched out of the kitchen toward the front door. It felt like the clown controlled his movements now. Like everything was finally falling back into place.

"Helen! I need to tell you something!"

Joe kicked the screen door open and emerged onto the porch. The blade glimmered in the sunlight. The clown nudged Joe down the steps to the lawn. He felt powerful again, for the first time in years.

His wife stood there, making change for one of the neighborhood dads. Terror filled their eyes as Joe charged, knife clenched tight in his fist. The clown laughed maniacally in the background.

Joe was almost upon them when a whistling sound came from behind him. The second neighborhood dad swung the driver and connected with the back of Joe's head. He went face first into the grass, the knife cartwheeling out of sight. The two men were on him in an instant, huffing and puffing as they swung their clubs. He could hear his bones snapping. His vision got blurry.

Joe turned his head to look at the clown. He was sitting on the front steps, elbows on his knees and his eyes on the ground. It sounded like he was sobbing. Joe didn't feel good about letting his old friend down, but there was nothing he could do.

The blood drained from his face and dripped from his lips. That's when Helen stepped in front of him. Joe concentrated on the pointy tip of her shoe as she drove it right between his eyes. The clown fell silent when the lights went out. Joe was finally free.

MYSTERIOUS WAYS

A Jake Diamond Mystery

J. L. Abramo

I sat at the reception desk of Diamond Investigations at nine on Monday morning. It was unusually early for me to be at the office.

My associate, Darlene Roman, who traditionally occupied the front-room desk, much more effectively, had taken off the previous afternoon for a sojourn in Las Vegas.

"What's in Vegas?" I had asked.

"I don't know, nobody is telling."

It was the first day of February, a typical San Francisco midwinter morning—forty-three degrees, humid, mostly cloudy, chance of light rain.

Darlene had taken care of all the first-of-the-month business required to keep the office functioning, lights operational, telephone on line, wolves from the door. She had left me very little to do other than sit at her desk testing a theory suggesting that if the phone bill was paid the thing might actually ring once in a while.

Or read a book.

At the moment I was halfway into *Great Expectations* and not feeling particularly optimistic.

Between page turns, I took a quick bite from a buttered hard roll and sipped from a gone-cold paper cup of coffee from the delicatessen below.

There was a rapping at the door.

Two tentative knocks.

I was about to rise, cross the room, and let my visitor into the office—but saw no reason to amend Darlene's customary protocol.

"It's open," I called.

The door swung into the room revealing a man of fifty or so—imposing, six-two, two-twenty, unthreatening. The grey suit was well-tailored but worn. The white shirt was wrinkle-free and the necktie was tight to the collar. The shoes were practical. He took a step across the threshold and stopped short. I nearly said *come in close the door take a seat*—but I stood and walked over to the stranger instead.

"Jake Diamond," I said, extending an arm.

"Henry Campbell," the man replied, accepting the hand-shake.

I gently guided Campbell clear of the entry way, shut the door, ushered him to the client chair and invited him to sit. I thought about offering a cup of coffee but remembered *no Darlene, none made.*

I moved around to the opposite side of the desk and sat.

Something in the man's demeanor, an absence of any air of superiority, inspired me to go *familiar.*

"So, Mr. Campbell—may I call you Henry?"

"Sure."

"Good. How can I help you, Henry?"

"My daughter, Elizabeth, twenty-six, registered nurse at St. Mary's, shares a flat with two other girls in the Upper Haight."

Campbell stopped there and turned his attention to his hands, which were neatly folded in his lap.

I gave him a few moments.

"Henry?"

Campbell looked up at me—then slowly looked around the room as if trying to recall where he was and why he was there.

"Someone has been using Elizabeth as a punching bag. It's been going on for a while. I noticed small signs weeks ago, but she explained them away—a spill from her bicycle, a low tree branch. When the injuries became more serious, she offered no explanation at all. When she showed up at my house Friday night, she could hardly walk. I'm a widower, she's my only child."

"Have you spoken to the police?"

"She won't tell me who is responsible and insists she will not talk to the police."

"Is it a boyfriend? Someone she's protecting?"

"It may have started that way but I think now she is frightened, afraid to talk. And *I'm* afraid if something isn't done to stop it she will suffer permanent injury or worse. I need to find out who is hurting my girl."

"And if you do?"

"I haven't thought that far ahead," Campbell said. "Try talking to the man, I suppose."

I shadowed Elizabeth Campbell for two days.

Late Wednesday afternoon I tailed her from St. Mary's to the Barrel Head Brewhouse on Fulton—a hop, skip and jump from the hospital.

I waited ten minutes before following her into the pub.

I spotted them sitting on adjoining stools at the bar and I took an empty seat at the far end.

He was a good-looking man, early thirties, who seemed to have a smile for everyone. At first glance, they may have been seen as a handsome couple. On closer inspection, she physically cowered beside him. At one point, when Elizabeth began to rise from her seat, he roughly grabbed her wrist and sat her down.

A bartender arrived. A nametag on her blue denim vest identified her as *Annie*. I ordered George Dickel—had to settle for Jack Daniels.

"Casanova, at the other end of the bar," I asked when she brought my drink. "Do you know his name?"

She took a quick look as she set the whiskey down.

"Never saw him before," she said, and walked off.

Twenty minutes later he literally dragged Elizabeth Campbell out of the place by her elbow. I thought about following but felt I still had a shot with Annie. I waved her over.

"Another?" she asked.

"I'm good," I said, dropping a twenty on the bar. "Can you help me out?"

"He's not a nice man and he would not be happy with anyone dropping his name."

"What he doesn't know can't hurt you," I said, sliding a hundred dollar bill her way.

"Richard Connor," Annie said. "Have a nice evening—somewhere else."

She quickly walked away and I left the pub.

I climbed into my car and pulled out my cell phone.

I was about to call my client, but decided I wanted to know a little more about Richard Connor before giving his name to Henry Campbell. I still had at least one favor coming from an SFPD Detective Sergeant. I called the Vallejo Street Station to see if Johnson was there.

We sat in front of a computer at the sergeant's desk in the police station.

"I don't suppose you are going to tell me why you are interested in this guy," Johnson said.

I treated it as a rhetorical question. He let it go.

"There had been talk going around that Connor played rough with the ladies, but no one ever came forward with a complaint. Then a young woman managed to walk herself into the Emergency Room at St. Francis Hospital, badly battered, claiming Richard Connor beat her and threw her out of his car. Connor was brought in for questioning and denied everything. A preliminary hearing was scheduled but before the date arrived the woman retracted her statement."

"Scared off?"

"Or bought off. This guy is literally Little Richie Rich. His old man is one of the most successful developers in the Bay Area. Lots of political clout, a ton of money, and very proficient at keeping junior on the street."

"So this maniac skates?"

"Unless someone without my constraints cancels his skating permit."

Suddenly we spotted Lieutenant Laura Lopez moving across the room to Johnson's desk. The sergeant killed the browser.

"Jake Diamond," she said, "why are you here?"

Lopez was seldom pleased to see me.

"I needed the sergeant's advice."

"About?"

"He's looking for a reliable and honest automobile mechanic," Johnson said.

"Aren't we all," Lopez said.

I thanked Johnson, said my goodbyes, and headed for my car.

I called Henry Campbell.

He said six words before ending the connection.

St. Mary's Hospital Intensive Care Unit.

I found him in the ICU.

He was standing beside the bed, looking down at his daughter. She was encased in a tangle of wires and tubes and bandages.

"Will she be alright?"

"Physically, eventually," Henry Campbell said, "emotionally, hopefully."

"I know how you must feel," I said, having no real idea. "If there is anything I can do."

"You can tell me who did this to my little girl."

"Henry, let the police handle this. They know about the guy, he has a history. There's a Detective Sergeant who will do whatever it takes to drop a net over the animal. If your daughter will come forward, other victims may do the same. He would be put away for a very long time."

"You say he has done this before?"

"Yes."

"He nearly killed her," Campbell said, "this time. What is his name?"

"His name is Richard Connor."

"I would like time alone with her now," he said, finally looking up at me. "What do I owe you?"

"Not a thing," I said.

And I left him standing at his daughter's side.

I'm not sure what brought me back to the Barrel Head, but there I was close to midnight draining my third drink.

Annie the bartender recommended I go with straight Kentucky bourbon as a Dickel substitute this go-around.

"Sorry if I was rude earlier," she said, "and thanks for the C-note. I need brakes for my car. Do you know any reliable, honest auto mechanics?"

"None," I said.

She poured another shot of Booker's, insisting it was on the house.

"He put her in the hospital."

"Who put who in the hospital?"

"Richard Connor. The girl he dragged out of here. He put her in the hospital."

"I'm sorry to hear that," Annie said.

"He nearly killed her."

"And you're wondering if things might have gone differently if you had followed them out."

"Yes. And why he wasn't locked up in a cage long ago."

"The answer to the first question is *probably not*. The answer to the second question is *there's no good reason*. Have you had anything to eat lately?"

"I don't recall."

Annie picked up the shot she had poured for me and knocked it down herself. She filled a tall glass with water and placed it in front of me.

"I'm done here in ten minutes," she said. "Drink the water, all of it. I'll take you out for breakfast."

Darlene would be back at her post early, so I was in no real hurry to get down to the office on Friday morning.

I sat in the large backyard of my house in the Presidio, drinking strong coffee, smoking a Camel non-filter, gazing at the Golden Gate Bridge partially obscured by clouds.

My cell phone shouted out The Beatles' *Hello, Goodbye*—something Darlene had arranged when she helped set up the voice mail.

It was Sergeant Johnson.

"Do you have time for breakfast?" he asked.

"Sure."

"Pat's Café work for you?"

"Sure, give me an hour."

I found Johnson at a small table near the front window looking out onto Taylor Street.

I sat and he got right to it.

"I thought you might be interested in knowing Richard

Connor was killed late last night."

"Murdered?"

"No. A traffic accident, but whoever hit him didn't stick around—so we're calling it a felony hit and run."

"Was Connor driving?"

"He was walking, crossing Frederick toward his apartment. According to toxicology Connor was pretty drunk— he probably forgot to look both ways, and the impact knocked him into next week."

"Witnesses?"

"It was after three in the morning. Two people saw it from a distance. It was a truck. Neither could make out a license plate or any markings. Both described it simply as a very large white truck. Funny."

"Funny?"

"Ironic, then," Johnson said. "Here's a guy who may have killed someone eventually, kept dodging bullets, and he steps in front of a truck."

"Fate works in mysterious ways," I said.

A waitress arrived to pour coffee and take our order.

"You should try the poached eggs with Hollandaise," Johnson said.

"The only way I can eat an egg is if it's scrambled and burned."

When I walked into the office, Darlene was behind her desk. Her trusty canine, Tug McGraw, was curled up at her feet.

"He missed me," she said.

"How was Las Vegas?"

"I was sworn to secrecy. Did Henry get in touch with you?"

"Henry?"

"We were drinking iced tea and he spotted one of your business cards on the kitchen counter. He said he had been looking to hire an investigator, asked if you were any good. I said you were okay and gave him the card."

"And how did *Henry* come to be in your kitchen?"

"Do you remember me telling you my refrigerator died?"

"Vaguely."

"The only solution I could think of was to pop for a new one, so I did. Henry delivered the new box on Saturday."

"Did he drive a truck?"

"A very large white truck."

"How's the new refrigerator?"

"Very cool."

STARK RAVING
Patricia Abbott

Less than year into her career as a mediator, Elsa Scotia saw
the unfamiliar names of Mr. Edward and Miss Alice Starkey
on the day planner. Mediating was a late-in-life career move
that had played well so far to her talent for problem-solving.
She assumed the Starkeys were coming in over a dispute
about the disposition of a will, her area of specialty. Mediation of wills was often contentious, but since it was about
possessions rather than people no swords had been drawn
yet in her office. If words could kill, however, there'd been
some near-misses.

"Husband and wife?" Elsa asked her assistant.

Doris fanned through the papers in the file. "Siblings.
Their attorneys recommended mediation rather than using a
court to settle their disagreement."

"A will is it then?"

"Yep." Doris said, coming up with the relevant page.
"There seems to be only one area of contention. Financial
matters, furniture, the house and cars—all that's complete."

"So what bequest's in question?"

Doris paused, scanning the page. "Alma Starkey's, collection of—Beanie Babies. Alma's their deceased mother."

"Her collection of what?"

"Beanie Babies." Doris looked up. "Kids collected them
in the nineties? My daughter had quite a…"

"I know what they are. But aren't the Starkeys adults?"

"Edward is fifty-four; Alice, fifty-two."

"Edward?" Elsa said with a frown. "A grown man who cares about dolls?" She walked over to her computer and googled, "beanie babies." She looked up. "They aren't valuable anymore. Not since around 2000."

"Perhaps our siblings think differently," Doris said.

Elsa shrugged. "Should be fun meeting these two."

"Or not," her clerk said.

"Or not," Elsa agreed.

The brother and sister who walked into her office a few hours later could've been twins—and twins of the same sex. Both had seen significant declines in whatever is was that differentiated them earlier. They were short, nearly the same height, round, and wore bobbed hair the color of hay. Their features were soft, their eyes nearly colorless.

Simultaneously, they thrust out right hands that could have been forged from the same cast. Without meaning to, Elsa pulled back, a bit repulsed. But the Starkeys seemed used to this reaction. They slipped into chairs at her table, waiting expectantly. Almost invariably any group entering Elsa's office took seats as far from each other as possible, but Edward and Alice Starkey sat side by side. Obviously, their relationship had survived the issue of the ownership of the Beanie Babies.

"The major portion of your mother's estate was settled without dispute," Elsa began.

Alice nodded. "The rest was just things. We've always lived in the house, shared the car, sat on the same furniture: Edward in the club chair, me on the loveseat. We will simply go on as we always have. He in the blue bedroom, me in the yellow."

The lyric "same as it ever was" ran through Elsa's head.

"Our last argument over household matters was when I wanted to paint my room apricot," Edward said. "Back in 1995, I think."

"It's always been blue," said his sister, "and still is."

Elsa took a cleansing breath as she imagined their life. "So what makes the Beanie Babies a particular source of friction?"

The siblings looked at each other at length. Finally Edward said, "We have different plans for the Beanies."

Perhaps one of them wanted to pass them along to a charity and the other to younger family members, Elsa thought. Dispositions could be fractious.

"I intend to play with them," Alice said. "I want to cut those darn tags off and put the Beanies in chairs, beds, a dollhouse. I've made clothes for them over the years, collected appropriate furniture." She paused. "The Beanies have been Mother's prisoners for twenty years. I was never once allowed to handle one."

Edward bristled visibly. "And I plan to maintain them just as Mother did. With their swish and tush tags intact, with their fur completely blemishless. That's what Mother expected when she left them to us. That's what we promised," Edward added, glaring at his sister.

"It was a promise she extracted under duress," Alice put in.

"How many Beanie Babies are we talking about?" Elsa asked, reminding herself that they'd been adults even when the craze began. It was much like her experience with Barbie Dolls. Regrettably, she'd been a teenager when Mattel introduced them.

"Over five hundred," Alice said." Every Beanie that Ty made. In triplicate at least."

"Ty was name of the manufacturer," Edward said. "Mother has—had—five Garcia, the Bears, for instance. And ten Princesses. She was extremely intuitive about which ones would increase in value."

"Mother even collected the counterfeit ones," Alice said. "She had quite a thing for Tabasco the Bull."

"But they have no value now, right," Elsa said. "None at

all."

"Exactly right," Alice said. "So why not play with them? I've been yearning to hold one in my hands for twenty years."

"Piffle," her brother said. "You were far too old even then to play with toys."

"And you're off the rails if you just mean to just stare at them forever. They're worthless, Edward. Mother made the wrong decision in collecting them." She looked at Elsa. "She did the same thing with Cabbage Patch Dolls. Her intuition, such as it was, was fallible in the long run."

"But if there're five hundred, why can't you both do what you want? Divide them in half." It seemed obvious to Elsa.

"They all want—or should want—to be played with," Alice said. "How would we decide which ones to keep encased? Or should I say imprisoned." She looked at Elsa. "The glass was even tinted. You could hardly get a decent look at them."

"Very few children were ever allowed to play with their Beanies. That's why so many still have their tags and are pristine. Beanies would be nothing more than a pile of dirty fur otherwise." Edward's sniffed. "If playing was all you wanted, ordinary toys would suffice."

"Beanies are ordinary toys now. They always were."

"Things come back in vogue, Alice," Edward said. "And why does a woman of your age want to play with stuffed animals?"

"Or why does a man of your age want to stare through glass at them?"

"Do you have any idea about how to settle this?" Elsa asked. It was suggested in her manual that she put this idea on the table. Let the contentious parties offer ideas.

"Indeed, we have," Edward said. "We want you to come to the house, build a bonfire, and burn every last one of them."

"It's the only thing to do," Alice said. "I can't bear seeing them in those dreadful cases and Edward can't bear seeing me handle them."

"I'm not sure Beanies will burn. Aren't the beans in plastic sacks?" Her five minutes' worth of googling had netted her this information.

The siblings looked at each other and shrugged.

"Look, I'll send someone to pick them up and dispose of them in an environmentally friendly way. Is that acceptable?" Both of the Starkey children nodded.

"It's only fair that Mother paid a price for her obsession," Alice told Edward a few days later. "For the last twenty years, she's used those Beanies to drive a wedge between us. Playing us off one against the other. Interfering with our relationship."

Edward nodded. "Watching that man carry the boxes out the door was one of the best moments in my life. That mediator will see to it that they are disposed of correctly. Even if they can't be burned."

"Yes, it was nearly as satisfying as watching Mother swallow that cup of tea." Alice watched as Edward smoothed the wrinkles in her skirt, his hand lingering familiarly. "Every sip was a step on the path to freedom. She could've outlived us both on pure vitriol. Evil woman."

"Speaking of tea, shall we have some. It's Oolong today," Edward lifted his cup and Alice tapped it lightly with hers.

Three weeks later five hundred Beanie Babies, their tags cut off by Doris to prevent future hoarding , were on their way to Afghanistan where Elsa's nephew handed them out to waiting village children. No one considered putting them behind glass.

"My aunt says the people who owned these toys wanted to burn them." said the soldier.

"Some people should be thrown in jail," said his companion, watching two little girls wrap their Beanies in keffiyehs. "Look at those smiling faces."

CREDITS AND DEBITS
Paul J. Garth

I'd been at work close to an hour and was halfway down straightening the dog food and motor oil aisle when Larnerd shouted through the cash opening over the counter and asked me what was wrong.

"What do you mean?"

He leaned down and pointed his mouth out of the hole in the glass that customers paid cash through. "Just that, usually, you sit back here with me, just texting and looking at dumb shit on your phone until a customer comes in. But today, it's like you're actually working. Just wondering what's up with that."

I finished zoning the off-brand of wet dog food and walked back to the counter. Eyed the Juicy Fruit and Orbit and packs of Starburst all sitting neatly in their thin cardboard boxes. I could feel him watching me through the glass. Knew if I looked up, I'd see his eyes moving up and down my arms, looking for puncture marks or cigarette burns, or checking my nose for powder. Knew he'd say it was decisions like those that were half the reason I was in the situation I was in—stuck working in a gas station, with no money and no idea how to make more.

"I don't have my phone," I said after a long time.

"Why's that?"

I looked up. "I just don't have my phone. Or. Actually I do. It's just it's turned off."

287

"Well, turn it on. We've got a charger. I mean, I'm glad you're actually doing something, but customers don't like seeing some sad dude mope around the store."

"I can't turn it on. It's the phone company that turned it off. Fucking Sprint."

We were both quiet for a while. Turned our heads to look out at the gas pumps surrounded by the cracked lot that bled into the county road in front of the station. It was a long time before a car passed. Not that it mattered. The credit card machine was broken anyway, and people always bitched when they had to get out of line and use the ATM in the corner. I turned, headed back to finish my job zoning the aisle I'd been working in, when Larnerd shouted to me, "Damn, Tucker. How does your phone get turned off?"

I tried to keep my temper in check.

It wasn't that Dan Larnerd was a bad guy. He never rode me about not working hard enough or showing up late. That afternoon actually, he'd told me he'd clock me in on time, whenever the time clock computer got fixed, even though I'd been close to twenty minutes late and had forgotten my shirt. It's just that he was smart. Too smart to do things like fall behind on bills or blow all his money at the bar on a Wednesday night, buying shots and sharing that last little baggie of crystal with a girl who would bat her eyes then pretend she was suddenly sick after she realized you're looking to fuck but willing to settle for a quick jerk-off in the parking lot.

Honestly, I had no idea why he stuck around town. He had a college degree from Kearney and could have gone off to Omaha or Lincoln or even Minneapolis or Denver. The idea of him wasting his life as an Assistant Manager at a Shell station made me sad *for* him. I could only imagine how he felt.

"It's pretty easy, Dan," I said. "You don't pay the bill."

Larnerd leaned back in his chair. Straightened his shirt. Adjusted his name tag. "Tuck," he said. "C'mon man. We've talked about this."

We had. A few months before, when my old piece of shit
'93 Taurus had finally given out, he'd gone on for the better
part of an hour, telling me in step by step detail how to get
the money together for a car loan. "You can't let that kind
of stuff just slide," he continued. "You've got to start building up a history. Letting people and companies know you're
good for your word when you say you are. And it's just you
right now, man. You're single. It's never going to get any
cheaper than now. You should be saving. Buying small
things with a credit card so you can get some history built
up."

"I know," I said. "I just. I had some shit come up."

"Like what?"

"Christ, Dan. Don't fucking ask me that. Stuff. You
know?" I turned and walked back toward the aisle I'd been
working, my arms suddenly itching. I tried to ignore it, went
back to straightening cans and pulling pouches of cat food
forward on their thin metal arms. The radio back by the beer
coolers was busted, so all I heard were the sounds of product
sliding on the shelves and the squeak of my shoes on the
floor until, from behind the glass, I heard Larnerd tell me he
was sorry.

A few hours later and I was getting antsy. I was out of cigarettes and cash, but it was another week until payday, and
with Larnerd behind the counter, I knew I couldn't pocket a
pack until he left, and he wasn't giving any indication he was
going anywhere until close.

There'd been a few customers in and out, a couple kids,
and some adults picking up beer to drink in the parking lot
of the high school before the football game started. Larnerd
talked to them all, making sure to express his support for the
Hastings Tigers as he rang them up, apologizing for the in-

sistence on cash. "Tuck," he asked. "Can you make sure the coolers are stocked? I'm thinking we're going to have a rush after the game."

I stocked beer while Larnerd worked the counter, his portable radio in the cashier cube giving us updates on the Tigers. Near the end of the game, he called me up. "Three minutes left in the fourth. Take your break now, if you want it. Probably gonna be busy for a while." He held out a pack of Camels, crushed at the top. I knew he'd pulled them out of the returns bin we were supposed to send back to the distributor, but was too grateful to complain. I thanked him and ran outside, around the corner of the building. The sun had dipped almost all the way gone and in the field behind the store I could see old beer bottles and witchgrass and a shopping cart throwing long, intertwining shadows. Out of habit I pulled out my phone, then put it back when I remembered. I wanted to cry then, but wouldn't let myself. Instead, I thought about Larnerd's suggestions for getting my life together as I smoked.

There was a rush after the game, just like Larnerd had said. For a solid hour, we ran both registers, the line in front of the cashier cube swelling to twenty or more customers deep, teenagers carrying bottles of soda and candy and twenty somethings my age buying beer and chew. If I saw someone I'd gone to school with, I looked down and made myself shrunken and invisible, my body turning in on itself until I was sure no one had recognized me.

When the rush ended, I hung out in the cashier cube with Larnerd, asking him questions about how to get my life back in order. He advised quitting smoking, of course, and suggested I stop whatever other shit I was into, but didn't lean too hard on it. Mostly, he said, I needed to save my money. Get a prepaid credit card. Go to the library and print myself up a nice looking resume. "Eventually you'll want to find another job," he said. "And the only way people will look past a gas station job is if you give them something nice to see first."

"Why are you still here, then?" I asked. "I mean, why are you in Hastings at all? Shouldn't you be working at the bank or something? Or in another city?"

Larnerd looked away. "I did once," he said quietly. "Got fired, actually. And probably couldn't get a job at a different one. But I can't leave Hastings. I've, you know, got family stuff." He smiled, then went back to me. "Anyway, like I was saying. It wouldn't take much. Even a thousand dollars could get you started."

We closed at midnight. I cleaned the soda fountains while Larnerd counted down the registers that were filled to the top with cash. About fifteen minutes later some cops rolled by and Larnerd let them in to take what they wanted from the uneaten hotdogs and taquitos. They came every night, mostly because the owner, Mr. Macfee, had worked out a deal with them for free food in exchange for once in a while drive-by, but also because they knew our little store didn't have any kind of security system. There were cameras, but everyone who worked there knew they didn't work, and Macfee said if the store ever got robbed, we were to try and take a picture with our phones of the car, so he could at least give the cops a license plate, otherwise, there was no way anyone was ever going to get caught.

While the cops were in the store, I worked the beer cooler, stocking and rotating cans and bottles onto the nearly empty shelves, wondering the whole time if, whenever I got my new life started, I'd still have the urge to hide from the police.

When they left, Larnerd asked if I'd need a ride home, or if I was going to walk. "It's a nice night," he said. "But I'd be happy to drive you."

"It's cool, man," I told him, patting the pack in my jeans. "I'd rather walk and smoke, you know?"

He gave me a teasing grin. "Last pack, right?"

"We'll see," I said, thinking about what he'd told me, that no one at a real job wanted to hire a smoker because of some bullshit about insurance. I followed him back into the cashier cube and watched as he bent over the safe. "Time computer's still busted," he said over his shoulder. "Should be fixed on Monday. Tell you what, I'll clock you in for an extra hour. Tell Mr. Macfee you came in a bit early. All the cash he made tonight, I doubt he'll care about nine dollars."

"He make a lot?"

Larnerd kind of snorted. "After that rush? It was around three and a half grand. No kidding."

"Holy shit."

"Yeah." He stood. Turned to the front of the cube and grabbed one of the register tills, then turned and crouched to put it all the way in the back of the safe, his head practically disappearing inside. "Hand me that other one would you?"

"Sure thing," I said, picking up the till. From my year or so working there, I knew exactly how much the till contained, twenty ones, eight fives, and two twenties, plus five dollars in assorted change. After my conversation with Dan, it felt strange to be holding even that small amount of cash. I started thinking about the rest of the money Larnerd said the store had made that night then. About how Mr. Macfee would let it sit, not bothering to fix the busted radio in the back or the cracked lot outside or the goddamn heater in the winter. I thought about how he had all that cash and just let it sit, then realized, if what Larnerd said was true, it was in his bank account, working for him, making him richer. I thought about how Larnerd said a thousand dollars would be enough to get a good start.

Larnerd was twisted half out of the safe. "You going to

hand that to me or not?"

The cash stared up at me, and I thought about my apartment. How the ceiling in the bathroom had collapsed over the toilet when the upstairs neighbor's bathtub had cracked. Thought about my lack of both a car and credit card. How I didn't even have cable, or a working cell phone. I remembered something I'd seen on TV once. How cops could track people by their phones. Some guy in California who'd killed his mistress had been caught just based on the pings his phone made on the towers as he drove around. But mine was off. It couldn't be tracked. As far as the cops could tell, I was just another piece of shit who maybe blipped on their radar a few times and then fell off, never to be seen again.

I knew I hadn't clocked in. That the timecard computer was broken. The only other person would could say I'd been there tonight was Larnerd. Other than that, the cops hadn't seen me, and there was no way in shit anyone in that line would recognize me from any other asshole they passed on the street. The till balanced in one hand, I reached down and gripped the door of the safe.

"Tucker?"

I thought through it all again. No phone. No time card. No security system. A safe full of cash. A once in a life time circumstance. A chance at starting over, just waiting for me in that cold steel box.

"Tucker. Earth to Tucker. You okay, man?" Larnerd asked, still half in the safe. "Are you going to—"

I slammed the safe as hard as I could, dropping the till so I could throw my full weight into it. From between the plates of steel, I heard Larnerd scream, because of the pain or the shock, I'm still not sure. I grabbed the safe door on the rebound and swung it again, using my hips to throw it harder. Saw it catch Larnerd on the side of the head, right on the ear. Saw his skull crack against the side of the safe and bounce back with a jerk. Blood lined the dark steel, spilled out on to the yellow-gray linoleum floor, and, next to me, Larnerd's feet jerked, kicking against the side of the cashier's cube.

I swung the safe's door again. Just to be sure. Once more. Twice.

When I was sure he was dead, I reached past Larnerd, grimacing as my hand touched blood and something soft and squishy, then pushed further back into the safe, where I touched plastic bags. I pulled them out, five of them squeezed in my hand, each full of cash.

"Holy shit."

On each bag, written in Larnerd's perfect rounded handwriting, was an amount. A total of almost five thousand dollars.

I stepped out of the cube, trying not to look at Larnerd's body, suddenly unsure of what I could do with that much money. And then I remembered his advice, his step by step guide to getting my credit back on track. A pre-paid credit card to build trust back up at the bank. A personal relationship with a lender there, who would get to know me. Automatic bill pay for the bastards at Sprint and the electric company.

I stepped back into the cube. Stood over his feet and the body that hung half out the safe. I opened the heavy door and reached back in, careful not to look down, and when I had taken all the cash from the tills, I thanked him for his friendship and advice, then took a fresh pack of Camels from the cigarette rack.

"Last pack," I said to Larnerd. "Promise."

ACKNOWLEDGMENTS

I want to express my thanks to the authors who contributed stories here. Each and every writer donated their story because they believed in the cause of reasoned and sensible gun legislation. These writers are working professionals and you can find more about them and their work online. Books are easily ordered from your favorite retailer or are available online.

Thank you to Down & Out Books for accepting this project and to Eric Campbell for guidance and support.

Thank you to http://ceasefireusa.org/ for working with us on this project and for your hard work and dedication to finding a solution to gun violence in America.

Thanks to those who can discuss the issue of guns without devolving into a shouting match or name calling. Thanks to those of you who do more than just complain about it. To the volunteers and organizers, to those who write their congresspeople, who speak out and who won't stay silent as more and more people die needlessly.

—Eric Beetner
January, 2016

ABOUT THE CONTRIBUTORS

PATRICIA ABBOTT is the author of *Concrete Angel* and the forthcoming *Shot in Detroit* (June 2016). More than 150 of her stories have appeared in print or online. She lives outside Detroit. She reviews movies for *Crimespree Magazine* and blogs at pattinase.blogspot.com.

J. L. ABRAMO was born in the seaside paradise of Brooklyn, New York on Raymond Chandler's fifty-ninth birthday. Abramo is the author of *Catching Water in a Net*, winner of the St. Martin's Press/Private Eye Writers of America prize for Best First Private Eye Novel; the subsequent Jake Diamond novels *Clutching at Straws, Counting to Infinity*, and *Circling the Runway; Chasing Charlie Chan*, a prequel to the Jake Diamond series; and the stand-alone, thriller *Gravesend*. Abramo's latest work is *Brooklyn Justice.* JLAbramo.com

TREY R. BARKER is the author of *2,000 Miles To Open Road, Exit Blood, Death is Not Forever*, and *Road Gig*, all published by Down & Out Books, as well as *Slow Bleed, The Cancer Chronicles*, and *Remembrance and Regrets.* He's published hundreds of short stories, plays, poems, and thousands of articles as a former journalist. Currently, he is a sergeant with the Bureau County Sheriff's Office, and an investigator with the Illinois Attorney General's Internet Crimes Against Children task force. TreyRBarker.com

ERIC BEETNER is the author of more than a dozen novels including *Rumrunners, The Devil Doesn't Want Me, Dig Two Graves, The Year I Died Seven Times.* He is co-author (with JB Kohl) of *One Too Many Blows To The Head, Bor-*

rowed Trouble and *Over Their Heads* and co-wrote *The Backlist* and *The Short List* with author Frank Zafiro. He lives in Los Angeles where he co-hosts the Noir At The Bar reading series. EricBeetner.com.

JOE CLIFFORD is acquisitions editor for Gutter Books, managing editor of *The Flash Fiction Offensive*, and producer of Lip Service West, a "gritty, real, raw" reading series in Oakland, CA. He is the author of several books, including *Junkie Love* and *Lamentation*, as well as editor of *Trouble in the Heartland: Crime Stories Based on the Songs of Bruce Springsteen*. His latest novel, *December Boys*, the second in the *Lamentation* series, is slated for release (Oceanview Publishing) June 2016. Joe's can be found at JoeClifford.com.

Called a hard-boiled poet by NPR and the noir poet laureate in the *Huffington Post*, **REED FARREL COLEMAN** is the *NY Times* Bestselling author of Robert B. Parker's Jesse Stone novels. He is a three-time recipient of the Shamus Award and a three-time Edgar Award nominee in three different categories. He has also won the Audie, Macavity, Barry, and Anthony awards. Brooklyn born and bred, Reed now resides on Long Island with his wife.

ALEC CIZAK is a writer from Indianapolis.

ANGEL LUIS COLÓN is the author of the novella, *The Fury of Blacky Jaguar*. His Derringer nominated fiction has appeared in multiple web and print journals and he's written for sites like My Bookish Ways, The Life Sentence, and The LA Review of Books. He's also an editor for *Shotgun Honey*, home of some of the best hard-boiled flash fiction on the web. AngelLuisColon.com

HILARY DAVIDSON has won the Anthony Award, the Derringer Award, the Crimespree Award and two Ellery Queen Reader's Choice Awards. Toronto-born and New York-based, Hilary uses her background as a travel journalist in her Lily Moore mystery series, setting stories in places such as Peru and Mexico. Her latest is the hardboiled *Blood Always Tells*, her first non-series novel. You can find out more at HilaryDavidson.com.

PAUL J. GARTH has had flash fiction published at Shotgun Honey in addition to other place. He had a story included in *Trouble in the Heartland* edited by Joe Clifford. Perpetually in transit between Nebraska and Texas, he can be found online at @pauljgarth.

Twice nominated for the Edgar and Anthony awards, **ALISON GAYLIN** is the USA Today bestselling author of nine books, including the Shamus award-winning Brenna Spector suspense series. *What Remains Of Me*, a standalone, is out now from William Morrow. AlisonGaylin.com.

KENT GOWRAN lives and works in Chicago. His stories have appeared in *Needle: A Magazine of Noir Fiction*, *Plots With Guns*, *Horror Garage*, *Beat to a Pulp*, and other wild venues. In 2011, he created the crime fiction webzine *Shotgun Honey*.

ROB HART is the author of *New Yorked*, *City of Rose*, and the upcoming *South Village*. His short stories have appeared in publications like *Needle*, *Thuglit*, *Joyland*, and *Helix Literary Magazine*. He's received both a Derringer Award nomination and honorable mention in Best American Mystery Stories 2015. Non-fiction has been published at *Salon*, *The Daily Beast*, *Nailed*, and *Birth.Movies.Death*. You can find his website at RobWHart.com.

JEFFERY HESS is the author of the novel, *Beachhead*, and the editor of the award-winning anthologies *Home of the Brave: Stories in Uniform* and *Home of the Brave: Somewhere in the Sand*. He served six years aboard the Navy's oldest and newest ships and has held writing positions at a daily newspaper, a Fortune 500 company, and a university-based research center. He lives in Florida, where he leads the DD-214 Writers' Workshop for military veterans.

GRANT JERKINS is the award-winning author of five novels, including *A Very Simple Crime*, *At the End of the Road*, and *The Ninth Step*. His new novel, *Abnormal Man* (originally rejected as "pretty distasteful" by his longtime publisher), is now available. He lives with his wife and son in the Atlanta area.

JOE R. LANSDALE is the author of more than three dozen novels, including *The Thicket*, *Edge Of Dark Water*, *The Bottoms* and *Cold In July* which was adapted into a feature film. He writes the popular Hap & Leonard series, now a series on Sundance TV. He has received the British Fantasy Award, the American Mystery award, the Edgar, the Grinzane Cavour Prize for Literature, and eight Bram Stoker Awards. He lives with his family in Nacogdoches, Texas.

S.W. LAUDEN'S debut novel, *Bad Citizen Corporation* (Greg Salem, Book 1), was published by Rare Bird Books in October 2015. *Grizzly Season* (Greg Salem, Book 2) will be published in September 2016. His novella, *Crosswise*, was published by Down & Out Books.

TIM O'MARA is the Barry-nominated (which means he didn't win) author of the Raymond Donne mystery series— *Sacrifice Fly*, *Crooked Numbers*, *Dead Red*—featuring ex-cop turned Brooklyn public school teacher, Raymond Donne.

His next in the Raymond series, *Nasty Cutter,* is scheduled to be published by Severn House this fall in England and this winter in the U.S. Tim is currently a NYC public school teacher, and lives with his wife and daughter in Manhattan's Hell's Kitchen. For more info, TimOMara.net.

JOYCE CAROL OATES is the author of more than 70 books, including novels, short story collections, poetry volumes, plays, essays, and criticism, including the national bestsellers *We Were the Mulvaneys* and *Blonde.* Among her many honors are the PEN/Malamud Award for Excellence in Short Fiction and the National Book Award. Oates is the Roger S. Berlind Distinguished Professor of the Humanities at Princeton University, and has been a member of the American Academy of Arts and Letters since 1978.

TOM PITTS received his education firsthand on the streets of San Francisco. He remains there, writing, working, and trying to survive. His shorts have been published in the usual spots by the usual suspects. His publications include *Hustle, Piggyback,* and *Knuckleball.* Tom is also co-editor at *Out of the Gutter.* Find out more atTomPittsAuthor.com.

THOMAS PLUCK is the author of *Blade of Dishonor,* which Mystery People called "The Raiders of the Lost Ark of pulp paperbacks." He has slung hash, worked the docks, and even cleaned the crappers of the Guggenheim (unfortunately, not as part of a clever heist). Hailing from Nutley, New Jersey, home to Martha Stewart and Richard Blake, he has so far evaded arrest. He shares his hideout with his sassy Louisiana wife and their two insane felines. ThomasPluck.com.

KEITH RAWSON is a little-known pulp writer whose short fiction, poetry, essays, reviews, and interviews have been widely published both online and in print. He is the author of the short story collection *The Chaos We Know* (Snub-Nose Press) and co-editor of the anthology *Crime Factory: The First Shift*. He lives in Southern Arizona with his wife and daughter.

RYAN SAYLES has over two dozen short stories in print, anthologies and online, including the Anthony-nominated collection *Trouble in the Heartland*. He is the author of *Subtle Art of Brutality*, *Warpath*, *Goldfinches* and *That Escalated Quickly!* He is a founding member of Zelmer Pulp. https://vitriolandbarbies.wordpress.com/

KELLI STANLEY is the Macavity Award-winning creator of the Miranda Corbie series (*City of Dragons*, *City of Secrets*, *City of Ghosts*), literary noir novels set in 1940 San. She is also a Bruce Alexander Award and Golden Nugget Award winner, and a *Los Angeles Times* Book Prize finalist. Kelli was named a literary heir of Dashiell Hammett by his granddaughter in a *Publisher's Weekly* article, and critics have compared her work to her icon Raymond Chandler. She was awarded a Certificate of Merit from the City and County of San Francisco for her contributions to literature. *City of Sharks* is her next novel. KelliStanley.com

HOLLY WEST is the author of the Mistress of Fortune series, set in 17th century London and featuring Isabel Wilde, a mistress to King Charles II who secretly makes her living as a fortuneteller. Her debut, *Mistress of Fortune*, was nominated for the Left Coast Crime Rosebud Award for Best First Novel. Her short fiction has appeared in numerous anthologies, including *The Big Book of Jack the Ripper*, edited by Otto Penzler, coming in Fall 2016 from Vintage Books. She lives in Northern California with her husband, Mick, and dog, Stella. HollyWest.com

On the following pages are a few
more great titles from the
Down & Out Books publishing family.

For a complete list of books and to
sign up for our newsletter,
go to DownAndOutBooks.com.

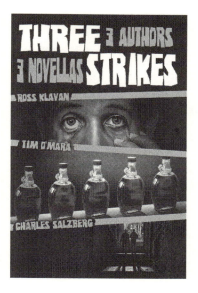

Three Strikes
Ross Klavan, Tim O'Mara and Charles Salzberg

Down & Out Books
September 2018
978-1-948235-25-9

I Take Care of Myself in Dreamland by Ross Klavan. A driver for the mob tells this tale, a guy who's heard it all. And when he begins a trip, it's almost always one-way.

Jammed by Tim O'Mara. Aggie's back. After barely escaping with his life in *Smoked*, Aggie disproves the old adage of "Once burned…"

The Maybrick Affair by Charles Salzberg. A couple weeks before the attack on Pearl Harbor and, as war rages in Europe, a young reporter, is assigned a routine human interest story.

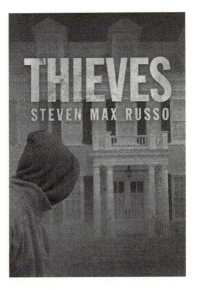

Thieves
Steven Max Russo

Down & Out Books
November 2018
978-1-948235-40-2

Dark, deadly and disturbing, *Thieves* will both horrify and delight you.

In his stunning debut thriller, Steven Max Russo teams a young cleaning girl with a psychopathic killer in a simple robbery that quickly escalates into a terrifying ordeal. Stuck in a deadly partnership, trapped by both circumstance and greed, a young girl is forced to play cat and mouse against her deadly partner in crime.

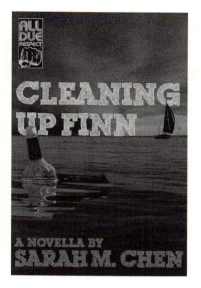

Cleaning Up Finn
Sarah M. Chen

All Due Respect, an imprint of
Down & Out Books
978-1-946502-49-0

Life is a constant party for restaurant manager, Finn Roose. When he seduces an underage woman on one of his booze cruises and loses her—literally, it sets off a massive search involving the police, her parents, and a private investigator. Finn is an expert manipulator but his endless lies only tighten the screws on himself and his unsuspecting best friend. Finn scrambles to make things right which may be too much to ask from a guy who can't resist a hot babe and a stiff drink.

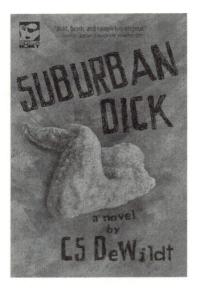

Suburban Dick
CS DeWildt

Shotgun Honey, an imprint of
Down & Out Books
May 2018
978-1-946502-72-8

When private eye/deadbeat dad Gus Harris catches a new case, he hopes it will not only save his failing PI agency, but also his family. However, a straight forward missing persons case quickly spirals into a dangerous world of high school wrestlers, embezzlement, and murder.

Solving the case isn't the issue, it's keeping his family safe from the fallout.

my stery
Unloaded
2016

1559232
Added 12/18

Made in the USA
Middletown, DE
16 November 2018